One Too Many

and Twelve Other Action-Packed Stories of the Wild West
by Frank Bonham

Edited by Martin H. Greenberg
and Bill Pronzini

BARRICADE BOOKS INC.
New York

"Tarzana Nights." © 1987 by Frank Bonham. First published in *Mystery Scene*.

"Burn Him Out." © 1949 by Popular Publications, Inc. First published in *Argosy*.

"River Magic." © 1944 by McCall Corporation. First published in *Blue Book*.

"Loaded." © 1949 by The Hawley Corporation. First published in *Zane Grey's Western Magazine*.

"One Ride Too Many." © 1950 by Popular Publications, Inc. First published in *Dime Western*.

"Trouble at Temescal." © 1949 by Popular Publications, Inc. First published in *Argosy*.

"Chivaree." © 1951 by Popular Publications, Inc. First published in *Star Western* as "Lovely Little Liar."

"I'll Take the High Road." © 1948 by McCall Corporation. First published in *Blue Book*.

"The Trail-Blazers." © 1944 by Popular Publications, Inc. First published in *Dime Western* as "Trail-Blazers of the Buckskin Empire."

"The Seventh Desert." © 1945 by Liberty Magazines, Inc. First published in *Liberty*.

"Plague Boat." © 1942 by Short Stories, Inc. First published in *Short Stories*.

"The Green Mustache." © 1946 byLiberty Magazines, Inc. First published in *Liberty*.

"Dusty Wheels—Bloody Trail." © 1949 by Popular Publications, Inc. First published in *Dime Western*.

Published by Barricade Books Inc., 150 Fifth Avenue, New York, NY 10011

Library of Congress Cataloging-In-Publication Data

Bonham, Frank.
   One ride too many and twelve other action stories of the Wild West
   / by Frank Bonham; edited by Martin H. Greenberg and Bill Pronzini.
      p. cm.
   ISBN 1-56980-034-0 (pbk)
   1. Frontier and pioneer life—West (U.S.)—Fiction. 2. West (U.S.)—
Social life and customs—Fiction. 3. Western stories. I. Greenberg, Martin
Harry. II. Pronzini, Bill. III. Title.
PS3503.04315A6
813'.54—dc20   94-46919
                                                    CIP

First Printing

Contents

Tarzana Nights

THE gosling author who spots the phrase, "Established Writer," in the classifieds is doomed to give a malarial shiver and read on. Certainly *I* shivered, and hurriedly rolled a letterhead into my Underwood #5, when I read the ad in the Glendale, California, newspaper one day in the late 'Thirties.

ESTABLISHED WRITER seeks secretary-collaborator. You write. I teach and sell. NO FEES. Box Q.

I was twenty-two years old, and as prolific as a hamster, often producing a short story a day. For two years I had written fiercely—one hundred and thirteen stories, seven sales —always fantasizing over just such a relationship. Now, perhaps, the sun was rising over the Underwood! I would write; Established Writer would teach and sell!

Mailing my response was like dropping the letter down a well—was there really a Box Q?—but he called and asked me to come to his apartment for an interview. That same day I drove over, and the established writer unfastened the safety chain and let me in. He seemed rather mousy and a little furtive, but in my eyes he had all the panache of a gaucho.

His nom de plume was Ed Oliver Ratt, and I had seen it in the Western magazines many times. It was famous from *Dime Western* to *Wild West Weekly*. Ratt explained that he also wrote Western movies for Republic Studios, and needed a collaborator to convert his scripts into short stories, which he would sell to his pulp markets. He showed me his name on a couple of scripts: *Ed Oliver Ratt.*

Okay? Okay!

I took two of the pink scripts home to transform them into fiction. But first I wrote to tell my agent the exciting news. Alas! In a few days I learned that the man was not the Ratt he claimed to be.

The real Ratt lived over in San Fernando Valley, and he had the same agent I did. Ratt—no nom de plume—drove over, scared off the fraud, who had stolen the scripts from the studio, and who wouldn't unlock the safety chain this time, and lingered to muse aloud that actually the con-man's idea wasn't so improbable, at that . . .

Except that, hmm, the magazines wouldn't appreciate being sold twice-told tales, so I'd have to come up with new material. Suppose he helped me develop the story lines, waved his wand over them to make them sound like his own prose, and sold them to the magazines under his name. We'd split the checks fifty-fifty.

Okay? Okay, okay! A happy ending after all, or at least —all I prayed for—a beginning.

In weeks I was turning out salable stories, and everything was aces and spades—as Ratt, a salty-talking Westerner from Pennsylvania, used to say. I was virtually guaranteed that most of what I produced would sell. So, although I earned only half the money per sale, I made a lot more sales.

But, as in any well-plotted pulp story, even the real Ratt was a hustler. Although I did not know it for some time, he had more ghosts than the Tower of London. Each ghost plotted and wrote his own stories. Ratt made them smell like the real thing by cramming in pounds of lurid modifiers; and later the checks were divided by two.

Before the partnership ended, I had accumulated the names of four other phantom writers, each of us generating approximately 40,000 words a month which sold in New York for about a cent a word. Through his branding pen passed at least

200,000 words per month, or about $2,000 worth. And in the meantime, Ed Oliver Ratt was earning good money writing B movies.

Each ghost had his own night to walk, I learned eventually. Mine was Thursday, and I recall with a thrill the first time I drove over to Tarzana, in San Fernando Valley, twittery and grateful, a short story in a folder. I stood to gain everything but fame, for all the fame and blame would accrue to that prolific earl of the pulps, Ed Oliver Ratt. But okay!

Ed was a tall, graying man with the air of a million-acre cattleman, and unusually full cheeks that gave him a squirrel-like appearance. He always said howdy as we shook, and when I left it was invariably adios. Years of writing Westerns had seasoned his speech and correspondence with a cowboy saltiness, as a cannery worker might pick up the smell of tuna.

The home place was a ranch-style spread with an elegant bunkhouse, and there were branding irons, spurs, and oxbows all over the living room. We went into a rustic den with at least a thousand pulp magazines on shelves lining the walls, and oil paintings of gunmen getting shot. As Ed sat down to skim my story, he handed me something of his own to read: a contract setting forth the terms of my indentured service.

He had composed it himself; it was even adorned with vivid adjectives and adverbs, and anyone with the slightest perspicacity would have perceived a story line as well. But I had no perspicacity whatever, and the story had to unroll in its own good time.

According to our covenant, I was to turn my entire literary production over to him, the checks to be split fifty-fifty. His task was to pay postage and "teach me the tricks" of writing, and "encourage" me. Either man could end the partnership at any time; but when that day came, all unsold copy remained Ratt's sole property. It would simplify the bookkeeping, he explained; and anyway all such relationships had to be built on trust. Trust started with my never once seeing one of those checks before it was divided.

But for the first year, the arrangement worked like a new marriage.

I was selling nearly all my work, and learning that a stitch in time saves nine, although an equally important axiom, that haste makes waste, would have to be learned later, after I was on my own.

Every week my girl friend and I would go over to Ed and Martha's, and the women would talk in the living room, among hide-rugs, animal traps, quirts and branding irons, while Ratt and I spun yarns in his den. He called me Panch', Pancho being Mexican for Frank, as in Frank Villa.

"Panch'," he said one night, "can you make that typewriter holler a little louder next week? *Horsecollar Western* wants a 40,000-worder by the 15th. We'll have to hump to make it."

I humped, and we made it. We always made it, though he kept assuring me that he had to wave his wand over the work considerably to make it sound like him. Sometimes he forgot to wave the wand, and an editor would write:

"Dear Ed: Sometimes you sound like you were two or three guys. . . ."

Because of their suspicion that he was in a soft bargaining position, editors began to take advantage of him. A story I had logged at 12,500 words might be paid off at 11,000. A magazine to which we had sold many stories at the regular figure of 1¢ a word would cut us to ¾ "because this one's a little sloppy and we'll have to tighten it up."

Actually, I knew my Ratty words and phrases by heart, and the wand was unnecessary, for I could write without flinching, "a bullet tore into his slab-muscled thigh." All his heroes, early-day Mr. Americas, had slab-muscled thighs.

Once a magazine made a typo and it came out "slab-muscled thing."

Hell of a place to get shot, pardner.

Another earmark of a Ratt story was that the heroes were usually referred to as kids, which, indeed, they were, many still in their teens. We would hunker down in the bunkhouse to spin a yarn, and Ed would toss out a teaser.

"Okay, the kid comes out of the saloon and somebody's sitting on his pony. What's that suggest?"

It suggested that the bartender should have asked to see his driver's license; but all right, his horse is being stolen.

"Um, he sees that the rider is a girl," I would say.

"Purty good, Where's it go from there?"

"She's um, the daughter of a sheepherder."

"Fine! Attaboy!"

And so we fed each other banalities, and came up with one grand cliché, which I wrote in the following week. Sometimes I itched to try something new, but Ratt rejected sternly my efforts to introduce anything less threadbare.

It was fun, though, when, as occasionally occurred, a genuine oil painting would arrive, the cover art for a coming issue, perhaps, of *Side-Saddle Western*. Match a story to it, an editor would write, and the painting was his. (Not mine. Read your contract, Panch'.)

Once it was a cowboy with lather on his face, shaving before a mirror hanging against a tree. In the mirror, you could see a rifleman taking aim on the cowboy's back. But in his right hand the cowboy held a Colt. What did that suggest? That he was a right-hander shaving left-handed, or a southpaw shooting right-handed.

I suppose it was vanity that began to poison our partnership, although it smelled like money to me. After over two years I was slamming out nearly a half-million words a year —but nobody knew my name. Everybody thought Ed Oliver

Ratt was a hell of a fertile writer, if a little uneven. So one Thursday night I suggested that, what if—well, time's awasting, Ed (I was now twenty-four), so how about I keep half my stuff to sell under my own name?

Ed didn't answer for a while. His plump squirrel-face was mournful. "What do you think?" I asked, uneasily. (My girlfriend and I were married now, a young couple with genuine food and utility bills, living in an apartment-house my wife's folks called "that tenement.")

"Well, I guess I'm a little hurt, Panch'," Ed said. "My button (boy) doesn't show any sign of wanting to carry on my brand (name), and I was figuring I'd leave it to you when I hung up my spurs (quit)."

"But I'd like to get a toehold, Ed, and—"

"It'd be kind of hard to keep track of the stuff in your corral, and the stuff in mine, Panch'," Ed said. "Hey, Rogers Terrill liked that novelette about what's-his-name—Buck Cordner. Let's cook up something along that line and call the kid, for instance, Cord Buckner. What do you think?"

Whatever I thought, it was clear what the stuff was in my corral. We were about to do a novelette about a kid named Cord Buckner. Under Ratt's brand.

Our word-rate dropped steadily, like the body temperature of a dead gunman, and my wife and I moved to my family's two-room cabin in the San Bernardino Mountains, where at least we would have no rent, and could chop wood for cooking and heating. On weekends we usually had friends up, and one weekend it was an *L.A. Times* columnist and his wife, and some other writing mavericks. This man, Lee Shippey, did a column the following week about our cabin in the pines, and the curious arrangement I had with a certain well-known Western writer. . . .

Ratt never referred to my breaking of the faith by telling somebody of our "arrangement," but a curious and frightening thing began to happen. Sales died like dogies at an alkali water-hole. And what sales we managed to achieve were at fire-sale prices.

"Mike Tilden said he was up to here on cavalry stories, Panch'," Ed would say, explaining a rejection. Or, "Gus knocked us down to a half-cent on 'Border Guns.'" Or, "Nobody's buying right now, pardner."

The hell they weren't. There were literally hundreds of pulp magazines on the stands, bulging with millions of juicy words—a lot of them my own until quite recently.

Finally I suggested that, since so little money was coming in, and he seldom had need to wave his wand over my stuff, I keep two-thirds of the proceeds. Ratt's eyes grew cold and hooded, like a hawk's.

"Wouldn't work, Panch'," he said flatly.

At last it was not okay. I had been told to sink or swim. It was our final visit to the bunkhouse in Tarzana.

No money came in, and I wrote a letter cancelling the contract. In the process, I presented Ratt with more than 80,000 words of unsold stories—several novelettes and a whole corral-full of short stories.

A couple of weeks later, however, I sold my own first story —for two cents a word, undivided with anyone. How proud my wife and I were of me! I had emerged from my chrysalis— no, no! won my spurs—strapped on my sixgun. Kid Panch' was finally in the saddle.

What had the horse cost him? About 1,440,000 words of fiction. I don't know how much money, but at least half of something like $15,000—Depression, exchangeable for silver.

What did I get out of it?

I learned how to divide by two. And I learned how to sit at a desk and write, against a deadline, day after day. My wife and I became able to distinguish between wants and necessities. I also developed some tricks of plotting and keeping a story running smoothly.

In short, I learned the ropes.

Of course it was outrageous the way he took advantage of me. I, Panch', would never do such a thing to a young writer. And yet—well, sometimes it tickles me to realize what a unique position I am in to help a young writer, now that I have written *and published* hundreds of short stories and novelettes, as well as forty-nine books—children's, mysteries, Westerns. My protegé—make that protegée—would be a young English teacher, perhaps, with oodles of unfocused talent but no experience . . . Needing an Established Writer to show her the ropes.

Fifty-fifty. Okay?

The dream unrolls. . . . It is Thursday night. I sharpen a few pencils, chill the wine, waiting for the doorbell to ring. . . .

Burn Him Out

WILL Starrett squatted before the campfire in the creek bottom, drinking his coffee and watching the other men over the rim of his tin cup. In the strong light from the fire, the sweat and the dirt and the weariness made harsh masks of their faces. They were tired men. But pushing up through their fatigue was a growing restlessness. Now and then, a man's face was lost in heavy shadow as he turned away to talk with a neighbor. A head nodded vigorously, and the buzz of talk grew louder. To Starrett, listening, it was like the hum a tin of water makes as it comes to a boil. The men were growing impatient now, and drawing confidence from each other. Snatches of talk rose clearly. Without the courtesy of direct address, they were telling Tim Urban what to do.

Starrett swirled his cup to raise the sugar from the bottom and studied Urban coldly. The man leaned against the wheel of a wagon, looking cornered. He held a cup of coffee in his hand and his puffy face was mottled with sweat and dirt. On his hands and forearms was the walnut stain of grasshopper excrement. He was a man for whom Starrett felt only mild contempt. Urban was afraid to make his own decisions, and yet unable to accept outside advice. The land on which he stood, and on which they had worked all day, was Urban's. The decision about the land was his, too. But because he hesitated, so obviously, other voices were growing strong with eagerness to make up his mind for him. Tom Cowper was the most full-throated of the twenty-five who had fought the grasshoppers since dawn.

"If the damned poison had only come!" he said. "We could

have been spreading it tonight and maybe had them stopped by noon. Since it ain't come, Tim—" He scowled and shook his head. "We're going to have to concoct some other poison just as strong."

"What would that be?" Starrett struck a match and shaped the orange light with his hands.

Cowper, a huge man with a purplish complexion, badger-gray hair and tufted sideburns, pondered without meeting Starrett's eyes, and answered without opening his mind.

"Well, we've got time to think of something, or they'll eat this country right down to bedrock. We're only three miles from your own land right now. The hoppers didn't pasture on Urban's grass because they liked the taste of it. They just happened to land here. Once they get a start, or a wind comes up, they'll sweep right down the valley. We've got to stop them here."

Will Starrett looked at him and saw a big angry-eyed man worrying about his land as he might have worried about any investment. To him, land was a thing to be handled like a share of railroad stock. You bought it when prices were low, you sold it when prices were high. Beyond this, there was nothing to say about it.

When Starrett did not answer him, Cowper asked, "What is there to do that we haven't already done? If we can't handle them here on Tim's place, how can we handle them on our own?"

They all knew the answer to that, Starrett thought. Yet they waited for someone else to say it. It was Tim Urban's place to speak, but he lacked the guts to do it. Starrett dropped the match and tilted his chin as he drew on the cigarette. The fire's crackling covered the far-off infinite rattling of the grasshoppers, the night covered the sight of them. But they were still there in every man's mind, a hated, crawling plague sifting the earth like gold-seekers.

They were there with their retching green smell and their racket, as of a herd of cattle in a dry cornfield. Across two miles of good bunch-grass land they had squirmed, eating all but a few weeds, stripping leaves and bark from the trees. They had dropped from the sky upon Urban's home place the night before, at the end of a hot July day. They had eaten every scrap of harness in the yard, gnawed fork-handles and corral bars, chewed the paint off his house and left holes where onions and turnips had been in his garden.

By night, four square miles of his land had been destroyed, his only stream was coffee-colored with hopper excrement. And the glistening brown insects called Mormon crickets were moving on toward the valley's heart as voraciously as though wagonloads of them had not been hauled to a coulee all day and cremated in brush fires. And no man knew when a new hatch of them might come across the hills.

Starrett frowned. He was a dark-faced cattleman with a look of seasoned toughness, a lean and sober man, who in his way was himself a creature of the land. "Well, there's one thing," he said.

"What's that?" Cowper asked.

"We could pray."

Cowper's features angered, but it was his foreman, Bill Hamp, who gave the retort. "Pray for seagulls, like the Mormons?"

"The Mormons claim they had pretty good luck."

With an angry flourish, Hamp flung the dregs of his coffee on the ground. He was a drawling, self-confident Missourian, with truculent pale eyes and a brown mustache. The story was that he had marshaled some cowtown a few years ago, or had been a gunman in one of them.

He had been Cowper's ramrod on his other ranches in New Mexico and Colorado, an itinerant foreman who suited Cowper. He did all Cowper asked of him—kept the cows alive until the ranch could be resold at a profit. To Hamp, a ranch was something you worked on, from month to month, for wages. Land, for him, had neither beauty nor dimension.

But he could find appreciation for something tangibly beautiful like Tom Cowper's daughter, Lynn. And because Starrett himself had shown interest in Lynn, Bill Hamp hated him —hated him because Starrett was in a position to meet her on her own level.

Hamp kept his eyes on Starrett. "If Urban ain't got the guts to say it," he declared, "I have. Set fires! Burn the hoppers out!" He made a sweeping gesture with his arm.

Around the fire, men began to nod. Urban's rabbity features quivered. "Bill, with the grass dry as it is I'd be burned out!"

Hamp shrugged. "If the fire don't get it, the hoppers will," he said.

Cowper sat there, slowly nodding his head. "Tim, I don't see any other way. We'll backfire and keep it from getting out of hand."

"I wouldn't count on that," Starrett said.

"It's take the risk or accept catastrophe," Cowper declared. "And as far as its getting out of hand goes, there's the county road where we could stop it in a pinch."

"Best to run off a strip with gangplows as soon as we set the fires," Hamp said. He looked at Starrett with a hint of humor. Downwind from Tim Urban's place at the head of the valley was Starrett's. Beyond that the other ranches sprawled over the prairie. Hamp was saying that there was no reason for anyone to buck this, because only Urban could lose by the fire.

Starrett said nothing and the opinions began to come.

Finally Cowper said, "I think we ought to take a vote. How many of you are in favor of setting fires? Let's see hands on it."

There were twenty men in the creek bottom. Cowper counted fourteen in favor. "The rest of you against?"

All but Starrett raised their hands. Hamp regarded him. "Not voting?"

"No. Maybe you'd like to vote on a proposition of mine."

"What's that?"

"That we set fire to Cowper's ranch house first."

Cowper's face contorted. "Starrett, we've got grief enough without listening to poor jokes!"

"Burning other men's grass is no joke. This is Urban's place, not yours or mine. I'm damned if any man would burn me out by taking a vote."

Bill Hamp sauntered to the wagon and placed his foot against a wheelhub. "Set by and let ourselves be eaten out — is that your idea?"

"Ourselves?" Starrett smiled.

Hamp flushed. "I may not own land, but I make my living from it."

"There's a difference, Hamp. You need to sweat ten years for a down payment before you know what owning an outfit really means. Then you'd know that if a man would rather be eaten out than burned out, it's his own business."

Hamp regarded him stonily and said, "Are you going to stand there and say we can't fire the place to save the rest?"

Starrett saw the the men's eyes in the firelight, some apprehensive, some eager, remembering the stories about Bill Hamp and his cedar-handled .45. "No," he said. "I didn't say that."

Hamp, after a moment, let a smile loosen his mouth. But Starrett was saying, "I've got nothing against firing, but everything against deciding it for somebody else. Nobody is going to make up Urban's mind for him, unless he agrees to it."

Urban asked quickly, "What would you do, Will?"

It was not the answer Starrett wanted. "I don't know," he said. "What are you going to do?"

Urban knew an ally when he saw one. He straightened, spat in the fire, and with his thumbs hooked in the riveted corners of his jeans pockets, stared at Cowper. "I'm going to wait till morning," he said. "If the poison don't come—and if it don't rain or the wind change—I may decide to fire. Or I may not."

Information passed from Cowper to Bill Hamp, traveling on a tilted eyebrow. Hamp straightened like a man stretching slowly and luxuriously. In doing so, his coat was pulled back and the firelight glinted on his cartridge belt. "Shall we take that vote again, now that Mr. Starrett's finished stumping?" he asked.

Starrett smiled. "Come right down to it, I'm even principled against such a vote."

Hamp's dark face was stiff. The ill-tempered eyes held the red catchlights of the fire. But he could not phrase his anger for a moment, and Starrett laughed. "Go ahead," he said. "I've always wondered how much of that talk was wind."

Cowper came in hastily. "All right, Bill! We've done all we can. It's Urban's land. As far as I'm concerned, he can fight the crickets himself." He looked at Starrett. "We'll know where to lay the blame if things go wrong."

He had brought seven men with him. They got up, weary, unshaven cowpunchers wearing jeans tied at the bottoms to keep the grasshoppers from crawling up their legs. Cowper found his horse and came back, mounted.

"You'll be too busy to come visit us for a while." His meaning was clear—he was speaking of his daughter. "As for the rest of it—I consider that a very dangerous principle you've laid down. I hope it never comes to a test when the hoppers have the land next to *mine*."

They slept a few hours. During the night a light rain fell briefly. Starrett lay with his head on his saddle, thinking of the men he had so nearly fought with.

Cowper would sacrifice other men's holdings to protect his own. That was his way. Urban would protest feebly over being ruined with such haste, but he would probably never fight. Hamp was more flexible. His actions were governed for the time by Cowper's. But if it came to a showdown, if the hoppers finished Urban and moved a few miles east onto Starrett's land, this dislike that had grown into a hate might have its airing.

Starrett wished Cowper had been here longer. Then the man might have understood what he was trying to say. That land was not shares of stock, not just dirt with grass growing on it. It was a bank, a feedlot, a reservoir. The money, the feed, the water were there as long as you used them wisely. But spend them prodigally, and they vanished. Your cattle gaunted down, your graze died. You were broke. But after you went back to punching cows or breaking horses, the grass came back, good as ever, for a wiser cowman to manage.

It was a sort of religion, this faith in the land. How could you explain it to a man who gypsied around taking up the slack in failing ranches by eliminating extra hands, dispensing with a useless horse-herd, and finally selling the thing at a profit?

Ranching was a business with Cowper and Hamp, not a way of life.

Just at dawn the wind died. The day cleared. An hour later, as they were riding, armed with shovels, into the blanket of squirming hoppers to shovel tons of them into the wagons and dozers, a strong wind rose. It was coming from the north, a warm, vigorous breeze that seemed to animate the grasshoppers. Little clouds of them rose and flew a few hundred yards and fell again. And slowly the earth began to shed them, the sky absorbed their rattling weight and they moved in a low cloud toward the hills. Soon the land was almost clean. Where they had passed in their crawling advance, the earth was naked, with only a few clumps of brush and skeletal trees left.

Urban leaned on the swell of his saddle by both elbows. He

swallowed a few times. Then he said softly, like a man con-
fessing a sin, "I prayed last night, Will. I prayed all night."

"Then figure this as the first installment on an answer. But
this is grasshopper weather. They're coming out of the earth
by the million. Men are going to be ruined if they come back
out of the brush, and if the wind changes, they will. Don't
turn down that poison if it comes."

That day Starrett rode into Antelope. From the station mas-
ter he learned that Tim Urban's poison had not come. A wire
had come instead, saying that the poison had proved too
dangerous to handle and suggesting that Urban try Epsom
salts. Starrett bought all the Epsom salts he could find—a
hundred pounds. Then he bought a ton of rock salt and
ordered it dumped along the county road at the southwest
border of his land.

He had just ridden out of the hot, shallow canyon of the
town and turned down toward the river when he saw a flash of
color on the bridge, among the elms. He came down the dusty
slope to see a girl in green standing at the rail. She stood
turning her parasol as she watched him drop the bridle-reins
and come toward her.

"Imagine!" Lynn smiled. "Two grown men fighting over
grasshoppers!"

Will held her hand, warm and small in the fragile net of her
glove. "Well, not exactly. We were really fighting over foremen. Hamp puts some of the dangedest ideas in Tom's head."

"The way I heard it some ideas were needed last night."

"Not that kind. Hamp was going to ram ruination down
Urban's throat."

"You have more tact than I thought," she told him. "It's nice
of you to keep saying, 'Hamp.' But isn't that the same as
saying 'Tom Cowper?'"

He watched the creek dimple in the rain of sunlight through
the leaves. "I've been hoping it wouldn't be much longer. I

could name a dozen men who'd make less fuss and get more done than Hamp. If Urban had made the same suggestion to your father, Hamp would have whipped him."

She frowned. "But if Urban had had the courage, he'd have suggested firing himself, wouldn't he? Was there any other way to protect the rest of us?"

"I don't think he was as much concerned about the rest of us as about himself. You've never seen wildfire, have you? I've watched it travel forty miles an hour. July grass is pure tinder. If we'd set fires last night, Tim would have been out of business this morning. And of course the hardest thing to replace would have been his last fifteen years."

"I know," she said. But he knew she didn't. She'd have an instinctive sympathy for Urban, he realized. She was that kind of woman. But she hadn't struggled with the land. She couldn't know what the loss of Urban's place would have meant to him.

"They won't come back, will they?" she asked.

He watched a rider slope unhurriedly down the hill toward them. "If they do, and hit me first, I hope to be ready for them. Or maybe they'll pass me up and land on Tom. . . . Or both of us. Why try to figure it?"

She collapsed the parasol and put her hands out to him. "Will—try to understand us, won't you? Dad doesn't want to be a rebel, but if he makes more fuss than you like it's only because he's feeling his way. He's never had a ranch resist him the way this one has. Of course, he bought it just at the start of a drought, and it hasn't really broken yet."

"I'll make you a bargain." Will smiled. "I'll try to understand the Cowpers if they'll do the same for me."

She looked up at him earnestly. "I do understand you—in most things. But then something happens like last night and I wonder if I understand you any better than I do some Comanche brave."

"Some Comanches," he said, "like their squaws blonde. That's the only resemblance I know of."

The horseman on the road came past a peninsula of cottonwoods and they saw it was Bill Hamp. Hamp's wide mouth pulled into a stiff line when he saw Starrett. He hauled his horse around, shifting his glance to Lynn. "Your father's looking all over town for you, Miss Lynn."

She smiled. "Isn't he always? Thanks, Bill." She opened the parasol and laid it back over her shoulder. "Think about it, Will. He can be handled, but not with a spade bit."

She started up the hill. Hamp lingered to roll a cigarette. He said, "One place he can't be handled is where she's concerned."

"He hasn't kicked up much fuss so far," said Starrett.

Hamp glanced at him, making an effort, Starrett thought, to hold the reasonless fury out of his eyes. "If you want peace with him as a neighbor, don't try to make a father-in-law out of him."

Starrett said, "Is this him talking, or you, Bill?"

"It's me that's giving the advice, yes," Hamp snapped. "I'd hate to ram it down your throat, but if you keep him riled up with your moonshining around . . ."

Starrett hitched his jeans up slowly, his eyes on the ramrod.

Lynn had stopped on the road to call to Hamp, and Hamp stared wordlessly at Will and turned to ride after her.

As he returned to the ranch, Starrett thought, *If there's any danger in him, it's because of her.*

Starrett spread the salt in a wide belt along the foothills. Every morning he studied the sky, but the low, dark cloud did not reappear. Once he and Cowper met in town and rather sheepishly had a drink. But Bill Hamp drank a little farther down the bar and did not look at Starrett.

Starrett rode home that evening feeling better. Well, you did not live at the standpoint of crisis, and it was not often that something as dramatic as a grasshopper invasion occurred to set neighbors at each other's throats. He felt almost calm, and had so thoroughly deceived himself that when he reached the cutoff and saw the dark smoke of locusts sifting down upon the foothills in the green afterlight he stared a full ten seconds without believing his eyes.

He turned his horse and rode at a lope to his home place. He shouted at the first puncher he saw, "Ride to Urban's for the dozers!" and sent the other three to the nearest ranches for help. Then he threw some food in a sack and, harnessing a team, drove toward the hills.

There was little they could do that night, other than prepare for the next day. The hoppers had landed in a broad and irregular mass like a pear-shaped birthmark on the earth, lapping into the foothills, touching the road, spreading across a curving mile-and-a half front over the corner of Will Starrett's land.

By morning, eighteen men had gathered, a futile breastplate to break the hoppers' spearhead. Over the undulating grassland spread the plague of Mormon crickets. They had already crossed the little area of salt Starrett had spread. If they had eaten it, it had not hurt them. They flowed on, crawling, briefly flying, swarming over trees to devour the leaves in a matter of moments, to break the branches by sheer weight and strip the bark away.

The men tied cords about the bottoms of their jeans, buttoned their shirt collars, and went out to shovel and curse. Fires were started in coulees. The dozers lumbered to them with their brown-bleeding loads of locusts. Wagonloads groaned up to the bank and punchers shoveled the squirming masses into the gully. Tom Cowper was there with Hamp and a few others.

He said tersely, "We'll lick them, Will." He was gray as weathered board.

But they all knew this was just a prelude to something else. That was as far as their knowledge went. They knew an army could not stop the grasshoppers. Only a comprehensive thing like fire could do that. . . .

They fought all day and until darkness slowed the hoppers' advance. Night brought them all to their knees. They slept, stifled by the smoke of grasshoppers sizzling in the coulees. In the morning Starrett kicked the campfire coals and threw on wood. Then he looked around.

They were still there. Only a high wind that was bringing a scud of rain clouds gave him hope. Rain might stop the hoppers until they could be raked and burned. But this rain might hold off for a week, or a wind might tear the clouds to rags.

There was rage in him. He wanted to fight them physically, to hurt these filthy invaders raping his land.

When he turned to harness his team, he saw Bill Hamp bending over the coffee pot, dumping in grounds. Hamp set the pot in the flames and looked up with a taunt in his eyes. Starrett had to discipline his anger to keep it from swerving foolishly against the ramrod.

The wind settled against the earth and the hoppers began to move more rapidly. The fighters lost a half-mile in two hours. They were becoming panicky now, fearing the locusts would fly again and cover the whole valley.

At noon they gathered briefly. Starrett heard Hamp talking to a puncher. He heard the word "gangplows" before the man turned and mounted his horse. He went over to Hamp. "What do we want with gangplows?"

"We might as well be prepared." Hamp spoke flatly.

"For what?" Cowper frowned.

"In case you decide to fire, Mr. Starrett," said Hamp, "and it gets out of hand."

"Shall we put it to a vote?" Starrett asked. An irrational fury was mounting through him, shaking his voice.

"Whenever you say." Hamp drew on his cigarette, enjoying both the smoke and the situation.

Starrett suddenly stepped into him, slugging him in the face. Hamp went down and turned over, reaching for his gun. Starrett knelt quickly with a knee in the middle of his back and wrenched the gun away. He moved back, and as the foreman came up he sank a hard blow into his belly. Hamp went down and lay writhing.

"If you've got anything to say, say it plain!" Starrett shouted. "Don't be campaigning against me the way you did Tim Urban! Don't be talking them into quitting before we've started."

He was ashamed then, and stared angrily about him at the faces of the other men. Tim Urban did not meet his eyes. "We've pretty well started, Will," he said. "You've had our patience for thirty-six hours, and it's yours as long as you need it."

Cowper looked puzzled. He stood regarding Hamp with dismay.

After a moment Starrett turned away. "Let's go," he said.

Cowper said, "How long are we going to keep it up? Do you think we're getting anywhere?"

Starrett climbed to the wagon seat. "I'll make up my mind without help, Tom. When I do I'll let you know."

The sky was lighter than it had been in the morning, the floating continents of cloud leveled to an even gray. It was the last hope Starrett had had, and it was gone. But for the rest of the afternoon he worked and saw to it that everyone else worked. There was something miraculous in blind, headlong labor. It had built railroads and republics, had saved them from ruin, and perhaps it might work a miracle once more.

But by night the hoppers had advanced through their lines. The men headed forward to get out of the stinking mass.

Driving his wagon, Starrett was the last to go. He drove his squirming load of hoppers to the coulee and dumped it. Then he mounted to the seat of the wagon once more and sat there with the lines slack in his hands, looking across the hills. He was finished. The plague had advanced to the point from which a sudden strong wind could drive the hoppers onto Cowper's land before even fire could stop them.

He turned the wagon and drove to the new campfire blazing in the dusk. As he drove up, he heard an angry voice in staccato harangue. Hamp stood with a blazing juniper branch in his hand, confronting the other men. He had his back to Starrett and did not hear him at first.

"It's your land, but my living is tied to it just as much as yours. This has got to stop somewhere, and right here is as good a piece as any! He can't buck all of you."

Starrett swung down. "We're licked," he said. "I'm obliged to all of you for the help. Go home and get ready for your own fights."

Hamp tilted the torch down so that the flames came up greedily toward his hand. "I'm saying it plain this time," he said slowly. "We start firing here—not tomorrow, but now!"

"Put that torch down," Starrett said.

"Drop it, Bill!" Tom Cowper commanded.

Hamp thrust the branch closer. "Catch hold, Mr. Starrett. Maybe you'd like to toss the first torch."

Starrett said, "I'm saying that none of you is going to set fire to my land. None of you! And you've got just ten seconds to throw that into the fire!"

Bill Hamp watched him, smiled, and walked past the wagons into the uncleared field, into the golden bunchgrass. His arm went back and he flung the torch. In the same movement he pivoted and was ready for the man who had come out behind him. The flames came up behind Hamp like an explosion. They made a sound like a sigh. They outlined the foreman's hunched body and poured a liquid spark along the barrel of his gun.

Will Starrett felt a sharp fear as Hamp's gun roared. He heard a loud smack beside him and felt the wheel stir. Then his arm took the recoil of his own gun and he was blinded for an instant by the gun-flash. His vision cleared and he saw Hamp on his hands and knees. The man slumped after a moment and lay on his back.

Starrett walked back to the fire. The men stood exactly where they had a moment before, bearded, dirty, expressionless. Taking a length of limb-wood, he thrust it into the flames and roasted it until it burned strongly. Then he strode back, stopped by Hamp's body, and flung the burning brand out into the deep grass, beyond the area of flame where Hamp's branch had fallen.

He came back. "Load my wagon with the rest of this wood," he said, "and get out. I'll take care of the rest of it. Cowper, another of our customs out here is that employers bury their own dead."

Halfway home, he looked back and saw the flames burst across another ridge. He saw little winking lights in the air that looked like fireflies. The hoppers were ending their feast in a pagan fire-revel. There would not be enough of them in the morning to damage Lynn Cowper's kitchen garden.

He unsaddled. Physically and spiritually exhausted, he leaned his head against a corral bar and closed his eyes. It had been the only thing left to do, for a man who loved the land as he did. But it was the last sacrifice he could make, and no gun-proud bunch-grasser like Hamp could make it look like a punishment and a humiliation.

Standing there, he felt moisture strike his hand and angrily straightened. Tears! Was he that far gone?

Starting toward the house, he felt the drops on his face. Another drop struck, and another. Then the flood let loose and there was no telling where one drop ended and the other began, as the July storm fell from the sky.

Starrett ran back to the corral. A crazy mixture of emotions was in his head—fear that the rain had come too soon; joy that it came at all. He rode out to catch the others and enlist their aid in raking the hoppers into heaps and cremating them with rock-oil before they were able to move again.

He had not gone over a mile when the rain changed to hail. He pulled up under a tree to wait it out. He sat, a hurting in his throat. The hopper hadn't crawled out of the earth that could stand that kind of pelting. In its way, it was as miraculous as seagulls.

Another rider appeared from the darkness and pulled a winded, skittish horse into the shelter of the elm. It was Tom Cowper.

"Will!" he said. "This—this does it, doesn't it?"

"It does," Starrett replied.

Cowper said, "Have you got a dry smoke on you?"

Starrett handed him tobacco and papers. He smoked broodingly.

"Starrett," he said, "I'll be damned if I'll ever understand a man like you. You shot Hamp to keep him from setting fire to your grass—no, he's not dead—and then you turned right around and did it yourself. Now, what was the difference?"

Starrett smiled. "I could explain it, but it would take about twenty years, and by that time you wouldn't need it. But it's something about burying your own dead, I suppose."

Cowper thought about it. "Maybe you have something," he said. "Well, if I were a preacher I'd be shouting at the top of my voice now."

"I'm shouting," Starrett admitted, "but I'll bet you can't hear me."

After a while, Cowper said, "Why don't you come along

— 24 —

with me, when the hail stops? Lynn and her mother will be up. There'll be something to eat, and we can have a talk. That wouldn't be violating one of your customs, would it?"

"It would be downright neighborly," Starrett said.

River Magic

BEYOND the window the sky was murky with leaden clouds shot through with the rusty-red of dawn. Bud lay heavily on his bunk, in a purgatory of sleep in which he was neither able to slip into sound slumber nor to waken. The strain of his long hitch at the wheel still lay on him like a weight.

River sounds and river odors came into the cabin—marsh-damp and the mustiness of oily bilge; the clank of machinery. The threshing of the *Nancy Hanks'* paddles were vibrating through every timber of the boat.

Someone came briskly down the texas and rapped on the door. Linn's voice came with a cheerfulness unbecoming the hour.

"On deck, shanty-man! You're taking over."

Bud looked at the clock. "Say that again in four hours," he growled.

"We're tying up," said Linn. "There's a lantern on the shore."

This was news to catapult Bud out of bed and put him to pulling on trousers and shoes. A lantern on the shore meant a wreck or a customer. Either possibility was exciting.

When he reached the pilot-house, Captain Yancey had the wheel tied down and was leaning by an elbow on the sill of the open window, squinting down at the muddy water ahead of the packet. Bud twisted a ball of pinepitch from a chip in the wood-box and popped it into his mouth as he took the wheel. The boat was prying slowly through the mist toward a timbered point that guarded the mouth of a creek. A bull's-eye lantern flashed and dimmed as someone on the shore signaled.

"All right," Yancey said. "Where are we?"

Bud was ready for this. He had already noted the shape of the spit of land and the moss-draped cypress at the tip of it. "Beartrap Point," he said. "That's Oyster Creek ahead."

This was one spot on the river that he would not forget. Not since a stormy day a year ago, when he was still considered by the old river man unfit to pilot a dinghy. That was the day he hung the *Nancy* high and dry on a sandbar. It was the day he learned the difference between a true reef and a wind-reef.

"Think you can take her in and hold her there while I make a bargain with them?"

"I reckon."

Yancey glanced at him critically, then again at the drab panorama stretching ahead. He pointed.

"How do you make that race yonder?"

"Snag."

"How you going to handle her?"

Bud swung the wheel a bit to larboard, shifting his cud of pine-pitch.

"It's too deep to touch us. I'm going over her."

"You hope!" Captain Yancey grunted that, and digging in his coat pocket for his pipe, left the wheelhouse. Bud saw him presently making his way through the freight piled on the bow.

He did not realize that Linn, Yancey's daughter, was still in the cabin until he heard her behind him. She stopped by the wheel, pulling on an old gray cardigan. He saw her face reflected in the glass, and the quickening of his pulses was as natural in him as the hunger for food. Two years he had lived on the *Nancy*, and the thrill of Linn's presence was still a sharply hurting thing. Seeing the faint smile on her lips, Bud was immediately on the defensive. He had been baited by her too often not to know the signs. By all the laws of the river, hers was the whip-hand, and she used it freely.

"Seems like you took us in here once before," she remarked, watching her father make his way through the gloom to the prow of the boat.

"Seems like I did."

"Had a little trouble that time, didn't we? Something about a reef and a two-hundred-dollar bill to be pulled out of the mud."

"I'm paying for it, ain't I? I reckon I keep this old teakettle rolling pretty steady nowadays."

"I look for a blowed boiler any day now," Linn remarked. "You know what they say—'Once a shantyboater, always a shantyboater.'"

"Is that what they say? Well, what I say is, clear out of my cabin before I cut off your pretty little ears and feed 'em to the rousters."

Linn laughed. She reached past him, tugged one of the bell-pulls, and was gone. Bud swore under his breath and shouted into the speaking tube, canceling the signal that would have sent them backing into mid-stream.

He thought darkly: "All that stands between me and desertin' this teakettle is not having my papers. The day I get them, so help me Sam Clemens, I'm finding a boat where a pilot gets a man's wages and a man's consideration!"

But his heart knew he wouldn't leave the *Nancy* as long as they would have him. This decaying hulk meant, to him, the first happiness he could remember, the first approach to a man's estate he had known.

From below came the rattle of oarlocks. Out of the reeds bearding the shore nosed a small catboat with a single oars-man on the thwart. The man waved and shouted. Captain Yancey gave back the greeting. His lanky form turned.

"You, Bud! Head up and hold her."

Bud let the rower come alongside. Mr. Wortley, the mate, made fast the painter while the man clambered over the ragged hempen bumpers. Bud rang quarter-speed, so that the boat breasted the sluggish current gently.

The lantern ceased its flashing.

He was a sturdy little man in red-checked shirt, corduroy breeches and laced boots. From the wheelhouse, all Bud Webster could tell of his face was that it was very red, and that he wore tufted sideburns that hung down his jowls like rabbit's feet. His voice came clearly above the slosh of the waves.

"Good of you to stop, Captain," he said. "Boats are mighty scarce on the river these days."

"What's your business, Mister?" Yancey demanded. With him, every man was a process-server until proved innocent.

"Lumber's my business," the stranger said promptly. "I'm Amos Henry." There was a pause, as if he expected the Captain to be familiar with the name. "You seem to be pretty well loaded, Captain. Therefore I shan't ask the favor I intended to; but I shall ask another."

Henry tucked his hands flat under his belt, cocked his head to one side as he asked: "Would a thousand dollars interest you?"

Would it interest him! thought Bud. It would practically incapacitate him. There hadn't been a month when they had lost less than a hundred dollars in the last year.

"Well, sir," said Yancey, "I never went in much for bankrobbery and kidnaping; but what's your proposition?"

At this point Amos Henry produced cigars. The steamboat man accepted one, biting off and commencing to chew one half, and putting the other into his pocket. Henry lighted up.

"These are hard times, Captain. I reckon nobody's been much harder hit than the lumber man. I lost my own mill two years ago. I guess I should have learned my lesson then. But dammit, I aint! Just a week ago I bought the old

Oyster Creek sawmill, and I'm all set to go back into production!"

"Where you going to sell your lumber? The yards in N' Orleans are stacked to the rafters. Nobody's building any more."

"Correct. But unless I, and all the prognosticators in New York, are wrong, those yards will soon be putting out lumber faster than the mills can replace it! Hard times are easing up at last. The stock market is coming back. As a business man, Captain, you know what that means. Folks are going to start buying again—buying and building. And when they do, it will be the man on the job who feathers his nest."

"How does that concern us, Mr. Henry?" Linn asked him.

"Miss," said Amos Henry, "I've got the yard full of rotting, warping lumber. I can't saw any new stuff until I make room for it. It's in my mind to push the old stock fast, even if it means taking a sacrifice. Haul that lumber to New Orleans, folks, sell it for what you can get, and half the take is yours."

"What's it worth?" Yancey asked quickly.

"The best of it will bring two thousand anywhere. The rest—for a second boatload—is worth up to twelve hundred. Those are sacrifice prices, mind. Any yard will pay you that." He held the cigar out from his body and tapped the ash. "Well, Captain?"

Mr. Wortley interposed a mate's objection. He was a sober man with an eye that could weigh a trip of freight as accurately as a dockmaster's scales. He stood by the rail, switching his thigh with the frayed end of the painter.

"We're already loaded to the guards. How we going to carry any lumber?"

"I can wait until you finish your trip and come back. Naturally, I can't guarantee that I won't proposition the next boat that comes along, too. But you've got a headstart, and it should bring you in first."

There was a silence; then Linn saying: "Why not, Pop? At the worst, we'd only be out our fuel."

Henry nodded. "That's right, miss. The old saw don't hold this time—nothing ventured, plenty gained!"

In the end, Captain Yancey could only put out his hand and seal the bargain. Henry shook it warmly, returned to his boat and pulled away. The mastiff-like features of Mr. Wortley, who was constitutionally opposed to optimism, remained glum.

Presently Linn and the Captain came up with a pot of coffee from the galley. Linn poured three cups. While the boat swung about and headed downstream, Yancey found a pencil and paper and began to figure.

"We can clear up all our debts as far down as Ironwood Bend," he announced. "Then we can get in on the fall freight at Cairo and Memphis. Be the first time I've looked the dockmaster at Memphis in the eye for two years!"

Yancey had a theory about loans: spread 'em out thin. That way, nobody got the hooks into you to the point where it was worth his trouble to foreclose. This plan of his had kept the *Nancy* in his name much longer than he had dared hope. But of late he had a feeling that some of his creditors up and down the river might be getting their heads together. For this reason he made his visits to the larger and more profitable towns extremely hurried.

"Yes sir!" said Yancey, leaning back in his chair and beginning to grin. "They'll soon be telling it like they used to—'Old Yancey's got the best pilots and the worst temper on the Mississipp'!'"

"Hard times never took the pepper out of your temper any," said Linn.

"But you'll grant the quality of my pilots aint increased," Yancey said, as though Bud were deaf or insensible to sarcasm. He gulped down the rest of his coffee and stood up. "Better catch some sleep, son," he said. "You'll be taking her into town tonight."

Bud's knuckles whitened on the spokes. He slipped the tie-down in place, and standing by the door, paused to ask: "Sure you aint taking too much of a risk, letting me pilot her into the harbor?"

Yancey looked surprised. "Why, you'll make out. Done it before, aint you?"

Bud's irony had gone far wide of its mark. He went out full of helpless rage. He heard Linn's laughter as he headed down the texas. He went into his cabin and slammed the door. But there was a darkness in him that was not all rancor. He knew that if Captain Yancey ever got a few hundred dollars ahead, he would get himself a lightning pilot quicker than an engineer's striker could center his engine. Men like Bill Trayner and Eli Hogg were a dime a dozen these days. You could get any of them for seventy-five a week.

The only thing that kept Bud Webster on the *Nancy* was that two years ago he had paid Yancey three hundred dollars to teach him piloting. Yancey couldn't fire him for a year without breaking their contract. But while there was security in knowing this there was no salve for a badly lacerated ego.

CHAPTER TWO

During the day black thunder-clouds rumbled across the green bottom-lands, and a wind came up. A cold rain was falling when the little stern wheeler warped in to the dock at New Orleans. In the dingy light of the fading September day she looked as bedraggled and spiritless as a wet dog.

On the freight-deck, rousters were gathering among the boxes and bales. It was just as Bud turned from the wheel that the shout came through the drumming of rain on the roof.

"Captain Yancey aboard?"

Yancey and Linn looked at each other with the alarm of those whose apocalypse includes a process-server. But it was Bud whose face showed the shock of a man who has stepped into an open cistern in the dark.

Yancey glanced cautiously out the window. Then he got the mate on the speaking-tube.

"Who is it, Ed?" he asked.

"Dunno, but he's no process-server. All duded up like a duke or somebody."

"All right. Send him up."

Presently the man who stood on the landing stage waved and came aboard. They heard him ascending the companion-way past the freight-deck, the main-deck, the hurricane. Just as the man started up the short flight to the glassed-in wheel-house, Bud Webster opened the door to the foredeck and stepped out. There was a look in his eyes like that in the face of a man who has been slugged hard over the heart. His legs were rubbery, as though the world were crumbling under him. And indeed, a very elaborate papier-mâché world was about to melt down into the lies of which he had constructed it. He sat against the wall, where he could hear without being seen.

The man who came into the cabin was obviously not of the river. He had the appearance of a great lump of flesh done up in wet gray broadcloth. He wore black button shoes and a fine silk shirt with a black stock; a gray beaver hat was thrust under his coat for protection from the rain. He took it out now and held it with a certain elegance in the crook of his arm. He produced a card from his pocket, and tendered it toward the pair standing by the great walnut wheel.

Ignoring it, Yancey said: "What's on your mind, Mister?"

"The name is Webster," the stranger said tartly. "Mr. Julius Barlow sends his regards."

Rancor came quickly to Yancey's eyes and he snapped: "Sure it aint a subpoena he sends?"

"As a matter of fact—" The fat man's hand went under the lapel of his box coat and emerged holding a folded document. He did not attempt to give it to the Captain, but tossed it on the table.

Captain Yancey snorted, unimpressed. "Scum! Why don't he come to a man and ask for his money?"

Webster said dryly: "I understand he has employed that device on a number of occasions without success."

"You can tell old Flint-eye Barlow," Yancey retorted doggedly, "that I'll be down tomorrow morning with his money, every last penny. If he thinks he can get the *Nancy* for a paltry three hundred—"

"I'm sure Mr. Barlow has no such notion," said Webster. "He is too shrewd a business man."

Yancey grabbed the subpoena. "Then what in Tophet is he subpoenaing me for?"

"If you will trouble yourself to glance at the paper," said Webster, "you will find Mr. Barlow's name does not appear at all. When I said he sent his regards, I meant just that. If you care to repay that long-outstanding loan, Captain Yancey, make the check payable to me. Mr. Barlow has had his money from me; I will have mine from you."

Captain Yancey, glancing at the document, suddenly emitted a choked sound. "Fifteen hundred!" he exclaimed, and peered closely at Webster. "Mister, what kind of trading is this?"

"You might," said Webster, looking very steadily into the steamboat man's eyes, "call it sharp trading. But no sharper than borrowing pittances up and down the river with no intention of ever repaying them!"

Linn said, "Pop!" and held Yancey by the arm. To Webster she said coldly: "I guess you don't know river folks, Mr.

Webster. You don't call them thieves if you value the set of your nose."

Webster's big shoulders shrugged. "Young woman, I don't care what you and your father call it. The fact remains, this kind of business borders on larceny. However, I have no intention of preferring charges. I am here to tell you that you have until midnight to raise the sum of those loans. Mr. Barlow's is only one of fifteen which I now hold."

"How'd you get them notes?" Yancey's voice betrayed uncertainty.

The fat man smiled. "I have—connections, Captain Yancey. It has taken some little time, of course, to track the loans down. But I believe I now hold the bulk of your notes."

Linn said sharply: "You're no river man. I'll bet you've never seen a stern-wheeler before. Why did you put yourself to all that trouble for a broken-down scow like this?"

Webster smiled. "You are a discerning young woman. Once more, may I offer my card?"

Linn read the little white square of pasteboard, and her eyes widened. "*Budford Quincy Webster II.*" Below the name, in discreet copperplate letters, "*Investments—Bonds—Securities. 74 Wall Street.*" She said suddenly: "Budford Quincy—you wouldn't be any relation of Bud Webster that left this cabin just a minute ago?"

"He happens," said Webster, "to be my son."

"But he aint braggin' on it!"

They turned, all of them, to see him standing in the doorway. There was fury in his eyes, and the turn of his mouth was sour. He looked older than his twenty-one years, and somehow desperate.

"So you found me," he said. "But it took you two years."

Webster champed his jaws like a bulldog. "You were followed every foot of the way. I chose not to come after you until you'd had a taste of the freedom you thought you wanted."

"I've had it," Bud said, "and I'm likin' it."

Yancey was suddenly yanking his greasy leather cap down on his brow and striding across the room. "Come along, girl. I'll see what Lawyer Reddey has to say about this kind of shenanigan."

Hesitating, Linn kept her eyes on Bud. Tears began to well in them. "At least we know he smelled out every note within eight hundred miles!" she said.

She turned to follow Yancey, but Bud was there with his hand on her arm. "I lied to you, Linn—all the way. But I had my reasons."

Linn did not turn her head, but her blonde hair tossed as she struck off his hand. "Did you think I didn't know you were lying from the day you came along with your wild story about being a down-and-out shanty-man? Your story had more holes than a sieve. I knew you were lying—but I guessed wrong about the reason."

Captain Yancey took Linn's arm, and she ran ahead of him down the stairs. Yancey's face was the last they saw of him as he disappeared down the stairway.

"I'll be back, Webster. And if I was you, you young mollycoddle's whelp, I wouldn't be within pistol range when I come in sight!"

With his departure, Bud and his father were left face to face, hostility lying like a chalk-line between them. Bud looked on him in contempt, seeing all the little trademarks of artificiality and power for which he despised the older man and the world he represented; the eyes incisive and suspicious, jowls padded and vein-shot from too easy living; and he was thinking of how they had tried to press him into the same mold.

Webster's mouth began to smile petulantly. "Well, boy,"

he said, "haven't you got a handshake and a hello for your dad?"

"Hello," Bud said dully.

Webster wagged his head. "A fine way to greet your father," he said. "I thought you would have got rid of some of those idiotic fancies of yours by now. After all, I've given you two years to get over them."

"Given me! I had to run away from New York to get them."

"Pah! I knew where you were, a month after you got to New Orleans."

Bud's eyes expressed his doubt. "You had no money," Webster stated. "All you had in your name was a few bonds. You cashed them in Nashville. Through a banker there, I traced you down the river. I've had regular reports on you ever since."

"As though I were on parole, eh?" In the brown hardness of his face, Bud's gray eyes were hostile.

"Call it whatever you like. It was for your own good." From a silver cigar-case Webster extracted a cigar. He snipped the end with a cutter depending from his watch-chain. Lighting it, he puffed a gray cloud of smoke about his head.

"I trust by now you're ready to come home and take your place in my organizaton. I have permitted you to waste two good years of your life because I knew you had to sweat this foolishness out of your system."

Bud looked at him with a sort of curiosity, not entirely hostile. "Why is it you can't keep your hands off other people's lives? Don't your bank and Lord-knows-how-many other businesses keep you busy enough?"

"In your case, Budford, I concern myself because I know what's best for you. Are you coming back with me or not?"

"I'm staying here — on the river."

"You're being a damned young idiot!" Webster snapped. He threw the cigar at the wall. Breathing hard, he glared at his son. Then he said, sourly: "Frankly, I expected this. And that is why I bought the boat. If staying on the river is what you want, I shall at least have the satisfaction of seeing you set up right before I leave. I'll have her entirely refitted and put in shape so that she can hold her own with anything on the river."

"That's great," said the younger Webster. "But it looks like you'll have to run the *Nancy* yourself. I'm going with Captain Yancey."

He slapped on his greasy leather cap and walked to the door. Webster barked after him:

"He won't have you! You know as well as I do that with licensed pilots going begging, no other boat in New Orleans will hire you!"

"We'll talk about that when he comes back," said Bud. "I'll be down in the texas where I can hear you hit the floor when he breaks your jaw."

CHAPTER THREE

Lamps came on in the steamboats that lay placidly, like stalled horses, in their slips along the Canal Street wharves. Bud Webster ate no dinner. He sat in his cabin, his telescope bag already packed, ears tuned to the sound of footfalls on the landing-stage.

It was after nine when he heard someone board the boat and mount to the hurricane. He went out and saw Linn hurrying up the deck. She did not notice him until he stepped into her path and demanded: "Where's Yancey?"

Linn tried to pass him, but Bud caught her by the shoulders and turned her so that the light from a street lamp was on her face, and then he saw that she was crying.

"We've lost the *Nancy*!" He blurted it out without realizing that "*we*" no longer meant the same thing to both of them.

She said, trying to control her voice: "No; you've just won the *Nancy*, Captain Webster!"

The title was sacrilege. "You're being a fool," he told her. "If Yancey's lost the boat, I'm going with him—wherever he goes. He's got a year to go on that contract. Where is he?"

"Right now he's probably at the Chateau Rouge; an hour ago he signed on as skipper of the *Island Belle*."

Bud stared. "That's a Blue Chimney boat!"

"But not a rival any more. The *Nancy Hanks* is our rival. Pop's on salary again. It should do a lot for him."

She brushed by him. Bud followed.

"Pack your things," he said. "I'll find Yancey's gear and go back with you. That old hoot-owl will listen to me if I have to hang him from the jackstaff."

They could see Yancey up in the cabin of the giant Blue Chimney boat when they came down the cobbled street an hour later. His scarecrow form was motionless beside the wheel. Just before they reached the landing-stage Bud stopped. He set down the bags and took Linn's from her, placing them on the wharf.

"Maybe you aren't interested," he said, "but you're going to listen to me for a minute: In the first place, I'm going to tell you about Budford Q. Webster, III. When you've got 'Third' after your name, you're apt to do a lot of funny things. Telling you I was a down-and-out shantyboater trying to learn a trade was just one of them I did.

"They've been trying to make a tycoon out of me ever since I could walk. Just because a Webster once made a fortune supplying the Revolutionary army with shoes, it's sort of become a habit with Webster men to make fortunes. I guess I'm a throwback. I like to hunt and fish and loaf, and to do hard work with my hands.

"Nobody's going to plant me behind a desk and say: 'Now, make money the way your dad did. Buy a railroad or something.' I got my craw full of that one day, and I left. I bummed my way down the Ohio. That's when I found out that I've got that scummy river water in my blood.

"I don't ever want to leave the river, Linn—even if I wind up broke and disgusted like your dad. Out here, a pilot's judged by how sharp his eyes are and how long his memory is, and how he stands up against trouble. Whether he's the 'Third' or the 'Tenth' doesn't make any difference to anybody but the census-taker."

Then he stopped for a breath.

"Linn, I—I want you to marry me!"

It came out so unexpectedly that she started. "Marry you—why?"

"Well—because I love you, for one thing. They tell me that's the best reason." He reached for her hands, but she put them quickly behind her.

"When I marry, it won't be a second-rate pilot's cub," she said distantly. "And it won't be a molly-coddle, either. It will be a man other river men will be proud to know. I guess that doesn't include you, Captain Webster."

Bud's eyes grew dark with anger. Linn marched across the gangplank onto the *Island Belle*. Bud muttered: "We'll see about *that*."

In the companionway he shouldered past her. He mounted to the wheelhouse. In the well-lighted cabin there was no sign of Yancey, but the door to the foredeck was open.

Bud found him there, leaning upon the rail enjoying a final evening's pipe. Yancey glanced over his shoulder. Then he laid his pipe carefully on the rail and straightened. From his bone-rack six-feet-three he looked down stolidly at the younger man.

"Listen to me, Yancey," said Bud. "I had nothing to do with what my dad has done. He followed me here. And I've quit him."

Still the old boatman had nothing to say. Bud felt his courage leaking but he went on:

"I'm sticking with you and Linn. Will you sign me on as second pilot?"

"No!"

"But Yancey, it's to your advantage! Why, if we pool our money—"

"Is that all you came here to say?"

The iron suddenly went out of Bud. The Midas-touch of his father might turn lead to gold, but of the worthwhile things, it made brass. "That's all," he said.

"Then," said Yancey, "this is what I've got to say to you."

He had Bud by the neck, suddenly, and his long arm was coming around like a loading-boom. His open palm exploded against the side of Bud Webster's head, and for the pilot's cub, the world became a slow pinwheel of stanchions, stars in a black sky, the tall stacks of near-by boats, and finally a sheen of dirty water reflecting the sky. He had a breathless sense of falling, which ended in blackness and cold and a roaring.

He came up struggling, freezing cold. The oily taste of the harbor was on his tongue. His clothes clung to him as he trod water, sputtering. A black hulk rose close beside him—the fantail of the *Island Belle*. He looked about and discerned the wharf.

He was conscious of no particular emotion until he stood shivering on the dock. Then a fury, born of his own misery and the laughter of the rousters, filled him. He felt the need of throwing that fury into action; a bale of cotton being the thing nearest him, he kicked it, and to the increased merriment of the laborers, walked off into the darkness. From the height of the *Belle's* wheelhouse he heard Yancey's roaring laughter.

Chapter Four

At breakfast Bud sat across from his father at a table in the empty saloon. The elder Webster had a critical eye for the mildewed tokens of the boat's former grandeur. The gilt mirrors had tarnished, and the crystal chandeliers had not known a dust-rag in ten years. There were worn spots in the red plush carpet. A single colored waiter took the place of the white-jacketed parade of yesteryear.

The years had not been kind to the *Nancy*. They had warped her planks and cracked her paint, rusted her towering chimneys until at night they glowed like incandescent screens. Newer, bigger river queens had relegated her to the position of a dowager. But Captain Yancey had always maintained that, given the proper pilots and engineers, he could still beat anything on the river.

Webster said presently: "I judge I was right. Yancey wouldn't have you. Not that you can blame him. That funnel outfit will give him the best pilots in New Orleans, and they won't cost him a cent. What are you going to do now?"

"Stay with the *Nancy Hanks*. Nobody will hire me without papers. At least, I'll still be on the river." His gaze went disconsolately through the window and along the docks to where the last of the *Island Belle's* cargo was being back-and-bellied aboard by the roustabouts.

His father leaned by one elbow on the table. "Why be pigheaded, son? Why not come back with me, let me fix you up in a little business of some kind?"

"Do we have to go through that again? You've spoon-fed me for the last time. I wouldn't be aboard if I thought I could land any other job."

"This," sighed Webster, "is the most idiotic of a long train of idiotic notions. But as long as you are determined to stay, you will of course act as my Captain."

"Captain!" snorted Bud. "A man that's only been on the river two years isn't fit to captain a gravy-boat."

"Is there anything criminal in being the youngest Captain on the river—so long as you know your business?"

"I don't."

"Then why in heaven's name do you want to stay?"

Bud looked out the window, trying to find an answer to the question. He said thoughtfully: "Well, you might call it romance—"

Webster's small blue eyes narrowed. "Ha! I *thought* that girl was ninety percent of the trouble."

Bud shrugged. "Well, she's part of it, I suppose. I asked her to marry me last night. She turned me down, of course." He chewed his lip, scowling. "Caste system. Here as everywhere. If I were a pilot, now— But that's not the kind of romance I meant. I'm thinking of the smells and the sounds; the heat and the cold. Of the way the river talks to you at night, whispering the way a girl would whisper in your ear. And I'm thinking about the times when you float along for weeks and it seems as though you're God Himself, just sitting up on a cloud watching the world struggle along."

His eyes began to burn. "And races! I don't guess you ever heard of the *Natchez*. Beat the *Princess* from New Orleans to Natchez in seventeen hours and eleven minutes. That's steamboating!"

Webster chewed a cigar. "Now that I've heard of it, I don't see where the owner was a dollar richer for possessing the faster boat."

Bud leaned back. "You might be interested to know that the *Natchez* carried more freight than any other boat on the river of her time, just because she got there first. Prestige and speed—that's what you make your money on."

Webster clamped his jaws together. "Now, that makes some sense. When do they have these races?"

"They don't 'have' them. They happen. As a matter of fact—" He pointed out the window. "See those barrels going aboard the *Island Belle*? That's rosin. Yancey's aiming to be first to the dock at Oyster Creek, in case anybody else has got wind of the pay-haul up there. Somebody stands to make an easy thousand on a load of lumber."

Webster's fingers began to drum on the tablecloth. "Is there anything to prevent us from beating him there?"

"Nothing in particular. Only that he's got a better boat. And that he's ready to start and we aren't."

Webster stood up, the old lure of easy money putting a flush in his cheeks. "Then why aren't we getting up steam?" he demanded. His finger stabbed at Bud. "I'll tell you what, boy—I've a mind to run this thing myself a few trips! I calculate I could make a profit out of a raft with an old shirt for a sail!"

Bud Webster's eyes sparkled with a wholly wicked light. "Now, *there*," he nodded, "is an idea! I'll run down to the fuel yard and get a load of rosin. Tell the engineer to touch 'em off."

He was at the door when his father's voice stayed him. "Make that half a load of rosin. I'll show you how to operate at a fraction of what that pigheaded old fool has been spending!"

The *Island Belle* was already in mid-channel when he returned with a flat-bed wagon loaded with rosin. Mr. Wortley watched in silence as the deck-hands rolled the barrels aboard. Leaning against a stanchion, he picked his wide-spaced square teeth with a splinter, his eyes puzzled. As Bud passed he removed his greasy cap and scratched his head.

"What's the rosin for—somebody's fiddle?"

"That's to get us to Oyster Creek before the *Island Belle*."

"Kinda skimpy, ain't it?"

"Maybe so."

Mr. Wortley spoke in a manner at once severe and fatherly.

"Listen to me, young feller. I don't know how it is with you and your dad, but I know how it is 'twixt you and me. You may be Captain of this tub, but to me you're still a third-rate pilot's cub that don't know shoal water from the deep sea."

Bud grinned. "Thanks for those kind words, Ed."

Mr. Wortley covered his surprise with a scowl. "They aint meant overkind," he pointed out. "I'm telling you two things, and you hark to 'em. First, I'm ready to quit the minute things don't go to suit me. Second place, wiser heads than yours have tried to figure how to cut operatin' costs on a stern-wheeler, and they've lost thousands saving pennies. That's what you're fixin' to do."

"No, Ed. My father's running this boat, as owner, Captain and underwriter. I'm still the third-rate pilot you mentioned. Between you and me, I don't think he'll last a month. Stick around. If you happen to have twenty-five or thirty dollars on hand, I reckon you can buy the *Nancy* from him and have enough left for a drink!"

A puzzled man, Mr. Wortley watched him go aloft.

Bud found his father pacing the floor. He had his coat off, and there were dark patches under the arms of his pleated white shirt. "Is this how we win races?" he demanded. "If that Blue Chimney boat is as fast as she's supposed to be, we're whipped already."

Bud took down the speaking-tube and shouted into the wide brass mouth: "Let's have some smoke!" He scanned the channel from the rear windows. Standing beside the wheel, he answered his father without looking at him.

"We'll take her before we make Barlow Light. The *Nancy's* faster in quiet water any day. After the current goes to work on us, it'll be different. We'll need all the steam the boilers will hold."

The *Nancy* got in motion slowly, like a rheumatic old crone resentful at being moved from her fireside. Through the clanking of rods and chow-chowing of the engines, a shout came up to the pilot-house.

"Room for another, *Nancy Hanks*?"

They looked down at a dapper figure on the wharf, clad in checked trousers, a belted brown coat and a Panama hat. The man was pointing a cane up at the wheelhouse.

"Take you as far as Oyster Creek," Bud called down.

"That'll help! Only going to Red Church. I'll pay twenty dollars."

Bud stopped the boat. His father swore in exasperation.

"If we lose this race, it will mean more than twenty dollars to us! Tell him to find another boat."

"You don't pass up twenty dollars' gravy on this river. Not these times."

But before they had reached Barlow Light, Bud was wishing he had let the stranger flag another boat. There was something about the man that put his temper on edge; something that whispered, "Fake!" from the moment he entered the cabin with his hand extended, announcing: "I'm Ward Sloan, gentlemen. Pleased to meet you."

In the brief glance Bud allowed himself from the river traffic he noted chiefly the man's busy bright eyes. They hugged the bridge of a beak nose that dominated a protruding lower lip. He had his Panama on the back of an almost completely bald head. He sat down on the creaking sofa and began to roll a cigarette.

"Oyster Creek, you said?" he remarked presently.

Bud did not answer, having given himself over to studying the dirty-brown wake of the *Island Belle*. He heard his father's grudging: "Yes. And fast."

Sloan chuckled. "Everybody's in a hurry these days, grubbing to turn an honest dollar—or otherwise."

"Which kind you out to turn?" Bud asked, not entirely in humor.

Ward Sloan laughed. "As honest as the times permit. I'm a lumber buyer, myself."

The elder Webster paused in the midst of lighting a cigar. "Lumber, eh? As a matter of fact, we're in something of the same business this trip. If we can nose out that packet, yonder, we stand to make a neat profit when we reach Oyster Creek."

"You boasting old fool!" thought Bud. *"Do you have to spill our business to everybody?"*

Sloan said, with excessive carelessness: "Freight rates must have gone up."

Bud listened in enraged silence while his father outlined the whole plan. "Maybe," he said acidly, "we could sell our lumber to you, Mr. Sloan. You look like a gullible sort."

"Maybe you could, at that." Sloan placed himself at a front window, watching the gap shorten between the big Blue Chimney boat and the little stern-wheeler. "I buy for Shippen Brothers, in Little Rock. There's big things a-doing in Little Rock since they opened up Oklahoma Territory. We're selling all the lumber we can buy to settlers traveling west. Maybe you can just drop me and your lumber off at the Arkansas and we'll both turn a good profit!"

"You're travelin' light," Bud said, "for a buyer that's just left New Orleans."

"Pshaw! Them blockhead woodmen of yours think their planks are gold plated. I couldn't pay them what they ask, freight my lumber to Little Rock, and sell at under forty-five a thousand feet. I heard of a little mill operating above Red Church. That's where I'm headed now."

"What do you pay a thousand?" asked Webster.

Sloan turned from the dun vista to smile at the other. "Suppose we wait till I see what kind of lumber you're selling."

"And suppose you both wait until we see whether we beat the *Island Belle* to the dock!" Bud snapped.

CHAPTER FIVE

Ahead, so close that they could hear her roustabouts singing and see the sparkling waterfall of her threshing paddles, the *Belle* went majestically into the full sweep of the river. Great clouds of black smoke vomited from her twin chimneys, bearing downwind upon the *Nancy Hanks*. Glistening curls of water rolled off her bullrails like milk-chocolate lathe-turnings. She was in her element now, and nothing but a blown drum would slow her down.

Webster stood beside the gleaming walnut wheel, measuring the distance between the boats. "I thought you said we'd take her before we passed the Light," he scowled.

"I didn't figure on Yancey pouring in the pitch by the bucket this early. We haven't got enough to try to match him."

"But if he gets away from us now," Webster complained, "we may never catch him."

Bud yanked the speaking-tube down. "Give me some more steam!" he shouted. To his father he said: "We can't keep it up, but it'll be a pretty race while it lasts; I hope that's what you want."

Beneath their feet the clanking of busy pitmans stepped up its tempo. The little *Nancy* shook like a dog casting off water and began to move ahead. On the head, the rousters were suddenly within insulting distance of those on the Blue Chimney boat's stern. Passengers clustered the river queen's decks to watch the down-at-heels freight boat draw alongside.

Now Bud could see the men in the *Island Belle's* pilot-house, looming fifteen feet above them. He thought he recognized Mark Patmore at the wheel, a name among pilots, in his gray beaver stovepipe and Prince Albert. He discerned Yancey's visage behind the glass, and then, with a tug at his heart, saw Linn.

He waved at her, trying to make it look light-hearted, and she waved back. But his heart was all gray inside, because this wasn't the way it should be at all: Yancey a hireling; Yancey beaten, going into old age with defeat mocking him. And him fighting Yancey instead of working with him.

It wasn't right with him and Linn, either. She should be at his side, ribbing him for letting a lubberly ark like the *Belle* show him her pintles. Nothing would have lifted his heavy soul more than to have her remind him of how he had scraped a sawyer or a sandbar the last time they passed this way; because it was in Bud's mind that she only wore this sarcastic armor of hers to keep him from knowing that it was the same with her as it was with him.

Bud Webster sighed and put his gaze back on the river. To the eternal shame of his pilot's soul, he didn't care whether he won the race or lost it. Not defeat, and not victory, would give him back Linn, and Yancey, and the old, threadbare, beautiful days on the *Nancy Hanks*.

Through that morning and into the afternoon, it was head down and wheel up. The *Island Belle* plowed regally up the wind-ruffled, beaten-brass river of midafternoon, her powerful cross-compound engines hammering away, bright-work flashing and white paint gleaming like porcelain. The *Nancy* puffed and panted along, holding together despite a beating such as she had not taken in fifteen years.

Once Captain Yancey leaned out the window as they wallowed along, bull-rail to bull-rail. "A hundred dollars you don't, Webster!"

Budford Q. Webster's florid cheeks purpled as he thrust his head out a window. "A hundred I do!"

"Done!" There was the sound of loud laughter aboard the *Belle*.

From the door, Wortley drawled: "I'll just take another hundred of your money, Captain."

Webster confronted him. "What do you mean?"

"I mean we just finished our rosin. We got two ricks of wood left, and then we stop at a wood-yard."

Webster's blotchy face worked. "I suppose that would mean we'd lost."

"I suppose it would."

Webster let himself into a chair. He put a cigar in his mouth and chewed on it, looking at his feet with two deep creases between his eyes. Abruptly he crushed the cigar in his hand and threw it at the wall.

"Well, haven't one of you smart riverboat men got a suggestion?" he demanded.

"I've got one," Bud remarked. "But it'll cost you money."

"Damn the expense!"

"All right. We've got a lot of good lumber right in front of our eyes. Look at that hurricane decking! Soaked with linseed. There's a cord and a half or better, right there."

Mr. Wortley's mouth slowly fell open. But Webster was on his feet with a grunt. "Put a crew on it with pry-bars! Have it sawed up and carried below. I'll show that blue-chimneyed washtub!"

The mate's hand was firm on the door-knob, as if for support. "Yes sir," he said. "And it might be a good idea to put the whisky bucket out for the firemen. They're plumb done in."

"Put it out, then," Webster said. "And send up a bottle for me. They're no more done in than I am!"

Now and again, as a crew of Negroes ripped up the planking, Bud stole a glance at the other boat. Passengers and crew gazed in astonishment. They began to understand, when the smaller boat slowly hammered out a lead of a hundred feet. This was the signal for increased belching of smoke by the packet, for heavier bow-waves to spill aside as she took up the slack.

When the *Island Belle* was nearly abreast, Webster grabbed the speaking-tube. "They aren't to pass us again, Mr. Wortley! See to it, if we have to burn up all but the wheel and the paddles."

The effect of this order was apparent when the wrecking crew appeared on the after-deck and began to tear up the texas. Down came the once-elegant crew's quarters, with the oil-paintings on the doors.

Webster began to pace the floor, stopping once to scan the river. "How much farther?" he demanded.

"Maybe six miles," Bud told him. "If we can hold them until we reach the creek, we've won. It's another mile to the mill, but there isn't room for a catfish to pass, once we're on Oyster Creek."

Ward Sloan had come up after dinner to get a pilot's-eye view of the race. Sitting on the lumpy sofa, he worked at his teeth with a gold toothpick.

"Be a fine show of gratitude," he chuckled, "if I was to buy that lumber right out from under you after we make the mill!"

Webster's eye was cold. "It would be a fine way, sir, for you to buy a punch in the nose."

Sloan laughed.

Suddenly Bud said: "There she is!"

Webster's fat hands gripped the window-sill. Sloan bounced to the window to stare with him. The familiar spit of sand, with its lone moss-draped cypress, indicated the mouth of Oyster Creek. From the *Island Belle* came a prolonged, hoarse whistle—one long note, two shorts, another long.

"That's their victory toot," Bud said.

Webster's face was moist; his eyes came to Bud in worried puzzlement. "But we're still ahead! They can't pass us now."

"They don't have to. They've got the inside track. I can't cross ahead of them. We'd foul them."

Webster's mouth twitched as though he were about to become sick. He looked forward, at the wreckage of the hurricane deck; he looked aft at the pile of rubble where the texas had stood. He looked up at Captain Yancey, who was leaning out the pilot-house window and shouting something that the whistle jumbled.

For the space of time it takes a match to burn, there was gloomy silence aboard the *Nancy*. Then, imperceptibly at first, the pulse of the gallant old boat began to quicken. Her bow lifted. The jets of steam from her 'scape-pipes merged into a solid plume. The Blue Chimney boat began to slide back.

There was no more whistling. The *Nancy Hanks* had been giving her all a moment before; she was giving something more than that now.

Webster glanced at his son for explanation, but the answer was not there: Bud was as puzzled as he. It was Ed Wortley, coming into the wheelhouse just then, who supplied the answer.

"Doing right nice, aint she? I was holding back a few buckets of rosin against a rainy day. I've got the safety-valve tied down and the drums a-groanin' with blue ruin!" He sat down and lighted his pipe. "I reckon," he said, "she'll just about do it."

Down on the head the rousters were delirious. There was desperation aboard the *Island Belle*. Only a hundred yards to go, and the smaller boat was set to swing across the moment she had clearance. Too late now for a last-minute spurt: A lady of the *Belle's* proportions did not indulge in such antics.

Bud looked back, gauging the moment when he could cross. Thirty seconds, he reckoned, would do it. At the point of

turning away, he saw Captain Yancey running up the hurricane deck, Linn behind him. He grinned, guessing the reason. He swung a bit to larboard, so that the bull-rails of the
two boats almost touched.

Yancey's scarecrow form came flying across the space
between them. Right behind him jumped Linn. They came
pounding up the stairs just as Bud Webster swung the wheel
and pointed up Oyster Creek.

Yancey stood there in the door with the fires of hell burning in his eyes.

"What kind of steamboatin' is this?" he charged. "You've
done twice the damage that winning the race will pay for!"

"May I point out, nevertheless," said Webster, "that we
bested you. I believe that was the object of the race." On his
fat lips was a smug smile.

Yancey turned away in disgust. He stood at a window and
watched the Blue Chimney boat swing off toward mid-channel. Bud knew his father had touched the quick: Yancey
would have burned the boat to the water's edge to win.

"Well, that finishes that," Yancey growled to Linn. "I'm
finished as far as captaining anybody's boat goes. Losing a
race and deserting all in the same day!"

Amos Henry, the red-faced lumber man, came panting up
the companionway the instant the *Nancy Hanks* was snubbed
against the spiles of the Oyster Creek mill dock.

"You look like you'd been running the Confederate lines,
Captain," he exclaimed. "I didn't mean you should tear your
boat to pieces to get back on time."

"Talk to Webster," Yancey growled. "The only interest I've
got in the boat now is a fatherly one. I've sold out."

"We had a bit of trouble," Webster admitted. "But I calculate we can still take care of your lumber nicely. I'm the new
owner of this craft."

Henry rubbed his hands. He said: "Fine, fine! I'll make

you the same proposition I made Captain Yancey — one-half of what you sell the lumber for."

Ward Sloan's unpleasant voice came into the conversation. "Would you be interested in a cash deal, Mr. Henry? Say, fifteen dollars a thousand feet?" He stood there confidently, his hat on the back of his head and his thumbs under his suspenders.

"See here!" That was Webster, facing Sloan angrily. "The arrangement is already closed. I'll have no pip-squeak buyer horning in on me."

"Anything written passed between you?" Sloan asked Henry.

Bud saw the delight in Yancey's face. Budford Q. Webster was being bested by a small-time tinhorn after doing two thousand dollars' damage to his boat to bring him here — and there was nothing he could do about it!

"Well —" Amos Henry rubbed his chin, tugged at a tufted sideburn. "Nothing downright binding, I reckon. Fifteen aint too bad. Cash in-hand, of course?"

"Of course!" Sloan had his check book out and was looking for a pen.

"Mr. Henry!" Webster thundered. "Do you realize I have all but ruined my boat to do you this favor? And now you want to back out!"

"Business is business, Mr. Webster. If you care to pay me the cash yourself, naturally, I'll give you preference."

"And take the risk of being stuck with your accursed lumber?" Webster watched in white-lipped fury as Sloan tendered the check to the lumber man.

Ward Sloan had his right hand in his coat pocket, casually, and he smiled brazenly into the other's eyes as the money changed hands. Then he made a move as unexplainable as it was swift. His hand flashed from his pocket and came down on Henry's wrist. There was a click. Amos Henry stared at the manacle on his wrist as the buyer snapped the other about his own.

"I suppose this is a joke," he said nervously. "If so, it's extremely ill-timed. Will you kindly take that thing off?"

Sloan flashed a marshal's star beneath his coat lapel. "Now, now, Mr. Henry! That wouldn't be sensible, would it, after me chasing you up and down the river for six months?"

Into Henry's voice edged a whining desperation. "Why should you chase me? I've done nothing but mind my own business."

"Yes, but such a business! You ought to be ashamed—using men like good Captain Webster as cat's-paws to sell lumber that wasn't yours."

"You mean he doesn't own this mill?" Webster asked.

"No more than he did the other four mills I've traced him through. He's caused more trouble in these inactive yards than a ton of termites. Now then, if you've got a cabin still standing somewhere that I could lock him in—"

Ed Wortley, muttering under his breath, led them away. Webster, the elder, sat down like a man in a coma.

During the hour before dinner, Bud sat in the pilot-house with Linn. She had little to say, beyond offering a commentary on pilots who could not win a race without sacrificing their boats. But Bud, who was coming to know the perverse heart of her, only laughed.

"You know what I think?" he asked. "I think you're in love with me."

"In love! A steamboat man's daughter in love with a brass-pounding cub pilot? That doesn't make sense, does it?"

"No, but neither do you. The first thing a man needs to know about women is that none of them make sense. After that it's clear sailing."

Linn's blonde head tossed as she went to the door. From the companionway she called back: "Better go easy. There may be a snag or two left."

It was over the dinner table that Budford Q. Webster spoke his first words after learning that he had been duped. After the trials of the day, he looked surprisingly composed.

"Gentlemen," he announced, "this is the first licking I've taken in thirty years. And I think it's done me some good. At least, I can promise you I'll never buy another steamboat. As a matter of fact, I'd be willing to sell this one mighty cheap."

He laid an envelope beside Captain Yancey's plate. "That's a bill of sale to the *Nancy Hanks*. I'm letting her go for a thousand, if you're interested. Payable as convenient."

"That's fine," Yancey growled. "But it aint going to do me much good in this condition."

"Well, I was meaning to take care of that too," Webster told him. "As a wedding present, I want to put the boat back in the shape I found it, plus a little capital to operate on. You can't whip those Blue Chimney tubs without the money to buy rosin and the like."

"I didn't know," Linn said loftily, "that anyone was being married."

"Why sure!" said Yancey. "Me and Bud—unless you'd rather have him. One of us has got to hook him, or I'll lose my chance to get the best cub pilot in New Orleans for nothing. Like Webster says, business is business."

Bud grinned, looking at Linn. He didn't need her answer to know that, with Yancey's okay, it was deep water and not a snag within a hundred miles!

Loaded

W H E N dawn broke, Coleman halted his wagon on a gravelly ridge commanding his back trail. He made sure there was not another traveler, white or red, between him and the yonder hills before he lay down under his wagon to sleep. Then it was a hair-trigger sleep.

They had told Charlie Coleman and his erstwhile partner, Pete Shank, that they might make a fortune in Arizona Territory, but they would never get out with it. Coleman, 12 years after reaching the Territory, was attempting to disprove it.

He had made his fortune. Once, even Pete Shank, the wildcatter and ladies' man, the bluff and the energetic, had counted six figures in his passbook. But Tombstone, the mirage that had deceived fifteen thousand miners and their host of camp followers, had tricked him, too. He had left his fortune in a thousand-foot shaft when the mines filled with water. But Charlie Coleman got out because his money was in purveying to the miners in his Big Store on Toughnut Street.

Eight years the town had sent the iron chatter of her stamp mills up to the skies, the headlong laughter of her saloons out over the desert. But after another two years the place was a ghost camp of chloriders drunk on whisky and dreams. The wealth was drowned in the mines. The girls in their net stockings and flounced skirts left approximately an hour after it was certain that the boom days were over.

Pete Shank still bunked in his suite at the New York House,

sharing it with pack rats who traded *ocotillo* twigs for cigar butts. He cooked his own meals with food from Charlie Coleman's store, staring furtively, and hungrily, at the big wooden safe whenever he was in. The dissolution of their partnership when Shank decided to go into mining had been mutual; but now he had begun to say, only half humorously:

"You're a sharp trader, Charlie. You talked me out of my share of the ranch slicker'n hog-fat, didn't you?"

So now it was Pete Shank, rather than the Apaches and Yaqui raiders, whom Charlie Coleman was keeping a lookout for . . .

When Coleman awoke he drowsed on one elbow while he gazed out over the stark, greasewood hills of southern Arizona. Haze choked the arroyos and the lean pockets of the hills. Seven o'clock, and already it was hitting 80. Charlie feared neither the heat nor the country, for he understood both. For six years he and Shank had ranched this area, raising cattle and hogs and planting maize, chili, and an occasional Apache.

The silver strike at Tombstone ended the partnership. It had not been too solid a thing from the beginning. The pact that had endured all the way from Missouri, thriving under the slashing attack of Indians, had wilted under the suns of boredom. While everyone else went crazy in the mines, Charlie Coleman still saw them as purveyors of hams and beeves to the miners. Shank's vision was of owning a mine, of wearing diamond studs and squiring the prettiest girl in town to the opera house in his own turnout. So Charlie bought him out, sold his ranch, finally, and concentrated on the Big Store.

He was a quiet man and no one knew whether he was making money or not. He was open-handed, grubstaking everyone who came along, buying drinks for the house when he visited a saloon. But no one ever got a look into his safe or his ledger. Those were his own secrets.

Under the sun, Charlie harnessed his four mules to the light spring wagon, chewed a piece of hardtack, and drove on. He glanced back periodically. He was nervous and in a hurry, for though he had left at night, he knew Pete had been watching him for weeks.

The wagon lunged across an arroyo and hit out across a flat. Near here, he and Pete had once fought off six Cochise bucks. That old .40-.40 Henry of Pete's had had a lot to do with it. Load it Sunday and fire all week. And he could hammer a tack at a hundred feet, three shots out of five.

Charlie's spine rippled. In that wilderness of boulders off to the left, Shank might be pulling a bead right now, licking his forefinger for windage, taking range with that eye like a scratch awl.

Six times in the last month—by count—Pete Shank had said:

"Nothing to hold a rich feller like you in Tombstone, Charlie. Why don't you get out?"

As much as anything, it was a taunt. *Try and do it!* he was saying.

It was hard to recapture any of his old affection for Pete. The affability, the resiliency, had faded like smoke on the horizon. Hard times had smelted all the goodness out of him and left a small, black cinder of ill-nature and greed. He would sit bitterly drinking whisky and thinking of the fortune he had had to abandon in his mine, and resenting the luck or foresight of men who had gotten off better.

Coleman nooned near Dragoon Spring, in a nest of boulders and runt pines. Some of the pressure was off. *If I make it through the pass*, he thought, *I'll know he started too late.*

He watered the mules. They were fine, strong young animals; by the time they arrived at El Paso, they would be gaunt and sore-eyed. The winds were in full fury on the desert. Through Texas Canyon, the slope was gentle, but the mules pulled strongly. For the crossing of the deserts, Coleman had dispensed with all but the necessities. A wooden water barrel sloshed at one side of the wagon; a tar bucket for doping the axles swung beneath.

The sun crested and slipped behind him, heating the faded blue shirt against his back. And now the tumbled boulders divulged a shallow valley ahead—Sulphur Springs Valley.

He thought, *Pete, you old son, I've showed you!*

He was in this sanguine frame of mind when one of the lead mules faltered, reared in the traces and went down kicking and making a startling amount of braying. Charlie stood up on the seat—and standing this way he saw the wound in the animal's shoulder. The report of the rifle came a moment later.

He had the sense to stand quietly. From a rounded gray cairn of rocks a horseman appeared. Pete Shank rode his horse down the rugged slope with a carbine in his hands and his pale eyes steadily on Charlie.

Charlie sat down. He was not a cowardly man, yet not one for heroics. The gun on the seat beside him might as well be four yards away. So he occupied himself with cramming tobacco into his pipe until Shank reached the wagon. The mule, shot in the heart, had ceased struggling.

Charlie glanced up. "That's a mighty fresh-looking hoss, Pete, to have come so far and so fast."

Shank was lean and brown and his eyes were pocketed deep under dark brows. "He ain't come so far," he said. "He's been staked out a few miles back for the last month. He's the third I've rode, Charlie."

Charlie slowly nodded. "Good planning, Pete. Better than you ever did when we were ranching." He looked at the Henry rifle in the other's hands, a short-barreled weapon with browned metal parts. "Same old car-been. And you can still handle it."

"She's a sweetheart," Shank said affectionately.

"About the only thing about you, Pete, that's still clean and shining, ain't she?"

Temper flared in Shank's face. "You dragooned me out of the ranch. You robbed me because you knew I had to have money quick to buy into my mine."

"It was your own price. Get to it, Pete. What do you want?"

Shank squinted along the rifle barrel. "Sure. I'll get to it. I've been doing some figuring. I figure you come out of the bust in pretty good shape. I figure some of it, say about two-thirds, ought to be mine."

His pale eyes came up quickly. Strange eyes which Coleman had never looked into quite so deep before. And he was afraid, for this man meant to kill him. All the talk was by way of whipping up a resentment to spike his resolve.

"How do you figure that?" Charlie asked mildly.

Shank retorted in sudden temper, "I didn't follow you to haggle! Going to trot it out?"

"You're pretty sure I'm rich, ain't you?"

"I'd be blind if I wasn't. If I've seen you set up the house once, I've seen you do it a hundred times. Backslapping and yarning with every white-collar man in town. Driving the best turnout in Tombstone, wearing the best clothes, and pampering yourself like a king! You ain't had time to spend the kind of pile you were making since. I put my money on the card that says you've got a hundred thousand if you've got a dime."

Charlie Coleman waved a hand at the gear crammed into the back of the wagon. "This will surprise you, Pete. There's all I've got in the world. Except this—" He pulled a chamois bag out of his pocket, opened it, and poured a handful of gold coins onto his palm.

"Six hundred dollars. There's my fortune. Your cut, according to your figuring, would be four hundred. Want I should count it out?"

Shank said, "Start throwing gear out. Open everything."

Charlie shrugged. He stepped over the seat into the poorly packed litter. He opened first a black india-rubber bag. Shank was not satisfied with a cursory look, though it was obvious that no fortune in gold could be concealed in it. Shirts, socks, straight razor, and a bachelor's miscellanea tumbled out of it onto the ground. Shank's eyes grubbed through it. He had not removed Charlie's Colt, but this was the reverse of comforting. It meant that Shank's intention was not to let his ex-partner live long enough to use it.

Charlie continued to throw articles onto the ground. His mind persisted in measuring, scheming, weighing. In a surprising length of time, he was finished. The wagon was empty, but not a double-eagle had shown up. Coleman regarded the paltry scatter of his possessions, and saw there, suddenly, the key Shank needed to be certain of his surmise that there was more than $600 to be had here—

Shank's voice shot up: "Where is it? You damned old scheming catamount—*where is it?*"

Coleman slowly shook his head, smiling. "You already named it, Pete. Didn't you know you had the answer? You said you'd seen me set up the house a hundred times. You bragged on my clothes and my buggies. Those things take money. Having a lot of friends is expensive business. But they're the best investment in the world, because nobody can steal them from you."

He said with a touch of wistfulness, "Those friends of mine, Pete—Pres Ramsey, Joe Ticknor, Scotty—they were my fortune. And if I ever need a hundred dollars and can get word to one of them, I know I'll be good for it. You knew them as well as I did. You should know that you don't pard around with men like that, champagne drinkers and diamond-stud

wearers, with nickels and dimes. They're my annuities, my
gold pieces, and my gilt-edge bonds. But they were worth the
price they cost me. Even," he said, "if knowing them meant
my winding up with no more goods than I could get into a
spring wagon."

Charlie had driven a small thistle of doubt into Shank's
hide. The lank features pulled into insecure lines. The gray
eyes again quested dubiously through the gear. Then they
flashed up as if to test Charlie's sincerity, as a man might test
a gold piece by biting down on it.

Gently, Charlie said, "They were great times, Pete. Remember Pres Ramsey's party at the Bird Cage? When he got so
drunk he fell out of his box? But they're over and done and
now all we've got is a lot of receipted bills and some memories
they can't take away from us."

The fire in Shank's eyes sank into embers. The story Coleman had recited was the story of nearly every man in Tombstone. They lived up to their income, and when there ceased
to be any income, they had only their clothes. Pete Shank
moved the barrel of the gun.

"I'll split the six with you. Throw three hundred on the
ground."

One by one, Charlie tossed 15 double-eagles onto the soft,
pebbly earth. Then he turned and painstakingly repacked the
wagon. Shank remounted, but kept an eye on him, as if any
moment a corner might be torn from a secret wrapping to
expose a brick of gleaming gold. It was then necessary to cut
the dead mule out of the traces. The merchant tied the other
animal of the lead team behind the wagon. He returned to the
seat. This was the moment he dreaded. He waved a hand at
Shank.

"So long, Pete. Better make it last. And no hard feelings."

Shank did not reply. Frowning, he was watching the two
mules go into the collars and with difficulty move the iron tires

out of the ruts they had made in the loose earth. The wheels ground forward grudgingly.

"What's a-matter with them mules of yours? Can't they pull a spring wagon and a canch of gear? You'd reckon they was pulling a load."

"They're tired," Charlie said. But on Shank's face he saw realization spreading like a brilliant red dawn; and now he threw himself forward over the dashboard to the ground, and when he rolled over his Colt was in his hand. He heard the stinging crack of Pete Shank's Henry, felt the gritty bite of gravel on his face.

He took time to make his shot good. Shank was spurring away, wanting distance, wanting a long-range battle so that his carbine would geld Charlie's Colt. But the storekeeper, astonishingly steady, let his shot go only when he was ready. It took Shank in the middle of the back, at the base of his neck, and he went forward against the saddle-swell and then slowly rolled out of the saddle.

Charlie Coleman camped a mile farther, after burying his ex-partner. The mules needed rest. He would have to replace the lost one. They were, after all, hauling a load of two hundred pounds of gold coin and three hundred pounds of silver. Nearly a hundred thousand dollars.

Friends were much to Coleman, but so was this money he had worked so long and so hard to earn. The friends were scattered, but the money reposed, layer upon layer, round upon round, under the false bed of the wagon, a flat, a shining, and a still-safe treasure.

He had made liars out of them all. He had made his fortune, and he was taking it home to an easier country to spend it.

One Ride Too Many

BARGEE had a bright and cunning mind, Smoke Alcorn thought. It was too bad it had to have that slight odor of decay. Pear-bodied and asthmatic, the cigar that dwelt in his mouth sagging, Tom Bargee sat on the edge of the hotel bed and talked about old times. For years, he had supplied bucking stock to the smaller rodeos in which Smoke rode.

"Remember Sam Moody?" Bargee said. "He's been out on the Coast since he quit ridin'. I'll never forget the run he gave you at Pendleton that last year!"

"What's he doing?" Smoke Alcorn asked.

"Oh, punching cows. He wanted twenty bucks. I gave him ten. Wife sick, or something." Bargee's face, dark and stubbled, brightened. "I guess you knew Red Cantrell cracked a vertebra at Albuquerque last week."

"There wasn't any show at Albuquerque last week," Smoke drawled.

"This was just a local ropin'. I put up some broomtails for the boys. Red had been sliding, last couple of seasons." Removing the cigar, Bargee inspected the fuming tip. "He was about the last of the old-timers. Except for you—"

Smoke pulled quietly on the cigarette, regarding Bargee drily. Smoke Alcorn made his living riding rodeo broncs and bulldogging steers. Bargee made his money supplying buckers for the rodeos. One side of Bargee's mouth twisted higher than the other, a cynical turn, thought Smoke, that kept anyone from mistaking him for Santa Claus—a mistake that would have shocked Bargee more than anyone else.

"Why all the talk about old times?" Smoke asked him.

"Why not? Us old timers . . . it's good to get together for a talk now and then." Bargee's greasy brown eyes crinkled. "Smoke, you were loafing on that Snaketrack horse this afternoon. What's the matter—gettin' old?"

"Are my varicose veins dragging again?" Smoke asked. He left his chair and found a pint of whiskey in the bureau drawer. He took a drink and handed the bottle to Bargee, whose eyes, even as he drank, never stopped watching the bronc stomper—this Smoke Alcorn, whose thorny body had been pummeled, kicked, gouged and sat on by more horses, perhaps, than that of any rodeo rider in history. Yet he had been coming back for more for fifteen years. They named saddle trees and kids after him. He had won more first-prize money than anyone still contesting. But Bargee knew Alcorn's retirement was overdue. And he knew no one crazy enough to ride broncs at thirty-six was crafty enough to save money.

Smoke read these things in the stockman's face and waited.

"What do you think of this Chap Freeman?" Bargee asked him.

"Good rider. He's local, isn't he?"

"And a natural. He's one of them riders that almost need help to walk. He came right close to qualifying at Pendleton last year. He's a good boy, all right, Smoke. Maybe the best in the contest."

Smoke sauntered over and sat beside Bargee on the bed. "Better than me?" he said.

"Maybe just as good. Everybody in town with a dollar is betting on him."

"At what odds?"

"One-to-three. I've covered six hundred of it myself."

"That's damned white of you, Tom, risking all that cash to protect my reputation. Do you give me much chance to win?"

"Four-to-one, or I wouldn't cover one-to-three money. But

how how about next time? Pendleton—or Salinas—or Cheyenne? Chap Freeman," he said, "is riding the same horse you were, fifteen years ago. It'll find its way to the top, Smoke, and you'll have to grin and like it."

"Some day, maybe."

"Some day soon!" Bargee snapped. "Get used to it, Smoke! It's come to every man who ever straddled leather, and it'll come to you. Then what will you do? Ride for ten-dollar prizes and crack your back, like Red Cantrell?"

Warmth invaded Alcorn's flat features. He stood—five-ten, wide through the upper body, devoid of hips—a not-young man who was a long way from being old. He said slowly, "I never took a good look at your face, before, Tom. I will, now, so I won't forget how it used to look."

Bargee grinned. "You wouldn't lay a hand on me—not on your future partner." He rose, as if to go. "What would Cantrell have given a month ago for a chance like this? 'Red Cantrell's Bucking Stock! The roughest toughest—'"

"What the hell are you talking about?" Smoke demanded, standing there very still, but already comprehending what the stockman meant, and starving to hear it.

"I mean I'm going to reach for some of the big money," Bargee said. "Been feeding buckers into little arenas like this too long. Now I've got everything lined up but the red paint, Smoke—and you're it. You're my Buffalo Bill. If your name will sell a saddle or a pair of spurs, why won't it rent stock?"

"A good question," said Smoke.

"If you can put up three thousand dollars, you'll pull ten per cent. Otherwise, five. You'll work with the show, of course, and move along ahead to arrange things."

"I put up the tents," Smoke said, "and get the corn popping."

Bargee shrugged. "I could get somebody else in on this thing, if it doesn't interest you."

Knowing Bargee, Smoke said, "Well, I reckon there's no rush. I'll let you know, Tom."

"Sure," Bargee said, starting out the door. "Only," he said, "let me know while you've still got something to bring into the partnership besides a memory book. I need a champion, not a has-been."

Smoke took off his shirt. Almost furtively, he removed a bottle of liniment from his straw suitcase and went to work on his shoulder. That Snaketrack! He was glad he'd drawn the brute the first day, not the last. But he'd ridden to the gun, somehow.

It struck him that he had hardly ridden a decent horse in years. His comrades had been savage mustangs, half-wild steers and murderous Brahmas. And somewhere, in some arena or hospital, he had lost his zest for the fight. Somewhere it had turned into a way of making a living.

But following the bloody-nose circuit was itself a wild horse you rode, only there was no flanker to take you off. You piled off the best you could. Broke, probably, like Sam Moody, or crippled like Red Cantrell. Having no three thousand bucks in the bank, Smoke sat down to figure up five per cent of a probable net. It did not make his mouth water. But it would do, at least for a few years, until he could get together a bucking string of his own, or pay something down on a small ranch.

But he knew he would have to finish the season as a current event, not as ancient history. And here he was, as early as July, up against one of the fanciest newcomers he had ridden against in years.

Smoke washed off the smell of liniment and went out to eat. . . .

Smoke encountered Chap Freeman at the bucking pens the next day. The stands were filling. Here, in corrals under dusty

oak trees, broncs for the day's riding were being cut out. Chap
sat on the top rail, figuring the horses. Smoke mounted beside
him to figure the boy.

"What's your pick?" Smoke asked.

Chap grinned. A young fellow of twenty, he was small
and compactly made, tow-headed and fair. He had a way of
thinking before he spoke, of being cautious without being
hesitant.

"I wouldn't pick that gray over yonder," Chap declared.
"Bargee says he found him in Mexico. Pancho Villa, he calls
him. He's got yellow eyes like a catamount. I've got a feeling
I've seen that horse. He looks a heap like one I saw at Albuquerque last month."

"The one that kicked Red Cantrell?"

"That's the one. Only that was a rosewood bay."

Smoke shrugged. "They all look mean, or they wouldn't be
here."

"Ever get hold of a real mean one?" Chap asked. "I mean a
killer?"

"I rode a bronc once," Smoke recalled, "that bit me
and clouted me with his head and finally rolled on me.
Then he kicked me. I was in the hospital six weeks. I'd call
him mean. And you'll fork one just as mean some day, if you
stay with it."

"I aim to," Chap said quietly. "I'll be at most of the shows
this season."

"Got entry money?"

Chap hesitated. "My old man's putting it up. He was a rider
once. He never got far."

"Hurt?"

Chap shrugged. "Just didn't have it, I reckon. He figures I
have."

"What do you figure?" Smoke asked, his eyes watching in
ironic amusement.

"I figure"—Chap smiled—"you won't do much coasting when I'm around."

"Chap," Smoke sighed, "you don't coast when *anybody's* around—not in this business. Not with the kind of critters we play with."

He climbed down the bars, hearing the call for bull-doggers behind the chutes. He had seen that this boy, Chap, believed in himself—you couldn't hear him speak five words without knowing that. He was good, and he knew it, but it didn't fuzz his brain; and this was the only kind of rider Smoke Alcorn feared.

He thought, Kid, I wish I'd ridden against you five years ago. It didn't matter so much then.

The wild riding of the first day had calmed down. The gamblers were out, outpointed or stove up. The veterans and the lucky remained. Through that hot New Mexico afternoon Smoke spurred his broncs to the gun. He spilled his calves and, in dust and crowd clamor, sprinted to make his ties. But waiting for his last saddle-bronc of the day, he felt the blunt hurting of his injured shoulder. He watched the handlers sorting through the stock for the bronc he had drawn. Again he saw the Pancho Villa horse. It reminded him of a cougar, pale-eyed and with its rump tucked under. It was like Bargee to have a bronc like that in his string—a horse just tame enough to risk using.

They shoved a Roman-nosed stallion named Black Bart into the chute and Smoke moved in to saddle him. The two of them spent ten minutes making it clear to each other that no one was going to enjoy this ride. He straddled the chute to fish for a stirrup. He kicked his boots home and accepted the fat cotton bucking rein.

"I got 'im!" he shouted.

Heavy springs yanked the barrier open. Smoke had a view of the pens at the far end of the field. Then he was foggily

staring back at the slot through which he had just come.
Another instant and he was heading downfield again, his hat
sliding over his eyes. The horse pinwheeled like a singed
moth. It squealed and grunted and came down stiff-legged
after each jump, as though it were trying to drive its legs into
the ground for posts. Smoke's leather-shod legs squeezed the
saddle.

Abruptly the black took off in a dodging chain of straightaway pitches. The horn slugged Smoke in the belly. The crowds
in the stands yelled at him, liking it.

He heard the field judge's gun pop and the flankers came
in. He reached an arm toward one, shifting his weight. Black
Bart gave a sidewise leap that covered eight feet. The flanker
yelled and Smoke grimly reached for him, but he was falling
between the horses.

He was down, rolling over and coming up and seeing the
dusty bulk of the black cannonading down upon him. The
horse was blind as a clay cat. It landed on four feet and its
head banged into Smoke's. Blood spurted from his nose. The
horse wheeled as if to kick. Stunned, Smoke struck out with
his fist, feeling the granite hardness of its head. Then a
flanker was crowding between them.

Something had happened to his hand. Smoke looked at the
queer cant of his fingers. He tried to flex them, but pain
blackened his vision. . . .

The doctor taped Smoke's broken hand flat on a board.
Smoke sat up, and still a little drugged, said, "That'll be nice
to tie calves with."

"You aren't going back with that hand," the doctor said
grimly.

Bargee stood by, punishing his cigar. "Hell, doc! Can't you
tape the fingers up for now? The boy's got to ride."

"And let him make a compound fracture out of it? Here
—I'll leave the thumb free. Though nobody but a damned

fool would ride with a broken hand in the first place."

"In the first place," said Smoke, "you've got to be a damned fool to ride at all."

They came out on the street. It was late dusk. Bargee growled, "Now you've fixed it right."

Smoke stared bitterly at the pristine gauze binding his fingers. He needed deftness as he had never needed it before, but now . . . Six weeks to heal, the doctor had said. Six weeks before I'm worth a damn! And the toughest shows of all ahead of me.

He realized suddenly that tomorrow was the biggest day for him since he had won his first big show. Tomorrow would tell him whether he would be in shape for Cheyenne and Pendleton. If he failed in those shows, he was merely another of the old-timers Tom Bargee had been talking about.

Bargee grunted. "Well, let's go get the results."

They walked down the cowtown street to rodeo headquarters, which were in the crowded back room of the Pastime Bar. Smoke shoved through the crowd of old friends and ancient rivals—those tough, bone-hard men he had contested against so long—to find the results on a blackboard.

A long shank of a rider named Bill Isham put a bottle in Smoke's hand. "Cut the dust, boy! You made mount money —and then some. Hard luck about the hand."

Smoke was ahead in the bronc-riding. He had taken second money in the calf-roping and third in the bull-dogging. A nice finish for the second day. But there he was with his hand in splints, and the finals coming up.

Other riders moved up to commiserate with him over his accident, trying not to let their relief show. In a far corner, a crap game was in progress. Chap Freeman was on his knees before a scatter of bills. He looked up at Smoke's greeting. Then he brought his lips together, all the friendliness of the morning gone. He glanced at Smoke's bandaged hand and said, "Tough."

For a while Smoke watched Chap. Then he squatted by him. "Buy you a drink, Chap. Come on out front."

Chap glanced at him. "With what in it? Cigar ash?"

Smoke's good hand clenched. Other riders were listening. "No," he said. "With anything in it you name. But don't let a few points between us make you think you've been swindled. Is that it?"

Chap slowly stood up. "Everybody listen. The champ's giving advice."

"Some more advice I could give you," Smoke snapped, "is to lay off whiskey if you can't handle it."

Chap plucked at the brassard on Smoke's arm. "Old Sixty-Eight. We're right honored to be riding against you, ain't we? And I reckon you'll keep on being top rider just as long as you've got a dollar to buy your way into the finals."

Trying to clench his fist, Smoke winced. He brought his left hand across Chap's mouth, and stood there.

Someone ordered, "Now, boys!" but Chap Freeman savagely pulled his right arm back. Smoke waited. Chap looked at his bandaged hand and slowly lowered his fist. Then he turned, scooped up his money and shoved out of the room.

"What's wrong with him?" Smoke demanded, glancing around.

"Maybe he don't like competition," Isham suggested.

Smoke stared after the boy a moment. "That's too bad," he drawled. "If he thinks he ain't going to get any just because I trimmed my nails, then he's going to be fooled tomorrow. That goes for a couple of boys."

In his hotel room, Smoke practiced making pigging-string ties on a brass bedpost. Once he cracked a finger against the post and sank to his knees in agony. Then he tried tying with his broken right hand, the twine clamped under his thumb. Failing, he went back to using his left hand. He stayed with it until he acquired proficiency.

He was down at the fair grounds next morning and wangled a calf out of a handler for a five-dollar bill. He put his rope horse after it and made a tie. He raised his arms. Then in slow and bitter disgust he watched the calf kick loose and lope off down the field.

Smoke did not deceive himself. No man could win on bronc riding alone. And he was seconds behind the worst of them when the calf left the barrier.

The finals started at one o'clock, and not long after that Smoke heard his name called for the calf roping and swung into the saddle.

He watched his calf cross the line and let his horse sprint after it. Making his throw was like dealing poker with a paddle. But the loop sailed clean and the pony set back for the shock. Smoke was after the calf savagely, spilling it and yanking the pigging-string from his teeth to secure three of the kicking legs. He tied and sprang back, got the flag and returned to his pony.

He heard the time, and then the surge of applause. Bargee was back of the judges' stand, sweating, and with a pulpy handshake for him.

"Always said you were a hard-luck champ! Make them all like that and I'll be seeing how you can operate a pen with that hand."

Smoke was cool with relief. But after that it was a stroll over a chasm on a slack rope, with pain, dust and heat obscuring the far bank. Suddenly it was late afternoon, and they were down to the last run of broncs. Smoke thought about points, and tried not to think about points.

He had not spoken to Chap all day, but now he found him, as the final Brahma was chased from the field, standing by the bucking pen once more. He stood by Chap. The boy did not look at him, but after a moment he said, "Sorry I jumped you, Smoke."

"That's all right."

In the corral, the gray horse, Pancho Villa, nervously stepped up and down the bars. "I'm sure about that horse now," Chap said. "I knew it was him. The one that put Cantrell in a cast."

"Bargee said it was a bay."

"What happens," Chap inquired, "to a rider who refuses a horse he's drawn?"

"He's out."

"Even if he's sure the horse they've given him is an outlaw?"

"It wouldn't make that gray in there a bay, would it?"

"No, but some dye might. Maybe I'm as crazy as that horse looks! I'd swear he's the same one! But if I squawk, and it's the wrong stud, then I'm disqualified." He turned to face Smoke. "How well do you know Bargee?"

"Well enough. We may go into partnership next season."

"That's what I heard. But I didn't believe you'd have any truck with him until last night."

Smoke's eyes squinted at the lean young face. "What happened last night?" he snapped. But Chap had moved away. An official was bawling his name through a megaphone.

Abruptly Smoke turned. Suddenly it was plain—Chap's behavior last night. *As long as you've got a dollar to buy your way into the finals!* Bargee! The greasy, bribing . . .

He faced the whitewashed maze of barriers. There were many places Tom Bargee could be. There was not enough time to cover them all. Smoke began to shoulder through the men coming up to the fence to watch Chap's final ride. Bargee was not on the judges' stand. He was not at the fence.

Smoke ran down the deserted alley of sandwich and drink stands, then turned. Slowly his glance traveled through the trees — and halted.

In the amber afternoon light, a wagonload of baled hay glistened near the trees. A man sat on a spilled bale with his knees spread and his elbows propped against his thighs, a gross figure in a dusty brown suit.

Smoke moved quickly between two stands. He seized Bargee by the shoulder.

"Where'd you get that Pancho Villa horse?"

Brown as leather, Bargee's eyes met Smoke's. "What's the difference to you? You're not riding him."

"No, by God — and neither is Chap! That's the bay that tried to kill Red Cantrell, isn't it?"

Bargee rose, his dark face alert. "Who told you that?"

"Chap. He recognized him. Only he's been to the hairdresser since then, and he came out gray." Smoke hauled Bargee around. "You're going over there and stop it. Tell them anything you damned please. But pull the horse before he goes out!"

Bargee struck his hand away. His voice was quick but low. "Look out, Smoke. He ain't going to get hurt. He just ain't going to stay aboard long. The one that's apt to get hurt is you. You want to win, don't you?"

Smoke moved in on him, and Bargee took a step back and collided with a bale of hay. "And who put that crack in the kid's mouth about me buying my way into the finals?" Smoke demanded. "Did you try to pay him to blow a stirrup today?"

"I'm telling you —" Bargee warned. But Smoke's good fist was traveling, and Bargee's hand flashed up with a glint of nickeled steel. The gun was small, but he rammed it into the bronc stomper's belly and shoved him back. "You can't do anything for some fellows, can you? I could have given a dozen men the break I offered you. All right, you don't want it. But don't think I'll pull that horse."

Smoke stood against him, his hands hanging. "You'll wish you'd pulled it, when we wash the paint off him."

Bargee grinned. "Doctor a horse in a show this big? I'd be more apt to doctor a horse in one the size of that other. One I was already leary of because he'd kicked hell out of a mustanger who sold him to me."

Smoke began to nod. "Tom, I wish I was as bright as you think you are. But if I was—" His knees moved. Bargee doubled up, groaning, and Smoke palmed the pistol and slapped Bargee in the face with the plated frame. "If I was," he repeated, "I wouldn't tackle men with a gun I was afraid to use."

He left Bargee lying on the ground.

As he turned, he heard the gate slam open and a hard, wild beat of hoofs. He heard Chap's soprano yell. He was too late.

Smoke ran across the earth toward the fence. The booming yell of the crowd was like a punch in his belly. It was a horrified mass-shout; he had heard it before. A breathless thought showed its face. *Smoke, Smoke, what's the matter with you? You want to win, don't you? A busted hand . . . A bad horse—what's the difference?* If Chap came out whole and drew a new horse, Smoke Alcorn probably drew a rocking chair. Then, with a snarl, Smoke pulled two men back from the fence and managed to climb the stout hogwire somehow, even with the splinted hand. He threw his legs over and dropped into the arena.

Chap and Pancho Villa were both coming up out of a roll of dust. The gray had tried to roll on him. Chap was backing away, flapping his hat at the horse. A flanker slashed in from the side. Rearing, the stallion struck at the rider, and the man ducked. The hoof struck his arm. Smoke saw the ripped cloth quickly stain with blood. The rider swayed. Around behind the horse come the other flanker, to pull the first from the saddle.

Hazers were sprinting from under the judges' stand, the rodeo clowns raced in—but Chap Freeman was alone with the outlaw bronc. He was backing steadily, pausing once to scoop up dirt to fling in the horse's eyes. Pancho Villa tossed his head, heaved his stringy forequarters off the ground and the small hoofs feinted.

Smoke brought the thirty-two revolver down. It was unsteady in his left hand. He let a shot go, seeing through the powder-smoke a puff of dust from the shoulder of the horse. The report was a small, ill-tempered crack. Pancho Villa came back to earth and twisted his head to bite at his shoulder. Chap turned to run. The horse swerved and moved after him. Again Smoke fired, emptying the five-shot pistol rapidly, his mind on the packed stands across the field. The gray slowed, stopped and tried again to bite at the silent hornets stinging the life out of him. For an instant he was standing there alone, blood-streaked and bewildered. Then a rope settled over his head and he was brought to earth. . . .

Chap Freeman went to draw for a new horse, and a clown in knee-length sheepskin chaps and a silk hat came out on a donkey to rope a wild cow. They called Smoke up for his last ride. He made an asset out of his grotesque white hand, scaring the bronc foolish with wild swings that sent it into the four-legged gymnastics that Smoke understood best.

Afterward, he watched Chap ride a straightaway bucker, and thought, Some day, son, you'll learn how to make even a rocking chair like that look good. But not today. . . .

At rodeo headquarters he saw his own guesses verified on the green board. He collected his purse, and for the first time since dropping the gray stallion he spoke to Chap and they went out together. The street was clearing of ranch people and riders who had come in for the show.

"Did you get a look at Bargee after the show?" Smoke asked Chap.

"For a minute. Somebody must have worked him over."

"He was my fourth bronc today," Smoke admitted. "He tried to bribe you to throw the show, didn't he?"

"You didn't know that till today?"

"No, and I didn't know Pancho Villa was really a gray, either. He was a dyed redhead at Albuquerque. Bargee knew he had an ace-in-the-hole there. He wanted to be sure he kept him. I reckon he had money on somebody else in the meet and he had to make certain Cantrell lost. Today it was you he picked—to lose."

Chap was silent as they walked. Then he breathed deeply. "I'll be damned!"

"How much did you clear?"

"Mount money, and better."

"You'll be ahead come fall. But you'll do some riding if you get ahead of me. I'm going to wind this season up right. I reckon if Bargee thought a Smoke Alcorn bucking string was good business, it must be. And if I was worth anything to him, I'd be worth twice as much to anybody else. Between now and December I'm going to find a partner with cash. Then I'll sit on the bars and watch you kids bust your clavicles while I get rich."

"You'll be back in the arena the first time you hear a saddle pop." Chap laughed.

"Maybe so. But it won't be because I need the money."

They moved on along the walk, a small and thorny man who had had more than he wanted of broncs, and a younger one who thought he could never get enough.

Trouble at Temescal

BEYOND the meadow he could see a vineyard, and beyond the vineyard the huge adobe building with sheds and outhouses huddled to it like hawk-frightened chicks around a hen. The lacy, round heads of pepper trees made shade everywhere.

"What they call a *hacienda*, I reckon," Hank Ashwood said. He whittled shavings for a fire, his big, horseman's hands easy and familiar with the Green River knife stroking off the long, even curls of wood.

From the gully beside their horse camp, Red Wolfe came swinging into view with the dripping water bags bearing him down. He poured some water into the Dutch oven and began crumbling jerky into it. "We sure come to the right place, Hank. There's money in this outfit. I hear these California *hacendados* are crazy for a blonde, whether it's a horse or a woman. I'm telling you what's the truth; we'll sell these yella horses at a hundred a head!"

"I'd feel surer of it if they were blonde women," Hank Ashwood said.

Chain-hobbled, the horse herd grazed tranquilly. Aside from the need for currying, they looked good—ex-Army mounts, most of them, bought cheaply in New Mexico and trailed to the pueblo of Los Angeles for resale.

Red threw a handful of dried vegetables into the kettle. He was a stretchy, middle-sized man of twenty-five who could never sit easy; he had to be busy all the time. Around a horse camp it came in handy.

He took a deep breath. "Smoke yonder must be the town.

Real hellroarer, what I heard." The thin dusting of freckles spread across his face with a quick smile. "You know what I'm going to do with my cut of these here plugs?"

"Blow it on craps, women, and whiskey—in two days. After five months on the trail."

Hank spoke gruffly and gave the stew a stir. But he smiled a little in his whisker stubble. Red would do all right. A mite wild, maybe, but his red head was screwed on tight enough when it counted. They had met in Santa Fe, when Hank was just out of the Army and Red was on the loose from some money-making project or another that hadn't paid off—Hank had never learned just what. Some horse talk over a bottle of whiskey had made them friends; Red knew his way around, and Hank had some back pay and poker winnings burning in his pocket. So they became partners. They finished the bottle and shook hands and went out to look over the Army mounts. Five months had brought them this far along the trail, and about as close as two men can get.

From his possible-sack Red had produced a steel mirror and was looking himself over. He bared his teeth and fingered a knife scar on his cheekbone. "Buddy, I'll strike a hard bargain with the *señoritas* hereabouts. They'll know how Red Wolfe likes his bacon before I leave. How 'bout you? What you figuring to do with your cut?"

"I'll find something," Hank said.

When the fire was going good, the smoke seemed to release something in both of them. They stood watching the sunset fume along the horizon, until Red noticed a covey of blackbirds strutting on the cropped grass a hundred feet away. Abruptly, he drew his Colt and fired into their midst. One of them exploded into feathers as the rest scurried off.

"What the hell was that for?" Hank said.

Red grinned devilishly at the smoking pistol, as he said: "Ain't you ever felt that way? So full of vinegar you could bust?

Man, what are you—a gelding or something?"

Hank smiled, but he pointed out across the gullied pasture. "If the people in that castle ain't used to gringos, they'll be putting furniture in front of the doors tonight."

"They ought to be used to 'em. If they ain't, they'll know about Yankees before we leave."

A few minutes later they heard the horseman coming across the field from the buildings. It was now late dusk, and the windows of the ranch house were orange with lamplight. There were the sounds of cows lowing to be milked, of sheep, and the family sounds of chickens going to roost. The fragrance of woodsmoke and food drifted past Hank Ashwood's nose. He would always think of charcoal fumes and frying chilis when he thought of Mexicans.

Red was shaving cake coffee into their cups, listening to the oncoming hoofbeats. His face gleamed with wicked expectancy.

Hank poured hot water. "Listen, kid," he said mildly. "Don't forget we're in somebody else's town, now. Have your fun, but remember you're a guest."

Red snorted. "The hell you say! This is California, ain't it? And California's a state of the Union now, ain't it? We licked them Mexes for fair. They get off the sidewalks for us."

"If it comes to that. But it don't have to come to it. These people were here a couple of hundred years before us. They never made trouble. Now, there's plenty of the kind of woman you're looking for, and plenty of places to raise hell, without riling up the decent folks—"

"What the hell's gone and got into you?" Red stared at him. "Why didn't you tell me you were a preacher? Why, hellfire, man, we could have had chapel every night!"

"For a fella your size that's a lot of mouth you're flapping—"

Red came up quickly, swirling the coffee in his cup, staring with open hostility. Across the fire from him Hank got to his feet, not quite casually.

"It's this way," he told the red-head. "We want some money out of these horses. We won't get it by going on the butt with our customers." His square, dark face said he was offering an explanation, nothing else.

After a moment, Red grunted. "Now, that makes sense."

They were sitting on the ground with their pie pans in their laps, eating halfcooked stew, when the horseman arrived.

He came like a flourish of trumpets. Loping his horse directly into the camp, he put it to a plowing halt on its hind legs and then, with a lift of his reins, hauled it over to the fire. Hank stared, not alarmed, just amazed. The man handled the magnificent horse like a god. He was a young Mexican with coppery skin.

He was furious. Hank was glad the Green River knife rested on his plate.

The Mexican said, "*Uenas noches, caballeros.*"

"Hi, Mex," Red said. He speared a bit of meat and took it in his teeth.

The face of the Mexican worked. He was blue-eyed, though Hank guessed him to be of Spanish blood. Whatever his blood, it was boiling.

Hank said gravely: "*A sus órdenes, amigo.*"

The courtesy tamed the man a little. He addressed his next remark to Hank. "*Han tirado un fúsil?*"

"Yeah, we shot a gun," Red said.

"*Porqué?*"

"*Porqué* you no speak English, if you understand it?" Red demanded.

Still speaking Spanish the man said, "I understand English, but I speak my own tongue. That is all right?"

"Sure. You talk Spik; we talk English."

Hank set his plate down and stood up, wiping his knife with two fingers. "*Señor,*" he said, "we're mustangers. We come a long way today and we're plumb glad to get here. My

partner took a shot at a bird, just because he felt good. I felt
the same way, but I just grinned. The shot didn't mean any
more than my grin. Only you heard it."

"Yes," the Mexican said. "We did."

Red walked around, looking at the horse. "You the
bossman? You look too green to boss much of anything."

He was grinning a little, but Hank knew that American
humor was not Mexican humor. The Californian's anger was
rising like the neck feathers of a fighting cock as he stiffly
watched Red circle the horse.

"I am Ramon Calder. This is Rancho Temescal, the de la
Torre ranch. I am a neighbor of the owner."

"Who's the owner, Ray?"

"Doña Julia de la Torre."

Red gave him that brash grin. "Prob'ly call her Julie, where
we come from. How old is she?"

"Old enough to hate gringos," snapped the Mexican.

Red frowned. "Maybe we ought to drop around and show
this lady how lovable we are."

Hank said quickly, "Cut it out, Red. Calder, all we want is
pasturage for some horses until we sell them. We figured to
pay our respects to the *patrón* and find out if we could leave
them here."

"You *figured*," the Californian said, "to squat here until you
could claim the land. Like the others in Pike's company."

"Pike? Who's Pike?"

Calder repeated softly, "Who is Pike!" He laughed without
humor.

Red's back stiffened.

Having stood between them long enough, Hank Ashwood
was now tired of it. He liked fun; he didn't mind fighting. But
he didn't like sarcasm.

"Calder," he declared, "we don't know Pike, and Pike don't
know us. I said we were mustangers, and that's the story on

us. They call me Hank Ashwood; this is my partner, Red
Wolfe. We'll be over to say howdy after we've eaten. Tell the
lady we're sorry about the shot. We don't know this fella, Pike,
and we don't aim to squat. Will you tell her that?"

"No," Ramon Calder said. "I will tell her that Pike has sent
two more squatters in. But that I ran them off."

"Well, listen to the boy!" Red took a twist of tobacco from
his hip pocket and broke off a chew with his teeth. He began
to work it up. "Calder," he said. "Ramon Calder. Got a gringo
daddy, eh? Reckon that would make you kind of a half-breed,
eh?"

There was a pistol at Calder's hip which Hank had not
noticed. He saw it now, gleaming in the firelight, rising from
the far side of the horse as the Mexican threw down on Red.

Red's gun was holstered at his feet, lying beside his saddle.
He dropped to his knees and clawed at the gun.

Hank's hand and wrist rolled in a blur of fluid movement.
The knife turned lazily in the air and hit Calder's wrist with
such force that the pistol was jarred from his grasp. It fell into
the grass.

Calder stared at his arm. The point of the knife had gone in
crookedly, tearing the shirt, ripping his flesh. As the blade
fell to the ground, blood flooded his sleeve.

Red had kept moving. He was across the fire, leaping at
Calder, pulling him to the ground. He had pumped four blows
into Calder's face before Hank dragged him off, dominating
him by sheer fury.

"You hard-mouthed little pint o' willow juice! Why didn't I
let you have it? We could have made a friend out of this boy,
maybe, but now you—" He shook his partner savagely.

Red twisted away. "He threw down on me, didn't he?"

"After you called him a breed." Hank turned to stare down
at the Mexican. The boy was stunned, and was bleeding
steadily.

With a clean bandana, Hank bound the injured wrist. "I'm sorry about this," he said.

But the Mexican's eyes remained stony. He did not say another word. When he finally left, he did not return to the rancho headquarters but quartered off northeast, toward his own ranch.

Red found a bottle of wine that he had acquired at a mission the day before. He lay back on his blankets and tilted the bottle to his lips.

"I'll buy him a drink in town," he offered, grinning. "Hell, we'll make a Christian out of that kid yet."

"The less we have to do with that fireeater," said Hank, "the better off everybody's going to be. If they're all as touchy as this one, we're going to have to go in with our hats in our hands before we get rid of these horses."

In the morning, a man from the ranch house rode to the horse camp. "Juan Soto, *mayordomo* of this ranch," he introduced himself. "At your orders, *señors*." He was slender and dark, with leathery skin and a gray mustache, an old man but a vigorous one.

"Glad to know you," Hank said. "Young Calder tell you what we wanted?"

"You desire pasturage, as I understand. *La Patroncita* will have to decide. Will you come to the *casa*?"

They rode through the vineyards. *La Patroncita*—the little boss. It was intriguing, and Hank wondered how she would look. Probably seventy-five, and have wooden pegs for teeth.

Soto led them into the courtyard. Two women stood in the doorway of the kitchen, watching them.

Directly in front of them, as they rode through the gate, was the two-story wall of the main building. A gallery ran along the full length of the upper floor. Vines trailed along the spidery woodwork, and behind it, standing in the sunlight, a girl was stroking her hair with a silver brush. Seeing them, she stood poised with the brush to her hair.

He would always remember her that way, Hank knew. When he thought of the Pueblo of Los Angeles, he would think of a girl on a balcony, brushing her black hair with a silver brush. In her vivid features was the same pride Ramon had thrust at them.

Even after she had called down, *"Momentito!"* Hank sat staring.

Red caught his glance. "By Godlins! Now there's a Mex filly I wouldn't mind putting my brand on!"

Soto growled something to the boys who came to take their horses. They walked toward the big, nail-studded front door. Walking slowly, a lanky-boned man with unkept dark hair, his sleeves too short and his face unshaven, Hank felt like a peddler about to invade a forbidden parlor.

Soto took them to the parlor. The furniture was heavy, home-made stuff, but handsome. The floor was red tile, patterned with hides.

The girl came down the stairs into the hall and entered the room. The tapping of her heels was light and feminine and throat-tightening. Both men bounced up.

"Los Americanos, señorita," Soto announced. "They would like to arrange for pasturage."

She met them without a smile. *"Bienvenidos, caballeros."* She was tiny, olive-skinned and slender, with eyes like black velvet. Her lips were very bright. She wore a high-necked gown of pale green merino, whose lowest hoop just brushed the floor.

And watching her move toward a chair, Hank decided his first impression in the courtyard had been right. She was the loveliest woman he had ever seen.

He started to sit down again, but she raised a slim hand toward him in a motion of annoyance and alarm.

"Oh, no, you mustn't! Please!" She hurried across the floor to remove an antimacassar-like cloth of petit-point from the back of Hank's chair. "It is very precious to me, you understand. My mother made it. And you Americans—the grease you put in your hair!"

Deliberately she laid it on the arm of a chair and sat in the center of the sofa, adjusting her skirt about her. Then she raised that lovely young face imperiously and allowed her eyes to say that she was ready for them to talk to her.

Hank ran his hand over his hair. There was dust in it, perhaps, that a creek bath hadn't removed completely, but there was no grease. He told her as much with his glance, but said nothing. This tramps-begging-at-the-back-door role which she had assigned to them got under his hide. He decided that she would speak first.

Finally she said, "I notice that you were in the army," glancing at his faded shirt.

"For a while."

"During the war?" And when he nodded: "Then you must have killed a great number of Mexicans?"

"Only the ones that were trying to kill me—"

"And won much medals. And honor." Her voice was scornful.

He said, "Can't we agree the war is finished? I don't know who started it, but I'm ready to forget it. Our business here is with horses."

"*Chapita*," Red chimed in boldly, "how'd you like a yella horse to set off that black hair of yours?"

"I fear the price would be too high."

Red laughed. "Wouldn't be a question of money at all, *Chapita*."

The girl flushed, from shame or anger, Hank could not tell.

"You Yankees! You think that is all there is to it—you come in here and think that you can treat us all like swine! And if we object, there are always your guns." She looked directly at Hank. "Or your knives."

"Now hold on," he said. "We got some horses to sell. We came a thousand miles to sell them, and the first night we get here a sprout tells us to break camp and move along, and pulls a gun on us."

"After he had been insulted!"

"That kid gave me a pretty good roasting first, *Chapita*," Red grinned at her.

"In California," said Julia de la Torre, "gentlemen call a lady by her proper name at the first meeting. After a while, names like Shorty might be permitted."

Red bit off the end of a cigar. "Us gringos work kinda fast. You'd be surprised to know how we treat ladies we take a shine to, on the *second* meeting."

Her lips went thin as she fought to contain her anger. "You have come to ask me for pasturage. What is it worth if I say yes? Will you and Pike leave me alone? Will—"

"Pike, Pike! That's all I hear," Hank said. "Who is Pike? Your pal Ramon Calder pulled the same thing on us. This Pike must be quite an hombre."

She sighed. "All right. I'll pretend that you are as innocent as you want me to think. Pike is an *empresario* who is camped with his squatters on my land. According to law, I can make him get off. According to practice, he can stay until the courts decide he ought to have the land, if he wants it so badly. Then he pays me a little money, and I have been satisfied."

"That really how it works?"

"When one's name is de la Torre. If it were—Smith, for instance, or Jones—it would go differently. My title would have been acknowledged four years ago and I could run off Pike before he ruins me."

Hank said easily, "Then why not throw him off—tie a can to his tail?"

He had forgotten the *mayordomo*, Soto, who spoke now from the doorway.

"Vincente Arvizu was fined five hundred dollars for throwing some squatters off his place. And then they brought their relatives. He lost everything."

In the silent parlor, guilt buzzed around the Americans. Even Red shifted on his chair.

Abruptly Hank rose. Carefully, he replaced the antimacassar. "I hope we didn't bring in any vermin, *señorita*. You go right on fighting the good fight. Enough females like you could send any army in the world home dragging its muskets."

Their eyes clashed.

"We—we have not arranged about your horses," the girl said quickly. "I shall buy all of them. I'll send the horse foreman back with you."

He smiled. "You really don't trust us, do you? You still figure maybe we got a connection with Pike. But give us a good hatful of money for our horses and we might listen to reason and ride off. Ain't that it?"

"Do not all Americans have a price?" she asked contemptuously.

"Not this one," Hank said.

That morning they drove the horses five miles north into some brown hills. Here, on scorched grass in a dusty live-oak grove, they settled the herd once more.

Then they ate hardtack and venison and sat among the low-branching trees sipping their coffee. Hank could discern the pattern of the vineyards and horse pastures, fruit orchards and truck gardens, of Julia de la Torre's Rancho Temescal.

Evidently Red had been studying it, too. "That there's a tolerable big outfit. Musta been fifty flunkeys around the *hacienda* this morning."

"No wonder pigs like this Pike try to grab the old ranchos off, eh?"

Hank knocked out his pipe and covered the sparks with loose dirt. "Well, we better curry the horses. I figure tomorrow we ought to move them into the plaza and advertise 'em. They must have a paper, town of this size."

Stretching, Red smiled like a lazy tomcat. "That ain't all they got, I reckon. You take care of the advertising, I'll track us down some sweet-smellin' . . . Hey!"

He grinned, ducking the rock Hank chucked in his direction. They got up and went to work.

With curry combs and dandy brushes, they burnished the golden horses. Hank wished the Torre girl could see them. She would gasp, and he would say "Take your pick. Nothing stingy about a Yankee, *Chapita*."

Of course, if she had formed her impression of them from an occupation army and one-mule 'croppers like Pike, you couldn't blame her. Yet every time he remembered the way she had treated him about dirtying the chair, he got warm in the neck. He found himself thinking, too, about this fellow Pike, and the kind of reputation a man like that brought to other Americans.

When they had finished with the horses, it was almost dark.

"I got Pike and his bunch spotted over in that wash where all the smoke is," Hank said. "Probably cooking a beef they stole."

"You figuring on riding over that way?" Red asked.

Hank nodded. "This may be just a cockeyed idea of mine. You don't have to get mixed up in it."

"We're partners, ain't we?" Red said.

They pulled out two mounts, tightened their saddle girths and rode out.

They encountered the fragrance of Pike's camp before they

found the camp itself. Rotting carcasses of sheep, rudely butchered for a few tender cuts, lay in the brush beside the trail. Soon they came in view of a campfire and saw deerhide tents among scattered oak trees. Riding in, they saw that a beef was being barbecued in a pit; a man was slopping sauce onto it with a mop-like affair. The scent of it was overpowering. They sat inhaling it and inspecting the sprawl of a half-dozen tents among gear of all sorts—plows, saddles, bucksaws, boxes.

A man spoke from the shade of a tree. "Howdy, boys. You the mustangers?"

Hank noticed the rifle in the crook of his arm. "Yep. Smelled your food."

"Plenty for everybody," said the man. He came forward to look at them. He was tall and well-made, youngish, not bad-looking, a supple man wearing a saucer-brimmed straw sombrero.

"Owen Pike," he said.

"Hank Ashwood," Hank said. "This is Red Wolfe, my pardner. Might take some of that boot-leather you're cookin'."

At the barbecue pit, they shook hands with the bald-headed little man with the mop. His name was Brown. There was another man named Flint who had unhappy gray eyes which watched with suspicion from beneath thick brows. Flint was very tall, with wide sagging shoulders. He had badly made false teeth which he rattled like a horse chewing a bit.

"Rest of the boys are in town," Owen Pike said, "gittin' fixed up." He chuckled.

All of these men, Hank perceived, had one thing in common, they were unconscionably lazy. They would do three days' work to get out of one.

"Aim to settle," Pike queried, "or move along?"

"*Quien sabe?*" Red shrugged. His teeth tore at a dripping slab of meat.

"Fix you up with a nice piece of land," said Pike.

"Horse traders," Hank sighed, "can't afford land like this."

"Bring me a couple of them titles," Pike told Flint.

Flint brought some impressive-looking documents. Pike frowned over one. "This is five hundred acres. Fifty acres of muscat grapes grow on it and a hundred orange trees. The rest will cultivate or raise stock."

"Nearby?" asked Hank, with interest.

"You're settin' next door to 'em. Both on Rancho Temescal."

"You own the land?"

"Fixin' to." Pike winked. "I'll sell either or both at a dollar an acre. Or trade for horses."

"What if this de la Torre woman makes trouble?"

"You got it wrong, friend. They don't make *us* trouble—we make *them* trouble. You could move in tomorrow."

"But how do I know these titles will stand up?"

Pike drew the cork from a jug of whiskey, laid the jug across his elbow while he drank, then stoppered it again. "I get it that every Mexican title in Los Angeles county is going to be throwed out. That makes the next titles in line good. And you know what they say about possession."

Hank drank deeply of the whiskey. After belching, he said mildly to Red, "Cover Brown and Flint."

Red pulled his gun and the squatters blinked at it. Pike stared, then roused up from his heels to reach for his rifle, cocked against an ox-cart. "Well, by God," he snarled. His face writhed, coming out evil as that of a cur.

But he froze when he saw the knife shining in Hank's hand. Hank reached forward to catch Pike's gun belt and cut it loose. The revolver fell to the ground.

"Get up," Hank told him.

Pike came up tall, like an Indian. He threw aside his hat and waited. His face was murderous; his eyes bored at Hank's.

"Up to you," he said. "But remember—in this town you can have a man killed for two bits, and git change."

Hank sheathed the knife and handed his Colt to Red. "You ain't worth two bits." His left hand flicked into Pike's face. His right crashed in when the squatter ducked. Pike covered his face and stumbled away. He went to one knee but lunged up again. As Hank came slashing in, he wiped the blood from his face and slanted into him, both arms swinging.

Hank ducked under the squatter's swings and butted him in the belly. He got his arms around him and ran backward.

The squatter, Flint, bawled, "*The pit, Owen!*"

Hank unlocked his arms and stopped short. Owen Pike stared at him, afraid to look back. At once he leaned, flailing, into Hank, swearing, calling up all the vicious profanity of two languages. Hank dodged and ducked and then feinted at Pike's crotch with his knee, and when Pike grunted and covered up he slammed him in the face with an overhand right. Pike's head jerked. He twisted backward and sprawled across the greasy, sweating carcass of the spitted veal. Screaming, he went ankledeep in the coals before he could haul himself out. Red was roaring with laughter. Hank just stood there with a grin, waiting to see whether the squatter had all the fight squeezed out of him.

Groaning, Pike held his feet for one moment, as he huddled on the ground. But an instant later he clawed his hands full of dirt and hurled it into Hank's face. Hank's eyes were full of the grit. He heard Red's angry bawl, "Duck, Hank—I'll give it to 'm!"

But the squatter was upon him, hammering one into his jaw, and as Hank went back, he felt Pike's hand clutching at his hip. Hank felt the knife slip out of the sheath. What had been only a rough fight was now deadly serious.

Pike was moving in like a cat. Hank considered ducking

away to give Red a shot at him. Yet he wanted to handle this himself, and he did not want anyone killed. He wanted Julia to know that he had been enough, barehanded, for a whole campful of squatters.

The knife cut the air before his belly, withdrew, slipped in toward his breast, retreated again. Hank backed slowly. Then Pike dived in with a straightforward lunge for the buckle of his belt. Hank jumped sidewise and brought a smashing fist down upon Owen Pike's forearm. The knife fell. Hank scooped it up and as the squatter went for his throat he brought it across the side of his head.

The tip of the squatter's ear fell to the dirt. Blood fountained over the side of his head and down his neck and shoulders. When Pike saw the bit of flesh in the dirt, he covered his ear with his hand and staggered away. He sat on a log with his palm against his ear, twisting his head back and forth in agony.

Hank saw to the disarming of the other squatters. He carried all their pistols in his hat. Mounted, he stopped beside Pike.

"You got all day tomorrow to pack and get. Be gone the next morning. Or all the two-bitses in Los Angeles won't keep you from losing the rest of that ear."

The pueblo called the Queen of the Angels was different from anything Hank had ever seen. It was a long haul from an eastern town, or even Santa Fe. Nothing seemed to matter to the natives. Even the air was soft and slow.

They had moved into town the day after the fight, and pitched camp in a vacant lot off the plaza, under a huge pepper tree dripping red. They corralled the horses in a rope enclosure and Hank put an ad in the *Star*, and the horses began to sell. They did not make a hundred a head, but they did well.

Red and Hank took their meals in a Mexican café on the plaza. In the evenings they would sit in the deep bay of the windows, smoking and watching the traffic come and go; and after a while, when it was dark, Red would say, "Got to find a gal, Hank. I'm great for dancing." With a laugh he would go out into the night.

After a couple of these nights he asked Hank, "What's eating you, *compadre*? All the *señoritas* you were going to swing, and you ain't done anything but eat and work since we hit town."

"Anything wrong with eating and working?"

"Nothing wrong with the fillies here, either. Tell you one thing—they ain't the angels they named the town after."

And Hank sighed and wished he could get the picture of a black-haired girl out of his mind.

At eight o'clock one night, as he was finishing his cigar before the café, Hank saw a turnout flash up to their camp and stop. He sauntered over, hopeful of a customer. A young fellow was walking nervously about the camp, looking at the horses, and as Hank came up he ducked to glance into the low deerhide tent.

"*Aquí estóy*," Hank called.

The man turned quickly. It was Ramon Calder. He came toward Hank with the stiff-legged strut of a small dog guarding a large yard. Hank smiled to himself but his hand was on the butt of his gun.

A girl spoke, close to him. "Ramon, you promised!"

A tingle chased itself along Hank's spine. Her voice—it was like a bell heard softly on a warm evening. He had heard it for days, saying things that tantalized and infuriated him. Now he did not turn to look at her, sitting in the rig, but watched the Californio come on. Ramon stopped three feet away with his hands on his hips. Just a kid, Hank thought. A

spoiled and hot-blooded kid, but a scrapper. He found himself liking him.

Before Ramon could say anything, Hank remarked, "Sorry
about the arm, Ramoncito. That pardner of mine—I blame
him as much as you."

"What's the plan now? To lay claim to the plaza?"

"Sell and git," Hank smiled. "Tell you what I'll do. Give
you your pick of the horses for half price."

"Would that apply to me, too?" asked Julia de la Torre.

Hank took his eyes off Ramon and let himself relax. The
night and her voice combined to disarm him. He heard his
voice say quite distinctly, "No, ma'am. I'll just give you one.
To set off that black hair of yours."

"Señor Ashwood," Julia said quietly. "Señor Ashwood, I
am sorry about the other day. But when you are about to lose
everything . . . I am going to accept the horse, with thanks.
Ramon, will you pick out one for me?"

"Be assured the horse won't be free," Ramon said darkly.

But the girl smiled and made a face at his concern, allying
herself by the small action with Hank. She got down from the
turnout, holding out her arm for him to take.

They stood close together. In the dying light he could see
that her lips were smooth as lacquer, that there was the slightest blemish near the corner of her mouth. And that her eyes
were very dark brown, with incredibly long lashes. Her nose
was delicate, perfectly fashioned. He was glad for that tiny
mole; without that to break the perfection, he had a feeling
that he would have choked on this lump in his throat. She was
sure something for a man to run smack into after five months
among the squirrels.

"I want to thank you for trying to frighten off my squatters,"
she said. "It was very brave of you."

He felt the movement of her hand in his and remembered

only then to release her. "It was very practical business, too," he told her. "Best way to show people here that I'm not like Pike, and that I want no part of Pike or his kind. My horse sales have been going well."

"Of course, *señor*. Good business, as you say. Pike and his men are still here, though. You must watch out for them."

"I'll take care of myself. Is that what you wanted to talk about, *señorita*?"

"To thank you, yes. And . . ." Her luminous eyes met his briefly, and he saw a doubt, a question in their depths. "Yes, there is something else. But I do not know if I can make you see."

She took a deep breath, swelling the merino gown. "This —this place is not what I remember from my childhood. What we had here before the war—it used to be so wonderful! The ranchos, the people—all of us living as we were meant to live. My grandfather would have fiestas you wouldn't believe! Those were the happy times, *señor!*" and she seemed to dream over it.

"And now we have the great ranchos being broken up, the land stolen from its owners. Did you know this town before, Señor Ashwood? The fine residential district of the North Side—it is now the infamous *Calle Desperar!*"

Hank had seen it—the lowest part of the worst section in town. The Alley of Despair. It was the bottom of the keg, where the lees went fetid. Drunkards and murderers roamed its sordid length.

"We did not have it before the Yankees came," she said. "I have heard they kill at least one man there every night. The big *hacendados* have the drunks rounded up by deputies and shanghaied to their ranches, work them until they drop and send them back with a dollar."

"All towns get worse as they get bigger," said Hank. "The

town will get sick to its stomach one of these days. It'll purge itself with a vigilante committee."

"We are losing what we had. The Rancho Temescal will be taken from me. Owen Pike and his squatters will claim still more of my land, or the survey commission will write a letter to Washington saying that my title was one of the fraudulent ones given when we were losing the war."

"It can't be that bad," he protested.

"It is," she said. "But there is a way for me still to protect what I have. If I marry an American."

For an instant he was shocked to silence. Then, "What kind of fool idea—"

"But of course! With a bona-fide American name—the wife of an American—my title would be accepted tomorrow. That is the established policy. But I could not marry a man I couldn't trust. He must live up to his part of the bargain, or I would be even worse off."

"Bargain?"

"I could not pretend there was love, when there is not," she told him. "I would want him to marry me and—and then leave. Go from California for at least a year, so that I could divorce him for desertion. By next week, when the survey commission leaves, my title would have been accepted."

His face grew bleak as he stared down at her. "You don't think much of us, do you?"

"But you see," Julia said quickly, "I would pay for his name. Two thousand dollars! For his name and his promise."

"Would a Mexican do that for an American woman?"

Her eyes, shifting quickly, gave him the answer to that.

"Of course not!" His voice lashed her. "He'd be too proud. But a Yankee!"

Before she could move, he pulled her roughly to him. His lips caught hers as she tried to shape a word of protest; she struggled, and then she relaxed against him. What had been meant to be a gesture of scorn did not remain one, and Hank released her, angry at himself.

He left her standing there, one hand held out as if to draw him back.

"Ramon!" he called. "You better come get the *señorita*. She's ready to go home."

He told Red about it that night. Red was feeling pretty good.

"You mean that nice piece of Mex fluff wanted you to marry her and you turned her down? I'm telling you what's the truth, Hank, you ain't got the brains God put into a billygoat. Saying no to something ripe as all that!"

Hank snorted. "It's not a real marriage. Some idea about a bargain—"

"Bargain's the word, sure." The redheaded mustanger smacked his lips theatrically. "It'd be legal—and *so-o-o-o* nice. So very, very nice. *Youe-e-e-e-ah!*"

"Damn it," Hank said, "a man that would do a thing like that would be so morally irresponsible he'd be a menace to society." His partner's refusal to be serious about it annoyed him. "He wouldn't only be making a pimp out of himself. He'd be making every other American in California look like one. Every Mexican widow, or single girl like this one, would be buying a Yankee husband and hustling him out of the state. Pretty soon we'd be stepping off the sidewalk for *them!*"

"Man, you're talking like a preacher again. Must be something this California air brings out in you." In the darkness of the tent Red's cigar glowed briefly. "All depends now, on who hustles who. There's nothing says a man's *got* to get out of the state once he's tied the knot legal to a Mex gal. A man could do himself right proud with one of these here ranchos. Maybe even turn it into cash. . . . Build himself a palace in San Francisco. . . ."

Red's voice trailed off. He began to snore. Hank got up, took Red's cigar out of his limp fingers and tossed it outside. He left the tent flap open to air out the heavy odor of the cheap whiskey that rose from his partner's body.

Sleep, for Hank, was a long time coming. He chased it down a lonely road, where the smells that came off the trees were the tantalizing odor of Julia's raven hair, where the hoof-beats beneath him were his own pounding heart.

In the morning, Red groaned and held his head as he struggled with his coffee. Some men from a livery stable came by to look at horses, and Hank was busy.

Sometime after noon, Red said morosely, "My stomach ain't speaking to my throat, Hank. I don't know what I was drinking last night but it sure peeled the lining. Nothing will fix a belly like mine but good whiskey. Hold 'er down while I'm gone, eh?"

Very late, Hank did not know when, Red was back. He was cold sober. He went right to sleep.

But the next morning Hank knew something was wrong. Red fooled with his breakfast until the mustachioed proprietor, cracking his knuckles asked, "*Demasiado pimienta, quizas?*"

"Nothing wrong with the chuck, Dad," Red said. "Something wrong with me."

"What's the matter?" Hank asked.

"Had a bellyful of town, that's all. I'm broke, Hank. Now I'm itching to travel."

"Where?"

The redhead hesitated. "Why—uh—up to the north. North California—the mines!"

"And you're leaving today. Is that it?"

"That's it. Sell you my interest in these plugs for a hundred dollars."

"Deal," Hank said. "Some advice, kid. Slow down. We worked like hell for that money. Save a little of the next you get and stick it in the bank. Or you'll wind up in *Calle Desperar*."

Out of the octagonal gold pieces Hank put down, Red tossed one back. "Make you a bet, *amigo*. Five years from now I'll be wearing better clothes than you are. And eating better."

Hank smiled. They drank a half bottle of wine on it, and shook hands.

And now it was a waiting game that began to drive Hank crazy, too. He all but gave away the last of the horses, retaining only the one he had earmarked for Julia. He stabled it and counted his money. He had thirty-two hundred dollars, gold. He clinked it in the chamois bag. Maybe money would grease a balky land title.

The office of the survey commission was in the Union Hotel. In a large room facing on the hotel corral, four men worked with maps and scrolls and drafting instruments. They looked harried, and at once Hank had sympathy for the big, gray-haired man who was in charge. Colonel Proctor must have had every landowner in California crying on his shoulder by now, honest or dishonest. There was a fat little man doing it when Hank arrived.

The Mexican had a cowhide volume under his arm. His eyes were black and miserable and desperate. "*Seguro Coronel*," he whined. "The name is different, but you see, my grandfather, he was unpopular after the revolution, and he change' his name. Then my father—he was *muy fiero!*—he change' it back! But when he married. . . ."

"It'll be looked into," Proctor said. "We're here to protect landowners, not rob them."

He began escorting the man to the door. "But I have

friends who have lost everything!" the Mexican protested.

Proctor shrugged. "We make mistakes."

After the old man had gone, the colonel looked at Hank. "What do you want?"

Hank knew at once that this man could not be bought. "What's the story on throwing squatters off your land?" he asked.

"That's up to the courts."

"But it's no different with a Mexican than an American, is it?"

"Well, what do you think? The case comes up before an American judge, and the squatter turns out to be a Yankee who fought for his country and brought his family out here to settle. But there's no place to settle. It's all big ranches forty miles square. Who's going to blame him if he squats?"

"That's right," Hank said. "What if he's single, though, just a drifter?"

"Every case is different," Proctor said. He opened a sheaf of papers, frowned at it, then growled, "What ranch is it you're interested in?"

"Rancho Temescal. Julia de la Torre."

"That's different. She's all right."

Hank blinked, "But she told me—"

"That was before she was married. Her husband was in to record the land in his name."

"Oh?" Hank said. "What's her name now?"

"Wolfe," the colonel said. "Mrs. George 'Red' Wolfe."

Hank went out and had a drink on it. Clinking the gold piece down on the bar reminded him of what he had intended doing with his poke. Get her title papers cleared for her —hand her Rancho Temescal all wrapped up in legal ribbons and say, "Here it is, a present. From a Yankee." A real gentlemanly thing to do, worthy of a grandee of Old Spain.

Hank stopped counting the drinks, and sometime later found himself in *Calle Desperar*, fighting with two drunken sailors who had tried to lift his wad. He beat them both into the ground, while other drunks howled wild encouragement. Hank was filled with pain and glory. It was like the Hell pictures in a Doré Bible. Much later he was sitting on a doorsill in front of a shop. It was dark. The street was quiet. His stomach, after a sleep, was tender as a boil. What had he been drinking—lye? He was sick, and came out of it shaken but sober.

Crawling through the low door of his tent, he halted, rigid. It stank of sweat—the sweetish, nervous odor you smelled on soldiers after a battle. Someone had been here, or was here, someone who was nervous from waiting.

Pike and his squatters, he thought.

He held himself unmoving, waiting for the first small sound that would tell him from which direction the attack would come. He had no way of knowing how many of them there were, and his ears strained for some indication. In his throat was the brassy taste of fear.

Breath hissed between set teeth. It was all the warning Hank had, but it was enough. He went sprawling forward to the small noise, one arm sweeping for his gun, the other held out before him, clutching. He touched something; knocked the man sprawling and they both went down in a tangle. There was no clear chance to use his gun; he hit the man in the crotch with his elbow and felt him convulse. They swore savagely, the words twisting into snarls of effort. Hank caught a blow against his shoulder and his hand was fast enough to grab the other's gun hand and turn it away from himself.

A sob of pain reached out to him, even as he realized the wrist he clutched was swathed in bandage.

"Goddammit!" Hank said. "Calder!"

"*Señor!*"

He felt the fight go out of Ramon instantly and held his own gun to one side, out of the way.

"What the hell you trying to do?" Hank released his grip. "You danged fool!"

"I am sorry, *señor*," the young Mexican said. "I did not know it was you."

"Thought you was Pike and his bunch."

"And I thought that you were your partner, Wolfe."

Hank shook his head. "You came to the wrong corral." He turned and led the way outside.

In the thin light Ramon's face was set in harsh, hard lines. "Did you know your partner has married Julia?"

"I found out today. Only you got it wrong, *amigo*. He ain't my partner now."

"I did not know that. I thought I might find him here."

Hank picked a spot beside the pepper tree. He sat down, got his pipe going. "You ain't looking for him to offer your congratulations, I reckon."

"No, *señor*. Julia should not marry an American," Calder said. "But she went through with it, and gave him the money she had promised. But he did not leave. He intends to keep the ranch for himself!"

"So?" Remembering what Red had said the other night, Hank was not too surprised. Legally, Julia could do nothing to stop him. In a way, the situation was funny.

"It is not for smiles, *señor*," Calder said hotly, watch ing Hank carefully. "Julia pleaded with him to keep his bar-gain—and he laughed at her. She offered him more money; he scorned it. Rancho Temescal is his now, he told her, and she could stay or leave, as she chose."

"He's pretty stubborn, when he sets his mind to it."

"I have offered Julia the sanctuary of my *hacienda*." The young Mexican spoke with careful severity. "Señor Wolfe shall not claim her, too. Soto says that Wolfe rode out this morning to look over his property, now that he is the *hacendado*. I searched but was unable to find him. I thought perhaps he came here."

"Ain't seen hide nor hair of 'im," Hank growled. "Like I told you, Red and I are quits."

"Good," said Calder. "Then it will not matter to you when I kill him."

Hank awakened to the sound of bells, the voice of every Mexican town he had ever been through. Near and far, they chimed and bonged and tinkled for an hour.

I wonder what I'd have done if I'd been her, he asked himself. If I knew I was heading for the street corner with nothing left but my clothes. Would I have been damn fool enough to have trusted any man on a deal like that? Couldn't she have seen that Red Wolfe was a hare-brained, devil-may-care gringo looking for all he could get?

It did no good to think about it. The thing for him to do was pack and git.

Accordingly, he busied himself throughout the morning, striking the deerhide tent, fashioning a bedroll that would sit easy behind his saddle. There were some things of Red's around and Hank made a separate bundle of them to take over to the Alta Vista Hotel.

"Hold these for Señor Wolfe," he told the proprietor. "If he should come in."

The man looked sourly at the blanket-wrapped bundle, muttering behind his mustache. Hank caught the words Temescal, and something about the damned gringo who probably would not need these things now that he was a big *hacendado*.

He supposed Red would be just one more reason, shortly, that the Mexicans could say so bitterly, "We had no *Calle Desperar* before the Americans came."

Yet weren't people like Julia de la Torre to blame, as well? With her "bargain" that was equally demeaning, and which offered such temptation?

But the argument made him feel no better, and by the time that he had downed two glasses of tequila in a *Calle Alameda* saloon, the strange compulsion that burned him made up his mind.

He went to the livery stable and got the horse which he had held out for her. Rope-trailing it behind his own mount, he took the road toward Rancho Temescal and Ramon Calder's *hacienda*.

He rode in late daylight through fields of dried mustard weed. He had expected to find the carts laboring in from the vineyards and truck gardens; there was no activity of any sort.

In the yard the silence was even more noticeable. The smell of charcoal smoke hung faintly in the air, yet there was not the frying food smell of supper. The quiet bothered him as he sat there, trying to get some taste out of a cigarette.

What the hell? he thought, and called out. "Hello!" waiting for a stableboy to come out to take his horse. But no one came. After another few minutes, Hank hitched the horses and went on inside through the stone arch that was the entrance.

Above the ringing of his boot heels on the tile floor he heard the murmur of voices in a high-vaulted room off to the left of the main hall. In there, he found the crowd of Mexicans, the men and women and children of the rancho, bunched like frightened cattle. Some of the women were sobbing openly, wringing their hands in their voluminous skirts; the men stood, slack-faced and bleak-eyed, their hats in their hands.

He caught the shoulder of the nearest man. "Señorita de la Torre—*adonde?*"

The man pulled away from him. "Gringo pig!" he spat.

Like a spark, the action seemed to ignite the crowd. A growing surge of anger ran through the room. Hank eased his hand to his holster instinctively.

"Hold!" someone commanded, pushing through the crowd. It was Soto, Julia's *mayordomo*.

"What do you want here?" he demanded.

"Where's Julie?"

"She does not want to see you, I am sure," the old man said. "Go from here now, *señor*, before there is more trouble."

"What's wrong?"

"There has been a shooting." The Mexican's eyes burned Hank's face. "Between your redheaded partner, and Ramon Calder. The doctor is inside with him now. I do not think he expects Señor Calder to live."

Even as he spoke a door opened at the far end of the room and Hank saw Julia de la Torre emerge. She wore a simple gown of gray, unrelieved by any ornamentation, and her face, as much as he could see of it, was white and drawn. Tears had stained her cheeks which she dabbed with a square of lace.

He could not hear what she said to those standing nearest her, but it did not take a wise man to guess. The women's sobs went just the least bit higher, rising on their indrawn breath, in the way it does when tragedy embraces them. The men passed the dread word, *"Muerta,"* softly.

Hank pushed his way through the press of bodies. He saw Julia look up at his approach, saw her eyes go larger with the briefest mark of hope, before the grief and disillusionment crumbled her face again. And then, as if it were the most natural thing in the world, she was in his arms, sobbing bitterly, her small body shaking beneath his hands.

"Chapita," he said softly into her hair, holding back nothing of the way he felt now, refusing to admit, in this moment

that brought them closer than a mere embrace, that it was too late. . . .

She put her lips up to his and he kissed her, a little stiffly at first, but suddenly bringing her hard against himself. His fingers moved along her back, up into her soft, dark hair; he felt an ache go all through him. He was kissing her and whispering her name.

After a while she moved away from him. But for themselves and a few ranch hands straggling through the door, they were alone in the big room.

Julia held his arms, looking up into his eyes, and he knew beyond a doubt this was the face he loved, this was the woman he wanted.

"*Pobrecito!*" she whispered. "There was my pride. You do not hate the Yankees all your life and then admit, even to yourself, that you are in love with one.

"Perhaps if there had been more time, I could have come to you as a woman, not as a frightened ranch owner who feared the Yankee law. But I did not know what to do. The day after I saw you, I had a visitor—Señor Wolfe. He said that you had told him you would not marry me. Your business here was finished. You and he were going away. He said he felt a great pity for me and so, before he left with you, he would do me the favor of this marriage which his partner would not."

He felt the moment of their nearness slipping from their grasp. "And you believed him."

"He was your friend, and he seemed so angry with you, for having refused. Yes, I believed him." The tears welled in her eyes. "Tell me how great a fool I was."

"You couldn't know."

"It is all my fault. But more than stupid. I am also guilty. Of Ramon's death." She started to sob again.

"I'm sorry for that." He put out his hands to comfort her,

then drew them back, opening and closing his fingers. "How did it happen?"

"This morning. I tried to stop him, but Ramon rode over to Rancho Temescal. He and Red argued. Señor Wolfe refused to go away. Ramon drew his gun. If it were not for my foolishness this awful thing would not have happened!"

"You're not all to blame," Hank said, so sharply that she was startled. "It's my fault, too."

He was not attempting gallantry, but examining the facts as he saw them now. "I brought Red Wolfe here as my partner. I told him about your offer of marriage, though I didn't think at the time he was figuring to do anything about it. And I'm the one who crippled Ramon's shooting hand. Whatever blame there is, I get some of it."

He reached for the hat he'd dropped when she had come into his arms. "I brought the horse. Perhaps you can ride it back to Rancho Temescal, when us gringos are gone."

"There will be little left to go back to when Wolfe leaves," she said sadly.

"Maybe not. I'll ride over there and see if I can talk Red into leaving with me tonight."

She studied the hard lines of his jaw. "You do not have to do this thing—"

"For you?" He shook his head. "No, *Chapita*, it is for me as well. And for the other Yankees who would be your friends. I don't think Red understands that in his own way he ain't any better than Owen Pike and his gang."

She twisted the small lace handkerchief in her hands. "But there will be more trouble, more shooting."

"Only if Red wants it that way," Hank said.

Julia wanted Soto to accompany him back to the Rancho Temescal, but Hank preferred to go alone. He did not like to think of what might happen if Red were drinking and in one of his ugly moods.

He rode with the soft night air pushing back his hat brim, washing his face with the clean sharp smells of the fields. They'd had some times, him and Red; some good, some not so good. Just last spring, when the bosque was sharp with the fragrance of new leaves and blossoms, and they were camped on the sand in the tunnel of cottonwoods along a river. They had hunted some horses which had strayed during a storm. There was venison and quail and wild turkey, and trout for the taking.

"A man'd have to be pretty used up, not to go for this," Red had said, and he spoke as if he wanted nothing else out of life. Then, a week later, a sandstorm caught them on the Jornada. They worked in a blinding, choking fury, struggling to keep the herd all in one piece, while their clothes tore to pieces on their bodies. "Anybody who tries to make a living this way should have his head patched for cracks, by Godlins!" Red moaned, forgetting the things he'd said a week before.

That was his way. Blowing hot one minute, cold the next. So maybe, Hank thought, he'll have changed his mind about making a big thing out of the Rancho Temescal, maybe something else will have struck his fancy by now.

The main house blazed with light, but like the Calder ranch it was quiet. Hank reined before the courtyard gate, which was closed. He had one leg out of the saddle when he heard the whine of a slug and felt his hat spin off into the darkness.

His mount shied, but Hank wasn't thrown; it was his own idea to leap from the stirrup and roll into the protection afforded by the thick wall, away from the doorway. Gun out, he waited, but there was no second shot.

"Red!" he called, changing position, just in case.

"Is that you, Hank? Well, hell, man!" Red Wolfe sang out.

Hank heard his footsteps in the courtyard, then the gate swung wide and Red stood framed in the light from inside.

"Hank! Sorry, *amigo*. I didn't know it was you."

"Man comes to pay a sociable call and gets shot at. You that touchy?"

The redhead grinned apologetically, putting up his gun. "Thought you might be Pike, or some of his boys. Ran into them this morning, up in the North Quarter, and they seemed downright unfriendly, way they were showing their hardware. I slipped them and got back here. . . . Well, come on in, come on in."

They went inside. "You all alone?" Hank asked.

Red studied him for a moment, as if trying to read the full intent behind the question.

"Yeah, Hank. Damn Mexes have been pulling out steady on me since I took over. I got some boys coming out from town. Shoulda been here today, matter of fact." He gave an imitation of the old, brash grin. "By the way, you ain't offered me congratulations on my wedding."

"That's right," Hank said. "I haven't."

Red turned and led the way into the parlor where they had first spoken to Julia de la Torre. Now, another girl — a young, pretty Mexican — got up from the sofa and stood there.

"Go get us some food, sweetheart," Red told her. "Two platters of enchiladas, and plenty of eggs."

He flopped on the sofa, while Hank took the seat he had used the last time. The antimacassar was gone, he noted. "You ain't been making friends right and left, have you?"

"Ain't it a fact, though. Tell you what's the truth, I can't understand how come a nice, lovable fella like me has got so many people looking down their noses at him." When Hank merely stared at him, he went on. "You can't blame a man for feathering his own nest, now, can you? Hell, if I hadn't grabbed off this place, the vultures like Pike would'a'."

"You were pulling out for the mines."

Red laughed. "This here can be a gold mine, Hank." He indicated a bottle of brandy on the low table between them. "Pour yourself a nugget."

They had a drink. Hank watched the redhead take two more in quick succession before he allowed his own glass to be refilled. Wolfe was struggling mightily to keep the light smile on his mouth, but Hank knew what the effort was costing him. This thing had not gone as easily or as well as Red thought it would.

Hank shifted in his chair. His holster hung free. "Ramon Calder died a little while ago."

Red frowned, started to say something and thought better of it. "Damn, I'm sorry." He rubbed his chin a while. "Hank, the straight of it—I didn't want to shoot him. God's honor. But the little hothead wouldn't give me a chance to talk. Went pawing for his iron. Hell-fire, what could I do?"

"You could have left, before any trouble started." He got to his feet, careful not to make a sudden movement of it. "I think it'll be better all ways round, if you and me just sorta mosey out of here."

Red's glance sidled up, and veiled itself. He smiled. "So that's what's on your mind. The way I been figuring, Hank, was you might be looking to go partners again. Now the girl —this Julie—she don't mean nothing to me. You know the way I am about women—one's about as good as the other. Just 'cause she happens to be my wife. . . ."

"Cut it," Hank said.

"Man, you got that preacher look again. Whenever you gonna relax and start enjoying life. This here spread is big enough for the both of us. We could live like kings."

"How long do you think you're gonna last around here?" Hank demanded angrily. "How long do you think it'll be before these people get sick and tired of the gringos pushing them around, robbing them blind, deaf and dumb? Red, get some sense."

Red laughed. "I don't want to live to be an old, old man. I just want to live *like* a man. Not like somebody sucking favors from a Mex gal, getting her ranch back for her from the big bad gringo and—"

"You're crazy!"

"No, Hank. You're the one's been nibbling that loco weed, if you think you can talk me into giving up all this. I ain't leaving. Now, if you propose to try and make me. . . ."

Red started to his feet. Hank's leg lashed out against the low table, skidding it across the tiles. It crashed into Red's knees and he swore, falling backward, his hand clasping his gun. Hank followed the table in a low dive. He and Red piled into the sofa and it went over backward, spilling them upon the floor. Hank's greater weight worked for him. He landed hard on Red and held him squirming, unable to reach his gun around.

"Drop it," Hank muttered.

Red struggled to get free. Hank ground an elbow and fore-arm against Red's throat, cutting off the flow of curses, chok-ing him.

Red dropped his gun and Hank picked it up.

"Let's go."

The redhead rubbed his throat. "I keep forgetting you're a knife man," he said wryly. "You knife men are just too damn sneaky to suit me."

"C'mon."

"You really mean it?" Red was amazed. "Hank, how the hell you fixing to keep me. Chain-hobble me or something?

I'm telling you, first chance I get I'm heading right back here to my good old rancho."

"Shut up," Hank said. "You get any ideas and I'll make Julie the happiest widow in California!"

They got as far as the door to the hall when the night erupted into violence. A fusillade of shots tore through the house; horse hooves pounded in the courtyard.

They heard the big, East-Texas voice of Owen Pike bawling to his riders, "Burn the bastard out! Burn it all! Wolfe, just show your mangy head!"

The did not know how many squatters Owen Pike had brought with him on this raid-and-ride, but it sounded like a regiment. The riders whooped their horses in different directions and slung firebrands that painted weird shadows in the hall behind where Hank and Red lay low. One torch crashed through a window in their room; it caught in the curtains. The dry cloth went up with a sudden, sizzling roar.

"He really means to burn the whole place out," Hank said.

Red grinned. "You know, I do think friend Pike is peeved 'cause I made Julie's title too legal to bust up."

"Helping me take part of his ear didn't make him love you none, either." Hank had Red's Colt out. "Partner, let's get back in business." He handed over the gun and clapped Red on the shoulder.

"Let's see if we can get the rest of that ear!" Red raced over and pulled down the flaming curtain, stamped it dark with his boots. He snapped a couple of shots out the window at the horsemen who were swinging back into the courtyard.

"You man enough to come and get me, Pike?" he hollered.

While Red backed down the wall from the doorway, Hank dropped to one knee behind a heavy table.

Outside, Pike's voice raised in a shout: "The bastard's in there, all right!"

– 115 –

A volley of shots drummed through the door. Pike came into the shadowy hall but did not enter the room at once. There was some conversation, and then two other men appeared, neither of whom Hank knew. Brown, who Hank had met previously, came in. Finally, bulwarked behind the other three, Owen Pike entered.

Pike had his gun out. So did Brown. The others merely had their hands on their holstered revolvers.

"Raise 'em boys," Hank said.

He guessed what Pike might do, and he was a move ahead of him. He had his gun barrel trained on the doorway, and when Pike fired wildly at the table top and lunged backward for the safety of the hall, Hank's shot caught him, splitting him in the middle. Pike, still moving, crashed against the wall opposite the door and slewed away.

The room was dense with smoke, but Hank saw Brown throwing down on him, and he ducked and slid away. The bullet ripped a gash in the table as it tore through. There was the thunder of his shot and the tumultuous, echoing roar of Red's Colt. Hank did not need to look to know that Brown was out of it.

"Look out!" Red called. "Behind you!"

Hank spun, the gun held sideways in his hand, throwing lead as if he were scything grass. Something burned him in his shoulder but he saw one of the squatters disappear before his fire, kneeling almost as if in prayer. The other squatter was fanning the hammer of his gun with the hard heel of his hand, and Red was answering, crouched low, weaving with each shot. They were within whispering distance of each other. Their bodies jerked as the bullets sped between them.

"Red!" Hank cried, "Red!" using his own gun on the squatter. He drove the man down, but he knew that it was too late. Red fell heavily before he could reach him, his face drained of color. The freckles stood out sharply, like rust spots touched to wax; and the boyish mouth, relieved of all strain, was younger than Hank had ever seen it.

Afterward, he worked with Soto and the other Mexican hands who had ridden over from the Calder ranch, attracted by the flames. They killed the fires in the main house, but two of the outbuildings were leveled to the ground.

Hank did not remember that he had been shot until he fell down in the courtyard. He crawled over and sat against the wall, and it was there that Julie found him when she rode up in the turnout.

"Pobrecito! Pobrecito!"

She lay her face against his cheek and he thought that she was crying, but he could not tell for sure. The night and all the people in it swirled in his vision. When he awakened she had removed his shirt and had bound his shoulder with clean cloth.

He pulled her to him and they sat together by the wall. High over the vineyards a half moon shone. There was a faint mist from the irrigated fields, a fragrance of wetness and vines that overrode the smell of charred wood.

The burial party filed past them. With his good arm Hank held Julie lightly, and silently they watched until Red's body was taken out through the entrance of Rancho Temescal.

Chivaree

IN the dark cabin Jim felt Nettie's body start and turn toward him. Her Injun blood, he reckoned—rousing on a sound no louder than the whicker of a horse. He held her tightly with one arm while he groped beside the bed for his rifle.

"Stay right here, Nettie," he whispered. "Keep the blankets about you."

"Jim! Jim!" she whispered. "What is it?" She had seen his bare arm hunting the rifle.

"Don't know," Jim Croft grunted, piling out into his boots and heaping the blankets on her. There was no telling what —but blankets would sometimes turn a bullet.

In his nightgown—which Nettie had made him and he had to wear—he slipped to the window. He had hardly reached it when the gunfire let loose. The bullets came in a slogging rhythm against the mud wall under the eaves. It was a shattering thing; but Jim understood, now, and was reassured.

He let the bullets run out; then he called to his wife: "Chivaree! Dress quick and rustle all the cups you can."

There was a blood-chilling sound, ripped through with a wild coyote yelling. There was some grunting, too—all the sounds which passed for Indian. He wondered if Nettie got it. If she didn't get it, Reuben Lightfoot—and the crowd he had brought along for the fun—would make it plain enough.

Again the guns blasted at the cabin; hoofs thudded in the corral and the chickens were squawking. Nettie came to him, pressing fearfully against his side. Her dark hair hung in two long braids over her shoulders. Her breast was soft against his arm, and Jim wanted poignantly to make it all smooth and easy for her, to keep her pride as shining as her eyes.

"What will they do, Jim?"

"Just horse around a bit. Don't let on you're scairt. But don't take anything from Rube Lightfoot, either. The others will be all right, unless—"

He watched her pull her flowered calico gown down over her nightdress. This dark-eyed wife of his—he loved her so much it was hard to bear. Nights, he couldn't squeeze her close enough; days, he'd make chores to take him back to the cabin. They were singing-happy, but inside they had both been waiting for the thing that would determine whether they would be neighbors or outlanders . . . whether a squawman and his half-breed wife would be accepted in this recently Indian country. And now Rube Lightfoot had brought it to them.

Jim opened the door. "When you lobos get done howling at the moon, come in and wet your whistles!" he shouted.

The gobbling and firing ended. Lightfoot's rainbarrel bass rumbled. "Well, she ain't scalped him yit, evidentally!"

Out of the sagebrush tromped a dozen men. Boots scuffing, smelling of man-sweat and horse-sweat, unshaven and brazen-eyed, they crowded into the cabin. On the table, Nettie Croft had placed a jug of corn whiskey and all the vessels which could pass for cups, including two small pottery pans.

"Missus Croft," Lightfoot said, "you set a mighty fine table." He took one of the pottery vessels.

The other men crowded in to the whiskey, cowpunchers who worked for Reuben Lightfoot and small ranchers like Jim. Lightfoot said, tossing a hand at the rumpled cot, "I see as you folks were in bed."

"Where else, at two o'clock in the morning?"

Nettie flushed. Jim's smile was varnish over the rough timber of his dislike. Lightfoot was a huge turkey-buzzard of a man, belligerent and bungling. He had got rich merely by getting onto this range first. It took more cleverness, now, but one day the likes of Lightfoot would be made to prove up on some of the range they claimed.

Lightfoot had a lofty nose and an oval-shaped black chinbeard. He inspected Nettie with a savoring curiosity. "I'm Rube Lightfoot, Missus Croft. I expect you've heard of me."

"I have, Mr. Lightfoot. You're quite famous."

Lightfoot rubbed whiskey from his chin. "Some of your people were quite famous, too, ma'am. I hope none of your lodge was at Little Rosebud. I lost a brother there."

"Those were Sioux, Mr. Lightfoot. My mother's people were Cherokee. My father, you know, was a Scotch trader."

Jim shoved between them. "Boys, you aren't drinking." He refilled Lightfoot's cup and started around. Suddenly he heard Nettie cry out; he whirled, the jug lying across the crook of his arm. Dave Banta had picked her up by the waist and was holding her so that her dark brushed hair was against the herringbone rip-rapping of the ceiling. A tall, skinny man in overalls, Banta had eyebrows and mustaches as yellow as chick fuzz.

"Always heard you couldn't creep up on an Injun!" he said. "Dang lie!"

The men in the cabin, Jim thought, would gag on their laughter. They slapped their legs and hooted, and tall John Porter howled and slapped his palm against his mouth, making the gobbling cry they had heard from the darkness.

Jim stood with a grin pasted on his face, despising them.

Banta set the girl down. She smoothed her dress over her hips.

"Of course I'm only half Indian, or I'd heard you coming,"

she said. Then: "I could make coffee and biscuits."

"Never mind," said Lightfoot. "I only come over on business anyhow. Directly we'll go along."

"Business?" asked Jim. "With me?"

"Two things, Croft," Lightfoot said. "You're overworking that Tres Piedras pasture of mine. You figuring to set up a Cherokee village for those papooses you'll be getting soon? I moved your stuff off it today."

"My deed says it's mine. I'll move them back tomorrow."

Lightfoot smiled, and a hard light came into his eyes. "It ain't the place of a guest to contend with his host. We'll talk about it when you're guest under my roof, which will be next week. I'm going to barbecue some goats o' Saturday. You and your squaw can come if you like."

Banta chuckled, and for a moment Jim's jaw muscles marbled and he was on the point of stepping into the rancher. But then he said drily, "Sure, Rube. We'll be there."

Lightfoot signaled that the fun was over by opening the door and herding the others toward it and out into the yard.

You could hear them cackling clean to Sierra County, thought Jim, and he stood there and watched them trudge off to their horses. Back from the darkness came Dave Banta's shout.

"So long, Jim! Hold onto your scalp!"

He went back, ashamed before his wife. He had drunk with these men and fought with one or two; fought beside them during the Texas trail invasion. But by taking a half-breed wife, he had made himself a stranger to them.

Nettie's arms slipped around his neck. She smiled. "It's all right, Jim. They're just testing us."

"It will be all right," said Jim grimly, "if I have to horsewhip every man in Sacaton County!"

"What about the women? No, Jim," she said. "If I can't

make them respect me for myself, your trouncing them won't help."

That was it, Jim realized. It was something he couldn't fight in the usual way. He snuffed the candle and punched a hole in the bolster with his head. "All right," he said. "I'll keep back. But if the big ox touches you, or his woman says any of the things they're askin' us over to say — I'll clean some plows right there."

"It wouldn't help, Jim. We could be proud and lonely, but I don't want to be lonely. I want friends, and friends for our children. I want them coming over to borrow things. I want neighbors, Jim, not next-door enemies."

Driving over Saturday morning, Jim kept tucking the blanket about her lap, making sure there wasn't space between them for a thickness of buckskin. It was March, with a few rags of snow under the junipers, brilliant against the red earth. The gray sky was slotted with bars of turquoise. Nettie's coloring was earthy, her lips vivid, her eyes pale blue against dark lashes. Her being so pretty, he thought, would make it no easier for her to get on with the women.

Out under the oaks in Reuben Lightfoot's canyon-bottom home place, the smoke fumed deliciously in barbecue pits. A small army of neighbors had collected — thirty or forty ranchers, their wives and children. In the rough way of the country, the Lightfoot place was grand. The house was large, a low adobe structure without plaster; the corrals were rambling and tight; there was a barn with a sheet metal roof.

Rube was the grand and mannerless host, keeping the whiskey flowing while his guests waited for the goats to cook through. Dave Banta lugged a gallon lard can around, smearing tart comeback sauce on the carcasses. Lightfoot roared greetings to the Crofts and a couple of other families just arriving. Mrs. Lightfoot, a small woman with a florid skin and the figure of a sack of potatoes, collected the women.

"Come along and fresh up, ladies," she said. "You might as well come, too, Mrs. Croft."

Jim stopped dead. He looked at Nettie. It had gone into her like a knife. For an instant he thought she would cry. Then he heard her saying gravely, "I'd like to. Won't you call me Nettie?"

"If you want," said Mrs. Lightfoot coldly.

While she was gone, he toured around among these men he had not seen since his marriage. They all wanted to know where he had captured his squaw, and he told them the same thing, "Off a reservation; where else?"

"Well, look out for her, ever she goes on the warpath," said tall John Porter.

"Look out for any of them, when that happens," said Jim.

The women came back, and now the barbecue was ready, the savor of it tremendous in the air. Rube stuffed a dishtowel under his belt, whipped an edge onto a carving knife, and began to carve. Coffee bubbled endlessly from blackened kettles. Horseshoes clanged against a stake somewhere, and men leaned against trees and wagons, with pie tins balanced on their palms. But their eyes were never off Jim and his half-breed wife, and rebellion built steadily in him.

He heard Mrs. Lightfoot say to Nettie, "Tell us about your life at the trading post, girl."

It was suddenly quiet. They waited, like beggars, for the meanest slip they could twist into something laughable or damning.

"Why, it was nice, but lonesome. We'd be snowed in so long, and just the same faces all the time. I was awfully glad when—when I came down here. Everyone's been so friendly."

"Did you ever have trouble with—with savages?" asked Mrs. Lightfoot.

"Indians, you mean? No, not at our post. They were friendly."

"I expect it's all in knowing how to handle them."

"Yes."

"How do you handle them?" Mrs. Lightfoot asked, and you could hear nothing but a horseshoe clanging against an iron stake.

"Just as you'd like to be handled yourself," Nettie said softly.

Mrs. Lightfoot was stopped for a moment. Lucy Banta simpered, "What was your real name, Nettie? Laughing Water, or something?"

One of the younger women tittered. Jim slung his coffee grounds into the pit. The steam flared hotly. He saw Lucy Banta start as he went slowly toward her.

"She was born a Christian, Lucy. By the way, I heard they're taking bids for a herd of beef at the Territorial prison. You ought to get Dave to bid—combine business and pleasure, as you might say."

Mrs. Banta's brother was making hair bridles in Santa Fe, having been caught with a small, select herd of whitefaces two years ago. Nettie arched an alarmed glance at Jim, but he would not back water. He stared Lucy Banta down.

Then he heard Rube Lightfoot's chuckle. "A cowthief," he said, "is just a nester that got caught. That's fine talk from you, Squawman."

Jim was seized with a cold and reckless fury. He turned quickly on Lightfoot, gripping the bosom of his buckskin shirt and ramming his back against a tree.

"That's one thing nobody calls me, Rube. Just nobody!"

The rancher grinned, his face larded with a bland satisfaction. "What do we call you—Gin'ral?"

"Anything except that." Jim was conscious that silence had invaded the yard. Everyone watched. Everyone listened.

Rube gathered his malice in his mouth like spittle. He said

softly, "Settin' yourself a big task, Jim, if you aim to whip every man that looks crostwise at you. I figure you don't make a thing something it ain't by telling other folks it's so. If it's there, they'll see it."

"If what's there?"

"What you want them to see."

"I don't want them to see squawman on me, Rube. That's what I'm saying. And you'd better not be talking about anybody else in my family."

The moment was thick; it ended with Mrs. Lightfoot's crying, "Well, land, we ain't touched the pies yet!"

Lightfoot, with a wink at Dave Banta, went to the house. Jim's shoulders made a settling motion, like a dog laying the hairs on his back. He hitched up his belt and looked around. At once he saw that he had blundered. Nettie was biting her lip to keep from crying. He had done what she had begged him not to. He had demanded something that could not be taken by force—respect for his wife. He had, by challenging Rube, merely shamed her.

He put aside the rest of his food and went to watch a horseshoe game.

The sun began to drift deeper into the hills. For hours, no one had stopped eating. Most of the men, including Lightfoot, had not stopped drinking. A lot of ranch wives would do the driving on the way home. He had a desperate desire to do something to make amends; he had this desire and at the same time wanted to crush them all with some supreme blow.

As it neared leaving time, Jim became aware that the men were ribbing Lightfoot up to something. When he was drunk, he always did feats of strength. He had already hoisted a calf over his head and wrestled down half the men in sight. Now, with Banta grinning at his side, he swaggered over to Jim.

"Injun-rassle you two out of three, Gin'ral," he said.

Nettie was shaking her head. Mrs. Lightfoot and the other ladies watched with cockfight eagerness behind their proper faces.

Jim looked Rube over. "Figure you can make it interesting for me?"

"Bet a long yearlin' you won't be bored."

Jim hitched up his pants and lay on the ground. Loaded with food and liquor, Lightfoot arranged his arms and legs for the best purchase. The men swarmed around them as they raised their legs on signal and began sparring. Rattlesnake-quick, Jim's foot caught Lightfoot's ankle. A single heave threwe the rancher out of position.

Jim laughed, while Rube swore and began claiming he had not been ready. Dave Banta laughed. "Ready as you'd ever be, Rube. Tally one for Jim."

Lightfoot's face was swollen with fury. He lay back. Banta called time and their legs went up. Cagey this time, Lightfoot feinted. Abruptly locking his knee about Jim's leg, he gave a sideward yank. Jim turned his leg and let the man's weight slough aside. With a surprised gasp, Rube rocked onto his side. He grunted, "Anybody can run!" and began to spar again.

Immediately Jim caught the fat leg with his heel and threw Lightfoot onto his face.

He sprang up. Banta and the others hooted at the rancher's protests. Lightfoot came up, looking sick and ugly.

"I hope all your kids are born with feathers in their hair, Croft," he said.

For a moment, Jim could almost feel his pulpy mouth on his knuckles. But after a moment his rage drained out of him. He was tired and defeated. He turned away, hating them all. He hated each one and he hated them as a clan. He despised them for the lonely years ahead of Nettie.

Remembering about the Tres Piedras pasture, he knew what he was going to say. He would tell Rube to keep the hell out, or there would be shooting trouble.

He was glad when the day finally ended. Darkness stifled the big ranchyard. Children began to fuss and livestock bawled in the pasture. Jim went to collect the pans in which Nettie had brought gooseberry pies. He found them in the kitchen, returning then to look for Nettie. But she had gone to the wagon in the trees.

As he entered the dark grove, Jim heard scuffling. He halted, listening. Nettie's voice came, low and taut. "Mr. Lightfoot! You aren't yourself."

The rancher's voice was choked with heat. "Don't be coy with old Rube, gal. I know Injun gals. Come on, now—"

Jim was striding through the dark. He heard Nettie sobbing with hurt and shame, "Mr. Lightfoot!"

Lightfoot was a hunched, bearish back. All Jim could see of Nettie was her face over his shoulder. Rube's mouth was pressed against the hollow of her throat. At the last instant he heard Jim. He swerved away and came slowly about.

Jim's fist collided with his cheekbone. It made a sharp, meaty slap.

Rube reeled back against a wagonshaft. Nettie cried out and came between them. The horse reared. Thrusting her aside, Jim met the rancher. Lightfoot's fist boomed against his chest. Jim hit him a savage chop on the ear. Lightfoot was driven to the ground, but he seized Jim's leg and pulled himself up.

A lantern was swinging in quick arcs through the trees. "What's all the rannikaboo, there, Rube?" someone shouted. Mrs. Lightfoot's cry came with a lacing of fear, "Reuben!"

Jim squared off, his fist cocked. Rube's face was a blank, bruised target. He looked scared. Jim savored the moment.

Lightfoot had had his day of shaming others, and now he was about to be shamed before his wife and guests. He would never again ride into town without seeing hands raised to whispering mouths.

But it was suddenly Nettie's face before Jim, and her hands were against his chest. "No, Jim!" she said urgently. Jim thrust her away. "Jim, please! For me! You promised . . ."

When Dave Banta arrived to hold his lantern above the men and the girl and the rearing horse, Jim stood with his long arms hanging. Rube looked drunk and foolish. The tableau lingered until Mrs. Lightfoot and the rest crowded in. Jim saw the shame and terror on her face. He was oddly touched —troubled that she must suffer, too.

Abruptly Nettie turned toward Rube. She touched his bruised cheekbone, exclaiming in sympathy. "Oh, it's going to blacken, Rube! We're so sorry—Jim," she cried, "I asked you not to use that horse. Why, he's just a half-trained bronc!"

Jim was stopped. Nettie pulled Rube away from the shafts. Dave Banta seized a cheekstrap to drag the horse down.

"Look out for him," Nettie cautioned. "He's a terror to club you with his head. Why, Rube was just harnessing him for me and he hit him without blinking an eye. He hit Jim only last week. On—on the right ear, wasn't it, Jim?"

Nettie's eyes were begging him. ". . . The left," said Jim. "I wouldn't have taken him, only he was handy. Rube, I reckon I owe you an apology." His mouth barely smiled.

Rube stirred out of his paralysis. "Sho'. I ought to know a skittish horse when I see one. My fault, Jim."

His wife, thought Jim, had the eyes of a grateful dog. She was looking gently at Nettie. "Don't feel sorry for the man," she said. "Maybe the horse just knows a drunken old fool when it sees one."

Jim shouted his laughter, and that was the end of it. Rube

took their banter, fussed with the harness, and finally the four of them were alone. Jim tucked the robe about Nettie, straight and dark-haired on the seat. As he put his foot up to mount, Mrs. Lightfoot spoke hesitantly.

"He—he does the most outlandish things when he's drinking, Nettie."

"Your husband's a great one to chivaree, that's all. He might have fooled me, only Jim told me beforehand, 'Rube's a great josher. But he's got a heart as good as gold'."

"Did Jim say that? Well, Rube's a diamond in the rough, only sometimes—"

Just as the wagon ground away, Rube called, "You go ahead and use that pasture, Jim. What's the use of good neighbors argifying over a little old buck-pasture like that'n?"

In the darkness, Nettie's eyes met Jim's, moist and laughing, and Jim knew it was over. They would come no more in the night, insinuating, and trying them. When they came, it would be as friends.

I'll Take the High Road

GINNY was drying her hair on the porch when Clark rode in. It was late afternoon of a day in May. Over the mountains soaring from the pasture the sun distilled an amber light which was just right for the leaves, for the grass, and for Ginny's hair. It was like twenty-four-carat gold, with sequins in the high lights. She heard his spurs on the walk and called to him.

"Did you catch him, Clark?"

Clark grunted. "We'll catch that horse when he's ready to be caught." Wearily, he let himself into a porch chair. Cocking his feet on the rail, he squinted at the light streaming through the fine mesh of her hair. "Blondes," he reflected, "are nice to come home to."

"But not nice enough to stay home with," Ginny said.

"Well, you see, horses are nice too." Clark had been gone four days on a wild-horse chase. He deserved the worst, but instead of tears and recriminations, he anticipated fried chicken with biscuits and gravy.

Ginny's eyes sparkled. They were blue; close up, they were the blue-gray of pine smoke. "So you wasted four days on that horse, and he's still his own man."

"We got so close to him this time that I could see the burrs in his tail. By George, that's a horse!"

"I'll bet! Fourteen years old, stringhalted, and he drags his chin unless he's standing on a ridge trying to impress you gullible cowpunchers. It takes good blood to make good stallions. That's what you said when we bought Red instead of the station wagon."

Clark smiled complacently. It was nice to know she was teasing. They both knew he wasted too much time on wild-horse chases and rodeos; yet she pretended to believe they were part of the business. Hunting and fishing weren't, of course, and neither was spending a couple of days a month with old Billy Hazard, up among the glaciers. Clark's philosophy was to give tomorrow its due, but not to sell today short, either. But Ginny never rode him for his derelictions. Theirs was a comfortable relationship which assumed devotion rather than demanded it.

After three years of marriage, they knew each other pretty well. They talked of making a fortune in quarter horses and whiteface cattle, but they knew they wouldn't. It didn't bother Clark, and he didn't think it bothered Ginny.

A car rumbled across the plank bridge. Dud Winter's pick-up swung into the yard. Dud flashed an envelope. "Telegram, Clark! Picked it up in town."

He lumbered up the steps and leaned his substantial hind-quarters against the railing while Clark opened the wire. Dud's big, simple face was avariciously inquisitive.

"Huh!" Clark said.

"Who's coming?" Ginny asked.

"Somebody named Lee Cushman. Wonder who he is?"

Ginny brightened and began tying a handkerchief about her hair. "Why, don't you remember? He was at the Salinas rodeo last year. He tried to buy Red. I think he said he was a horse trainer for the movies."

She caught the iron look of warning suddenly rising to Clark's eyes. "Or something," she added.

"Don't think you never mentioned him to me," Dud said.

Of Dud Winter, Billy Hazard had once remarked: "Dud ain't got the sense to pour whisky out of a boot, but he can smell a horse sale two counties off."

Clark laughed offhandedly. "You know those movie people!

Lots of talk, but nothing behind it. I think he runs a boarding stable near Hollywood."

Dud's round blue eyes turned to Ginny. "I thought you said he trained broncs?"

"I was just guessing."

"What do you suppose he wants?"

Clark put the wire in his pocket. "He's wasting his time if he still thinks he can buy Red. Four hundred, he offered!"

"When's he coming?" Dud asked. He ran a horse ranch just east of Clark's, and it was no trouble at all to drop over any old time.

"Saturday." The wire said Thursday. It said: "*Have opportunity for you to supply colts to movie trade. Your price.*"

Dud drove away with a pleased and thoughtful expression.

Lee Cushman drove up on Thursday. He was a likable man in his early forties, deeply tanned and with tightly waved gray hair and a mustache three hairs wide. He dressed casually in wrinkled slacks, a field jacket, and scuffed boots.

After lunch they went out to the corral. All the horses had been curried to the fine sheen of oiled silk. Cushman could not keep his hands off them. They were highly bred and responsive, and he was a quarter-horse man, one of the fraternity which held that a pony capable of roping cows on weekdays and beating Olhaverry in the quarter-mile on Sunday was a lot of horse.

After Clark let him ride Morocco, a half-trained bay, he regarded it respectfully. "That's the finest Technicolor stud I've seen in years!"

"What's the difference between a Technicolor stud and any other?" Clark laughed.

"About two hundred dollars. It used to be color was just something to wrap a horse up in. Consequently there's people raising buckskins, blue roans, and grays everywhere; but try to find somebody you can count on for bays and chestnuts!"

"You can count on me," Clark said. He hardly knew whether to take Cushman seriously or not. "There hasn't been a cold color in this line for generations. It just happened, but we can try to keep it that way, if it matters."

Cushman wanted to try the horses out. They rode five miles up Spanish Creek. It was a spectacular country of breath-taking extremes. Behind and below them were the flat gray desert and the burnt-sienna hills hiding the smoking ugliness of Death Valley. Before them the Sierras presented towering façades of granite, lofty rims where the snows never melted.

Clark was pleased to observe Cushman responding to it. Yet there was a drop of the motion-picture producer in Cushman's enjoyment.

"You ought to run dudes here, Clark," he said seriously.

But Clark shuddered. "I've always avoided anything that requires special feeding."

They rode on up to Jawbone Lake, a splinter of emerald caught in giant boulders. Clark had a stone corral here. From the branch of a twisted oak hung branding irons and scraps of harness. Lee Cushman said again: "With a spot like this, it's a crime not to capitalize on it!"

Clark let it lie. In a windy dusk, they rode back to the ranch.

It was cool enough that night for a fire. With one of Ginny's fine meals under his belt and a drink in his hand, Cushman relaxed. The big living room was as informal as a bunkhouse. The floor was of rubbed tile; the tawny adobe walls pointed up the bright Mexican rugs. The house was Ginny's hobby—one of those hobbies women have before the children come and after they leave.

Cushman got down to business. He was training eight or ten horses a year. He could use all the Steeldusts Clark could raise. Anything that did not come up, he could sell as a saddle mount.

"You see, I'm tired of following up leads. I hear about a horse in Arizona, but by the time I get there he's just being loaded into a trailer. And maybe he's got Thoroughbred blood in him, anyway, and a gunshot would send him into hysterics. I'll pay you 25 per cent more than you'll get anywhere else, just to know the horses will be right and ready. How about it?"

Clark glanced at Ginny, and if she did not speak the small tight smile on her lips talked a plain language. *If the money means more to you than your mountains, go ahead.*

He got up and poured Cushman another drink. He was rather surprised to discover that he was excited. Not over the money, but over the idea of going into horses big; of having a show ranch. He saw it in redwood: "The Travis Quarter-Horse Ranch." And of course the material things were pleasant to contemplate too, the fine trappings of prosperity. But it would mean the end of wild-horse chases for a while.

"Well—" he said, finally; and then hesitated. "Well, how about it, Ginny?"

"You're the businessman," Ginny said. She wasn't helping any.

Clark drained his glass and spun the ice in the bottom of it, and set the glass down and pressed it against the coaster an instant. "I guess we'll try it."

"Fine!" Cushman smiled, but didn't get excited. He spoke to Ginny. "I have been trying to interest Clark in taking some paying guests, Mrs. Travis. Somebody's always asking me about a ranch where they don't dress for dinner or go on tours. They wouldn't want anything but good food and horses. I'd say you have the perfect set-up. And if you charged less than twenty dollars a day, they'd feel cheated."

Ginny laid a finger on her cheek. "It sounds wonderful! I suppose I could fix up the storerooms and partition the bunkhouse."

Clark looked startled. "Sure that's what you want to do, hon?"

"Why not? You 'tend to your horses, and I'll 'tend to my dudes!"

After Cushman went to his room Clark said: "You aren't sore about the deal with Cushman, are you?"

Ginny sat on the rug before the fireplace. "No. A little worried, I guess. Because if this is another of your enthusiasms, Clark, it will be the most expensive one you've had."

He didn't like the word "enthusiasms." It made him think of an elderly playboy cavorting through his love affairs. He was nearly thirty, a little old for whimsies. "It's no enthusiasm," he said shortly. "It's time we got an angle, and I think this is it."

His last thought that night, an irrelevant thought called up by a subconscious calendar in his mind, was: I'll have to get some leaders soaking for the opening next week. It was a pleasant thought to go to sleep on; but a small stern-lipped objection showed its face just as he fell asleep: You won't have time for the opening. You have those ponies to get ready. . . .

As Cushman was leaving the next morning, Dud Winter rode in on his palomino. Clark noticed that the big quarter horse, Dutch, had been curried until it gleamed like greased gold. Cushman turned from the car to stare at it.

Dud, grinning fatly, dismounted. "Just thought I'd stop by, Clark, in case you wanted anything from town."

"Pretty long ride," Clark said, "when you could have taken the pick-up."

Cushman hadn't even seen Dud, yet. He walked around the great golden horse. "Got any more of these?" he asked Dud.

"You kinda favor palominos?" Dud asked coyly.

"Haven't, up to now." Cushman rubbed his chin. "Might

– 135 –

be something in it, though. That's a good-looking stud."

Dud turned the stirrup and remounted. "Glad to help you any time I can. Be seeing you, Clark. Glad to've met you, Mr. Cushman."

Cushman drove off, and a few minutes later Clark saw Dud swing his horse east and start for home. "I hope that crockhead breaks a leg," he told Ginny. "If it rained pennies over here, Dud would be on hand with a piggy bank."

It was hard to tell whether this was an end or a beginning. It was the end of loafing and inviting one's soul. It was the beginning of working with horses, instead of what Clark used to call "fooling with broncs." He attended endless horse auctions, for there was no magic that would give him more colts without buying more mares.

At the same time, Ginny seemed possessed of an urge to turn Spanish Fork into a trading post. She brought in carloads of rugs, hides, and furniture. She hung ollas from the beams of the porch. Window boxes appeared, and all the walks were traced with whitewashed stones. Clark began to suspect she was taking advantage of a situation.

One day Billy Hazard came rambling in on his red mule. Clark, working with a horse in the corral, saw him stop short and peer at the ranch house. In a city, he would have checked the address. Billy scratched his head and sat uncertainly on the mule.

Clark went out. "What drove you out?" he asked. "Fire?"

Billy had been born in the hills, offspring, so the legend ran, of a glacier and a mountain goat. His features were narrow, flat, and brown, and he wore an Army campaign hat that made him look like William S. Hart. Billy lived on a Spanish-American War pension. He could have made good money guiding sportsmen, but he contended a hunting dog wasn't made to run with poodles. He had a fine Thoreau-like philosophy that was like whisky to Clark's soul.

"What the hell's going on around here?" Billy demanded.

Clark hedged. "Oh, Ginny's getting ready for guests. A woman gets lonesome, you know, out like this."

"Lonesome!" Billy looked around. The trees were still there. The creek was talking its usual good sense, for whoever wanted to listen. The mountains hadn't moved away.

"For company," Clark said.

"Oh!" Billy accepted it without trying to understand. Women were said to be necessary; but God help the man who tried to understand them. He glanced into the corral. "What are you trying to do—corner the horse market?"

"I've made a deal with a fellow to take all the horses I can raise. Pretty good money in it."

Billy looked concerned. "You hard up, Clark? I've got a bit put by."

Clark wished he had rehearsed this scene. "We're going all right, Billy, but I've got to think about the future. I've got to save for the children, when they come along, and—well, a lot of things."

Billy peered at him, and finally dismissed the whole matter by spitting in the dust. His eyes freshened. "Better saddle up, Clark. I've got old Silvertip spotted. He's got his mares in Icehouse Cañon. We'll shore put a halter on him this time!"

A cool, clean breeze entered Clark's mind, scattering the hundred vague worries of the past weeks. It brought the green fragrance of the pines. It rang with the silver music of a stallion's call.

Sternly the worries reassembled. "Billy, I'm going to have to skip it this time. I've got three horses to get ready before next week. Some folks are coming, and they'll want to ride. Besides," he said, "what would we have if we did catch him? A cold-blooded, wall-eyed outlaw."

"Then why have we been chasing him all over Inyo County?" Billy demanded.

"For the same reason we hunted that lost gold mine last summer—an enthusiasm."

Billy scratched the mule's neck. Finally he swung around. "Come on up after you turn this nut house back into a ranch."

It was unreasonable, and Clark frowned after him. But that night, when the darkness flowed down from Billy Hazard's mountains, he had a tingle as he thought of Billy setting his trap to catch the stallion.

On the 3rd of July, Cushman arrived with two guests: a good-looking young fellow dressed like Roy Rogers, and a sultry-eyed brunette. The Roy Rogers character was an up-coming Western actor named Barry Carter. The girl, Lois Lane, also played in Westerns, although there was nothing homespun about her in a belted tan skirt and a diaphanous blouse which she filled marvelously. She had dark, earthy-red lips, and an undeceived look in her eyes.

Clark installed them in their rooms and saddled the horses. It seemed that every time he rounded a corner he fell over Barry and Lois.

In the afternoon, they went out for a ride. Ginny stayed to attend to dinner. As Lois started to mount, Clark said quietly: "Look out, Miss Lane. You're going up backward."

Lois discovered she had the wrong foot in the stirrup. She laughed. "They always give me a ladder, in my pictures."

Cushman wanted to show Barry Jawbone Lake as a possible location. They were a couple of miles below it when Lois pointed at a cliff west of the trail. "Isn't that a cave over there?"

"It's called Painted Cave," Clark told her. "There're some Indian pictographs in it.

Lois insisted that they look for Indian pots. Cushman shook

his head. "You and Clark go on. I want Barry to see this other spot."

It was an hour over a rough trail to the cave. Once they were there, Lois showed only mild interest in pots. They sat in the shade to smoke. She was a pleasant companion; but somehow the subject was always some oblique aspect of sex. They got around to the old questions of why men had excelled in every field of endeavor.

"The only place we've beaten you," she deplored, "is in having babies!"

"You girls have done pretty well in acting," Clark said.

Lois laughed lightly and touched his hand. "Mr. Travis, you're gal-lahnt!"

She had, he thought, the most personal eyes he had ever looked into. An instinct from his bachelor days caused him to glance at her hand. No rings. He changed the subject to horses. . . .

It was nearly dark when the two reached the ranch house. The others' horses were already in the corral. As he entered the back door, Clark tried to whistle away a little ghost of guilt. He was not reassured to see a heap of overdone biscuits in the sink. The Indian woman was putting a fresh pan into the oven; and Ginny, at the sink, was starting to make a fresh pot of coffee.

"You two didn't need to rush," she told him. "I can always warm things over and make more biscuits."

"She wanted to see Painted Cave," Clark grunted.

Ginny trilled a little laugh. "Remember the time you brought me up here before we were married? I had to see it, too—after you dragged me there by the hair."

"No, look—" Clark began.

Ginny brushed past him. "Later," she said.

In their room that night, she demanded to see his handker-chief. She studied it on both sides. "No lipstick," she decided.

"So maybe you have changed your habits. Just the same, I think you can see how it looks to other people to be sneaking off with lady guests."

"I told you it was her idea!" Clark protested. "The others could have gone along if they'd wanted to. Good Lord, if you're going to walk up the walls every time I saddle a lady's horse—"

She kicked off her shoes. "It's not that I'm jealous, Clark—"

Clark said: "Ha!"

Her chin went up. "It's just that any woman that's married to a—a playboy, doesn't know what to expect."

She saw the effect of it in his face, and said quickly: "Clark, don't be silly. You know what I meant. You aren't a *playboy*, any more than Billy Hazard is. But you're certainly a nonconformist. I only meant—"

"Forget it."

"I won't forget it! I've got a right to make myself clear." She sounded something more than earnest. There was a small shadow of fright in her eyes.

He went into the bathroom and showered. When he returned, the light was out. He got in bed carefully, but in a moment he heard her say: "I wish every horse on the place would get the epizootic. And that goes for the dudes, too!"

Cushman and his dudes left, new bunches came up, and Clark sent his first batch of horses down to become Triggers or Silvers or merely dusty animals in a sheriff's posse. Whatever they became, they brought the money in. Clark looked at the figures in his passbook, and wondered what had become of the thrill he was to feel.

It was July, now, and high in the thousand lakes wedged in crevices of the mountains the fish were gliding shadows. Clark decided he had to have a week off. The night before he was to leave, a mare dropped a premature foal. He lost it, saved the mare, and wondered where he could find another colt to take the dead one's place.

Then Dud stopped by in his pick-up. He and Dutch were on their way to Salinas. "Ain't missing the big un, are you, Clark? They say ol' Bob Crosby may be there."

"Wish I could. Pretty busy right now." Clark tried to sound as if he were too busy getting rich, but what he felt was the ache of a boy kept in after school the day of the game.

Good old Dud did not fail to stop on his way back. Yes, sir, it had been the hottest thing yet! He and Dutch walked off with two hundred dollars' roping money, and there was a new record set in the team tying.

Clark noticed a new horse in the double trailer. "Buy yourself a plug?"

Dud smiled, a little embarrassedly. "Little ol' mare. Cost too much, but I'll get the money back. I—uh—Cushman was there, Clark. He's going to take a colt now and then."

Clark laid down the bridle he had been repairing. "Look! Is this my market or yours?"

"Cushman says there's room for both of us."

Clark snapped. "Stop kidding yourself. Your tongue's been hanging out ever since you saw that Hollywood address. This thing may last ten years, and it may end tomorrow. The movie public is deciding that—not Cushman. While it does last, it's my baby."

Dud's light blue eyes toughened. "You got a patent on selling horses?"

"I'm appealing to your sense of sportsmanship. You know what I've got sunk in this outfit. And you know that every horse you sell him is one I won't."

Dud glanced at the trailer. "I've got two thousand dollars in that mare, Clark."

"Why, you damned fool!"

Suddenly Clark saw the whole thing. Lee Cushman was the only man who would walk out of this mess with a profit. Unconsciously or otherwise, he had pitted them against each other. All that could come out of the situation was price cutting. That was one step farther than Clark would go to make a dollar.

In Dud's face, some inkling of it began to dawn. "If I hadn't bought that mare— You see, I had to borrow money to get her."

They sat on the running board. Clark said: "How much sporting blood have you got, Dud? Willing to stake Dutch against Red in a match race?"

"That's pretty steep!" Dud rubbed his neck.

"If we keep on competing with each other," Clark reminded him, "we're both going to lose more than just a stallion. We'll be giving horses away, and working like fools to do it."

Even Dud could see that. He took a deep breath and began to nod. "Okay, Clark. Okay."

They decided on the Labor Day rodeo at Bishop for the match. Clark did not tell Ginny about it. Quietly he set out to get Red into shape.

Cushman brought up some dudes for Labor Day week end. On Sunday they all drove down to Bishop. Clark took Red along in the trailer. The town was an hour away, a cool vista of trees along a creek, with the desert for a doormat and the mountains for a back yard. The day was hot, but under the trees at the fairground the broken shade was cool.

Cushman found Clark unloading the stallion. He frowned. "You're not going to rope with *him!*"

"Going to race him."

"What's the idea? If anything happens to Red, our deal's off."

The stallion stepped off the ramp, and Clark held him by the cheek strap. "As a matter of fact," he said, "I'm racing Dud's palomino."

Cushman began to comprehend. "Clark, you're not sore about my arrangement with Dud?"

"I'm not singing carols about it. You've put us in competition with each other. Since neither of us can make a living cutting prices, we're settling it this way. Winner takes both studs."

Cushman was still standing there when he led the horse away. . . .

A few minutes later Ginny hurried over to where he was walking the horse. Cushman had told her about the race. Clark had done a lot of wild things in their married life, but nothing had upset her the way this did. He pointed out to her the same things he had told Dud, but his logic did not reassure her.

"If you lose Red," she told him, "you may never find another horse like him. Clark, you've worked so hard!"

"But I don't intend to lose him, Ginny."

He led the horse through the trees and worked him until the kinks were out. The race was for two o'clock. He heard the loud-speakers announcing the results of the first round of bronc-stomping. With a cold, nervous vacancy in him, he rode back toward the track.

The barrier had been moved to the end of the chute, the tail on the oval track which provided a quarter-mile straightaway. Dud was behind the barrier on his palomino. He said, "H'are yuh, boy?" with forced gaiety.

By now, Clark thought, he must realize he had been maneuvered into a wrong race. Dutch was too light in the hindquarters for a winning start, unless he was running out of his class and Red was way off.

The track was a clean set of lines converging near the trees.

Above them the mountains beckoned, lean and blue and ribbed with granite. This time of day the fish lay deep and lazy, where only the trout flies of such giants as Billy Hazard could rouse them. The wild flowers would be a light on the ground. In the morning, now, there might be a glint of frost in the air.

The starter was waiting. It seemed to Clark that the bay was excessively nervous. Clark dismounted, loosened the cinch a bit, and then realized it was not the horse that had the jitters, but himself. He remounted and brought Red up to the barrier. As the stands quieted, the timers looked at their watches. Then, automatically, Clark and Dud raised their whips. The barrier banged open.

There was a surge that pulled Clark back against the cantle, and then the horse was in long and easy stride down the track. You could ride all your life, Clark thought, but riding one like Red was forever a thrill. For a while you were freed from the slow prison of gravity, riding a breeze as strong and as sweet as a prairie wind.

Dud was right there beside him, lying along the neck of his horse, quirting fiercely and pleading. He and Clark were of a weight, but Dud's was mostly in the seat of his pants. He could distribute himself any way he wanted; the load remained that of a sack of wheat. Gradually he began to slip out of Clark's view, until it was no longer Dud beside him, but the head of his mount.

They were streaking past the bleachers now, breasting an almost tangible roar. They're yelling for you, Clark thought. You lucky stiff! You're winning the best palomino in Inyo County. Ten years, and you'll own the finest Steeldust herd in California, plus a bank roll, a paunch, and a face that turns purple every time you lift a bale of hay.

He glanced back at Dud. There were tears in Dud's eyes and his big clock face was a strangled red as he tried desperately to ride the whip to victory. And somehow the golden horse was beginning to close it up. The stands saw it and came to their feet with a shout. Dud began to quirt like a madman.

But Clark let Red reach, stretching along the horse's neck and giving him the whip, and the thin shadow line of the wire lay across the track just ahead. When they streaked across it, there were a bare six inches of dark-red muzzle between the palomino and the finish.

Clark and Ginny sat on the tailgate of the trailer, drinking beer from cans beaded with cold. Ginny's eyes were still moist.

"Oh, Clark, I'm so happy! It was a beautiful race."

Clark looked at her. She had something of the enameled brilliancy of a party girl, flinging roses riotously, but not fooling anyone.

"You are, are you?" he said. "You look like the face on the mortuary floor. If you really wanted Red to lose, why didn't you say so?"

There were tears in her eyes then, and she said gently: "Oh, darling. I did want him to win—but I wanted us to win too, and I guess we couldn't both, could we?"

Clark squeezed the beer can and felt the cold sting of it in his hand. "I suppose not," he said. . . . "You know, we used to have a lot of fun up there, didn't we?"

Ginny sighed. "We'll never get over it."

"Well, is there any reason why we shouldn't have fun again?" Clark demanded.

"None that I can think of."

Clark finished his beer and jumped off the trailer. "I'll be back," he said. She watched him until he disappeared into the crowd.

Just before sundown they drove out of town with the empty

trailer booming along behind them. "Dud like to broke down," Clark chuckled. "He thought I was doing him a favor. He pays me a thousand apiece for the horses, and 25 per cent of his net from Cushman for two years."

Ginny laughed. "That was mean. But he'll probably make a fortune out of them, at that."

"Serve him right if he does."

She sat close to him as they drove through the warm, rocky hills. "When do you think you'll be back?"

"About a week. And I'll have a rope around that broomtail's neck this time!" He said: "Why don't you have some friends up?"

"Maybe I will. We do have plenty of room, now, don't we?"

"Plenty." Room to kiss your wife. Room to dream. As they turned up the road toward the mountains, Clark began to whistle.

The Trail-Blazers

CHAPTER ONE

King of the Fur Trails

Smallwood looked at his watch. Eleven o'clock in the morning, and already the mountain men who had come rowdying into Widow Parker's Tavern last night, filling the place with the noise of their debauchery until dawn were at it again. They had fallen in bed or burrowed into the hay barn for a few hours' sleep, with their companions, the soldiers, bullwhackers, steamboat roustabouts, and other frontier offscourings who swarmed the red-mud streets of Independence this busy spring.

Jim Smallwood brushed his fawn-colored box coat and fastened the buckles of his trouser-straps. There was, of course, no mirror, but he managed to get a view of himself in the glazed window. He was a tall, well-turned out, slightly cynical looking young man, with "Easterner" written in big letters on him. He adjusted his cravat, purely from habit; neither the unwashed throngs of Independence nor the Widow Parker would know whether the knot was correct.

Below the window, mist still obscured the river, but he heard the hoarse blast of a packet's whistle. Wagons struggled through the cloying mud, top-heavy with baled buffalo hides and merchandise. And on the board sidewalks, just out of reach of the ever-present mud, swarmed the cosmopolitan traffic of the city. Soldiers from Fort Leavenworth mingling

– 147 –

with gangs of ragged looking volunteers outfitting for an excursion against the Mexicans at Santa Fé. Shawnee and Kaws from the Territory drifted about in their bright robes. On the west side of town caravans of white-tilted Conestoga wagons were lined up for outfitting.

Smallwood took a deep breath and went downstairs, taking in the mix of smells and noises of the large dirt-floored room.

Between him and the festivities was a section given to merchandise, with kettles and guns and traps and blankets hanging from wall or ceiling hooks, and beyond were the bar and tables. The man called Old Black, who ran the bar and rolled out the drunks for Widow Parker, was drawing rum—the raw dynamite they called Taos Lightning—from a keg. The trappers, odorous and colorful in their buckskins and moccasins, with all kinds of gear stowed about their persons—embroidered pipe cases and powderhorns, bullet pouches and whetstones, the deadly Green River knife—were playing a game on the floor, with horsehide cards.

There was a great adobe fireplace in one wall, with a dozen kettles on cranes, and here the Widow Parker was busy making some kind of a stew. Her dark-eyed daughter, Allie, sat there in her thin white blouse and short skirt, furrowing her brow over their accounts. Jim Smallwood seated himself opposite the girl.

Allie Parker looked up, smiling quickly when she recognized him. She was for the raw frontier, a pretty girl, thought Smallwood, with her small nose, red lips, and curly black hair hanging down her back and upon her shoulders. But what a difference from the girls he knew in Cincinnati—from Cyn, for instance! He would wager ten dollars that a grizzly bear couldn't cause Allie to faint, where a mouse sent Cyn to bed for a week.

"Morning, Jim," Allie said. And she added, with another smile: "You'll have to excuse the familiarity. It's the custom. Here you call everybody that you aren't fighting with by his first name."

"I'm glad you aren't fighting with me, then," Jim Smallwood said with a smile. "I'll have a cup of coffee—Boston."

Allie said: "Boston?"

"Lots of cream," Jim explained.

"I don't know about the cream," Allie said. She brought him a gray-black mixture in a brown pottery cup, which he downed only because he needed it.

"Mr. Hugh Morgan hasn't come in yet, I take it," he said.

"If Mr. Morgan was here," Allie told him, "you'd know it. He likes to fight, drink, and laugh, and he doesn't do any of them quietly. A real mountain man." She mentioned, dropping her glance, "I'm sort of engaged to him, I guess."

"You guess!" It startled Jim, coming from a place where an engagement called for a ball.

"Well, he hasn't rightly spoken for me. But heaven help the man who slips an arm about my waist when Hugh's around!"

Jim was quiet a moment, frowning into the coffee cup. Beaver pelts had brought him out here, and he had wasted three weeks inspecting the plews the mountain men brought in, and seen nothing his father would care to buy. The big companies were getting the cream, taking the finest furs from the trappers before they ever saw a town, and in these days of waning beaver popularity, only the best of furs was worth buying. Jim had decided to see one more trader.

The man Morgan was one of the few remaining free trappers. Had his own crew, in fact—outfitting them every season, taking them into the river country, and getting first call on their best pelts. Morgan would be the man to see, if he could get to him first. And he had Allie's word that Widow Parker's was always his first stop.

Jim interrupted the girl's figuring once more. "I wonder," he said. "You buy and sell a few furs, don't you?"

She nodded, and they went to the rear of the place. Old Black, a short, humped man, with a black, silver-streaked beard, dragged three bales of beaver furs onto the floor.

Old Black opened a bale and held up two plews for Jim's inspection. "Damn good plews," he said. "Prime."

Jim inspected the backs of the hides. He blew into the silky hairs, searching for bald patches or scars. "Good enough," he said. Then he turned to Allie. "How much?"

"Four dollars apiece."

Jim said: "Good Lord, girl! I can't pay over three and make a profit. And these aren't top furs."

Allie was unmoved. "You won't do any better in Independence, Jim. We take them from the trappers in trade; we've got to make our profit, too. The best furs just aren't coming in any more. Maybe you can strike a bargain with Hugh Morgan. But not at two-forty a bale."

"I'm afraid we'd lose money on these," said Jim. "We sell to the finest hatters in the country. But if Morgan doesn't come tomorrow I may have to take them. I've taken passage on the *Belle Fourche*. My father can't spare me any longer."

Old Black grunted as he shoved the bales back against the wall. "All the money's in outfittin' anyhow," he volunteered, and started off.

"Wait a minute," Jim said. "Outfitting what?"

Old Black showed him his impatient frown. He was a mountain man himself, but icy streams, Assiniboine arrows and carrying heavy loads on his back had taken the spring from his body. "Outfittin' emigrants," he said. "That and tradin' has got all the money. Take a post along the Picketwire or the Snake. Man'd make money."

Allie laughed. "Everybody's cracked on some subject,"

she said. "That's his. All he wants is to get back in the mountains."

The front door banged open, and a big voice rolled through the tavern: "Hide your women and tie down your hair! Hugh Morgan's in town!"

Allie laughed and, taking Jim's arm, moved him toward the front. "Here's your man!" she said.

He came into the middle of the room, a great, golden giant of a man in beaded buckskins, his hair worn long, a possible sack over his shoulder. His chest was like a drum, and the way he walked, like a panther moving, was magnificent. He wore a short yellow beard. Jim Smallwood had not seen such sublime confidence, such thumping vanity, in any man before.

Morgan saw Allie. The possible sack crashed on the packet dirt and he strode across the floor and picked her up in his arms, kissing her resoundingly on the lips. He swung her around, skirts flying, and then he put her down and held her at arms' length to look at her.

"Why does beaver go to the mountains," he said, "when there's fluff like this in the towns?"

"Because he loves the mountains more than the fluff," Allie said, smiling.

Hugh Morgan kissed her again. Jim was both embarrassed and, in an odd way, angry.

Allie Parker said: "Hold on, now, wild man. Here's a man has been waiting two days to see you. This is Jim Smallwood, Hugh."

The mountain man looked at Jim, in his tan coat and trousers with their brown velvet turnbacks, and he smiled, as one does at a little dressed-up poodle. He struck him on the shoulder and said, "Howdy, Jim," and then he turned and went to the bar, where his dozen trappers were clamoring for rum and making a general uproar.

His hand came without warning against the side of a man's head, knocking him against his companion and felling the two of them. They began to swear, getting to their feet, and Morgan said: "Get them furs carried into the barn, hear now? First the work and then the play."

The men went grumbling into the yard. The bourgeois followed them. They could hear his voice bulling them through the job. Jim Smallwood drew a long breath; it was as though he had been completely captivated by some monstrous display of natural force—a waterfall, or a hurricane. And yet he was in a way repulsed by the man, and it surprised him that a girl like Allie, who seemed sensible, should be taken in by his noisy pomp, his cocksureness.

Jim looked at some of the furs. They were prime plews —worth four-fifty each in Independence. In Philadelphia, John Stetson or another big hatter would make them into high-crowned beaver stovepipes that the dandies of New York and New Orleans would pay dearly for, at any rate, this year. Heaven knew when beaver would go out completely. Already there was considerable vogue for silk.

Later he sat at a table with Allie and the Widow Parker, watching Hugh Morgan and his clerk, Rube Hammond, stuff the Widow's stew into their mouths.

Allie said to Morgan: "Jim, here, has been looking at your furs. Have you sold 'em yet?"

"Had some offers," Morgan said. "What you payin, Jim?"

"Four-fifty," Jim Smallwood told him.

Morgan, with a mouth full of food, threw back his head and roared his laughter. "Lordy, man," he said. "Them wasn't polecat hides you were looking at. Them was prime beaver plew—and worth six apiece! What do you take me for—a worm?"

Jim said flatly: "Then I've had my wait for nothing. Six dollars is out of the question."

CHAPTER TWO

With Knife and Guts

Hugh Morgan stopped chuckling. He put a hard and disapproving stare on the Easterner. "You city men," he said, "think you get furs by goin' out in the woods with a saucer of milk and sayin', 'Pussy, pussy!' He pulled his shrunken leather sleeve back and showed blue scars in the flesh, like the marks of giant teeth. "Trap done that," he said. "I got more scars I wouldn't be showin' with ladies present. All of them I got trappin' beaver. I lost two men by pneumony this year; another lost his hair. And you mince and dicker about a dollar and a half!"

Jim felt the disapproval of the whole room. Things had been considerably quieter since the trapper arrived; they all listened for his jokes, ready to laugh with him.

"Four dollars is the going price," he told Morgan. "I think that has always been considered enough to pay for your risks."

Rube Hammond, Morgan's clerk, snorted. He was an undersized, black-haired man with an odor of rancid tallow about him. He held up a hand with a missing index finger. "Does four or six or ten, even, buy me back that finger?" he asked. "No. But I keep on trappin', so that you and your fancy city friends can have hats that the ladies *oh* and *ah* at!"

"Perhaps you are in the wrong business," Jim suggested tartly. "In time you may continue to lose parts of your body until there is nothing left but your mouth. I presume that will be the last to go."

Hugh Morgan laughed, but Rube Hammond flushed angrily.

"As a matter o' fact," said Hugh Morgan, "I reckon I'll get out of the trade sooner or later anyhow. Beaver ain't what it was. Bill Sublette's takin' him a party of invalids to Brown's

Hole for their health. That's what he thinks of beaver. Jim Clyman's guidin'. I been thinking some of running supplies for Genr'l Kearny."

"You show good sense, Hugh," Widow Parker said. "Old Black thinks I should get into outfitting."

Allie came in quickly. "You know, Ma, he may be right. The Santa Fé trail is busy as the Mississippi these days, and it'll be busier. If we had a post—"

"Child," said her mother, "trading posts take money. Lots of money. We'll keep our tavern."

Allie's black eyes went with some daring to Jim Smallwood's face. Jim's got money," she said. "He could write a check for ten thousand, I'll bet, did he want to back us. His dad is Christopher Smallwood, of Cincinnati."

Jim shrugged. "I wonder how much profit there is in such a venture?"

Morgan struck the table with his fist. "Jim," he said, "if you're anyways interested in being a trader, I'll make you a deal. You set me up, and I'll run 'er so you clear twenty thousand a year!"

Jim resented the way he intruded himself into whatever pleased his fancy. "I don't know whether I'm interested or not," he said. "But if I am, Miss Parker has first call on my investing money."

Morgan's mouth smiled, but he let contempt turn his lips. "Well, laddy, I may be going into the business, at that. After I sell these furs I'll have something of a stake, myself. That's if I can talk the boys into investing their fur money in me. Which," he smiled, "I reckon I can."

Jim knew it was madness, but he found himself taking a pencil out of his pocket and an old envelope. He asked Allie, "Can you give me a rough idea of the expense such an undertaking would involve, Miss Allie?"

Hugh Morgan opened the embroidered case that hung

against his breast and produced a blackened stone pipe, which he filled with twist tobacco. While the girl talked and Jim Smallwood wrote down figures, he smoked thoughtfully.

"Mostly," Allie said, "we'd need wagon parts and the things that wagon outfits would be needing after three-four hundred miles. We'd need Indian trading goods—cloth and beads and knives. . . ."

Jim finished totalling the figures she had given him. He said, "I get around nine thousand five hundred dollars. Do you think that would cover all the small details which would come up later?"

Allie's cheeks were flushed, and it was obvious that excitement ran strong in her. "I made the figures big," she said. "Ma, if Jim decides to do it, would you have any objection?"

The older woman had her sharp blue eyes on the Easterner, trying to read a type of man she did not know. "I suppose it would be the wise thing," she said, "to have such an investment, provided all is as represented. But we can talk about that later." She arose and went out the back to the kitchen garden.

Allie leaned her elbows on the table. "Well, Jim?"

Hugh Morgan and Rube Hammond, and even Old Black kept their eyes on Jim Smallwood. Jim put the paper in his pocket and met their gaze levelly.

"It will require some thought," he said. "Suppose I tell you after dinner."

Allie walked back through the merchandise room with him. She talked with him a moment, painting the picture a little brighter, and Jim watched the movement of her lips and the shine of her teeth, the healthy glow of her face. Beyond her he saw Hugh Morgan scowling at them, still at the table. Jim had one of those impulses like the perverse desire to jump from a high place.

"Miss Allie," he smiled, "this isn't part of the bargain, but—"

He had her face in his hands, and he pressed his mouth against hers; and suddenly desire caused him to slip his arm about her waist and hold her slim, rounded body against his.

Allie gasped. She pulled away, and glancing over her shoulder he saw Hugh Morgan staring, his bearded jaw agape.

"Jim!" she said. "Oh, Jim—!"

Jim Smallwood laughed. "Don't worry," he said. "It was worth it to me, even if your fiancé thinks it necessary to challenge me to a round of fisticuffs."

He walked upstairs, his heart thumping.

It was Jim Smallwood's way, when his mind was confused, to set his thoughts down on paper, and thus see, as if in a diagram, where the rub came. He did that now, in the form of a letter to his father:

My Dear Father:

I write this from the Widow Parker's Tavern, in Independence. My boat sails tomorrow, but I very much fear I shall not be on it. A strange thing has happened.

Furs—good furs—are extremely scarce. Those available are priced beyond reason. I think we may as well strike them off our list. A proposal has been made to me by Miss Allie, daughter of my landlady, that Smallwood and Son back her in a trading post venture on the Santa Fé trail.

As you know, there is a great movement of soldiers and settlers West. It is undoubtedly true that there would be good profit in such an undertaking, and a sum of $9,500 should finance it. I am therefore drawing on our account for this amount, and will accompany the train West to see the post well established.

I hope to be home within six or eight months. Tell
Cynthia. . . .

But when he tried to cast the next sentence, his pencil
trembled. Allie's face came between him and the vision of
Cynthia, his almost-betrothed. Jim's heart pounded, but san-
ity would not come to him.

"In love! Good heavens!" he thought.

Young gentlemen of substance did not fall in love with
tavern-keepers' daughters. Certainly not over a few days'
acquaintance and a single kiss! But he had to call it something, this racing fever within him, this madness of desire. So
he called it infatuation. There was comfort in the word. Infatuation was a fire ignited by a beautiful face and a teasing
laugh, the soft curve of a young waist, but soon common sense
would always extinguish it.

So he wrote:

Tell Cynthia I shall be grieving until I see her. I shall
write when time permits. Your obedient son, James.

He had dinner at the long table in the dining room, jostled
by Old Black on his right and Rube Hammond on the left.
Hugh Morgan sat at one end of the table and the Widow
Parker at the other, and Allie was at the trapper's side. Dinner
was a bedlam. The mountain men were half drunk; their
heavy voices rang through the whole tavern.

After the food was done with, Allie leaned across the table.
"Well, Jim?" she said.

Jim knew the whole table was listening. "I believe," he
said, "that Smallwood and Son is interested in your offer."

Old Black's palm thundered against his back. The mountain man let out a roar that sounded like something from a
bear's throat. He was no longer the close-mouthed, scowling
outcast from the mountain country.

"Jim," he said, "your stick floats true! I could take you to the spot with my eyes closed. Right under Johnson's Bluff, on the Picketwire!"

But the Widow Parker remained calm and unimpressed. "Just what sort of financial arrangement do you have in mind?" she asked Jim.

"Share and share," the Ohioan said. "We will bear the initial expense of setting up the port; you will pay us back through the profits of the first, say, five years."

"I should think that was fair enough," said Widow Parker. "Old Black and Allie will go with you, of course. I may sell the tavern and join you. But I'm an old woman for that trail."

For the first time Hugh Morgan spoke, twisting a strand of his short blond beard and smiling at Jim. "Here's a strange thing," he said. "I sold my furs today at a profit, but not like last year. Like I told you, the money's not in trappin' any more. I thinks to myself, 'I'll just set up a little trading post.' And would you believe it, Jim—Johnson's Bluff is the spot I decided on!"

Old Black rumbled in his chest. "There ain't room for two posts there," he said. "Nor in that corner of the country. One'd rob the other."

"Well, now," Morgan countered, "I'm a man that's plumb stubborn in his mind. I'm puttin' out for the Picketwire Saturday."

Allie gave Jim a quick little glance as he was about to speak; she said to the trapper: "That's not fair, Hugh. We've already made our plans. There's other spots on the Purgatoire."

"But none where three main trails converge. The beaver at Johnson's Bluff is the beaver that'll get the yaller stuff."

Jim saw the whole show; saw Morgan's jealousy behind it all. He could play the game, too. He borrowed one of Old Black's phrases.

"If that's how the stick floats, Morgan, are you man enough to gamble the point? Winner takes the Bluff. Loser has the rest of the frontier to chose from—but no closer than fifty miles."

Rube Hammond cackled a thin laugh. "Is he man enough? I reckon he's got a game you ain't got the insides to play with him."

A fight it is! Jim thought, and though he knew he was outpointed for size, he was not afraid. He had done fencing at M. Carondelet's in Cincinnati; he had shot many a round from balanced duelling pistols, though not in anger; and he reckoned he was fast enough to keep out of the way of Morgan's fists in a rough and tumble.

"Name your game," he said to the bourgeois.

Allie gasped, "No, Jim!" and her eyes were large and dark.

Hugh Morgan slipped his Green River knife from his belt, tossing it up so that it fell back point first upon the table. "Split Finger's my game," he said. "Two out of three."

Old Black had his fists clenched, where they rested on the edge of the table. "The boy's new to the West," he said. "You're givin' him no chance, Hugh."

"He can back out, if he's afeard," said Morgan, his tawny eyes hard and level. "Only I'll take Johnson's, o' course."

Jim stood up, removing his coat to stand in his pleated white silk shirt. "If you'll explain the rules," he said, "we can get at it."

CHAPTER THREE

Morgan's Game

Morgan's face had a hard brightness as he cleared the lower end of the table. The mountain men crowded behind him and

Jim as they took seats across from each other. Morgan, turning his skinning knife in his fingers, expounded to Jim Smallwood the rules of the ancient and honorable game of Split-Finger.

"The idee is to drive the point of the knife into the back of the other beaver's hand," he said. "Say I win the toss and take the first crack. You slap your hand down on the table and I hold the knife above it—no lower'n six inches. When I'm minded to, I stab—and you pull your hand out of the way, if you're quick. If I miss, it's your turn. Two out of three cuts give you the game."

They were watching Jim, waiting for him to blanch and back out. But all he said was: "I'll be needing a knife."

Old Black produced his Green River. There was considerable noise, so that only Jim heard him say: "Watch the eyes —it'll be in them when he's going to strike!"

Morgan rolled up his sleeve to the elbow, exhibiting a forearm banded with muscle. Rube Hammond flipped a bit-piece and Morgan said: "Heads!" and it was heads that lay under the dim lamp-light.

Jim placed his hand before the trapper. Morgan held the knife above it. Jim kept his gaze on the pale eyes. The flat, bearded face was not at rest; a muscle tautened at the corner of his mouth and the heavy brows pulled in. There was cruelty in the face, in the turn of his lips. Jim Smallwood saw the lower eyelids pull up a trifle; he was ready when the blade flashed.

Hugh Morgan sat there looking stupidly at the bare table-top, into which he had driven the sharp point a full inch. Jim interrupted his slow grappling of the situation.

"My turn, I believe."

Morgan took a deep breath and laid his hand in position. Jim raised the knife, conscious of the smells of liquor and sweat on the mountain men, of the snapping of coals on the hearth. Morgan suddenly caught his breath and pulled his hand away; but the knife had not moved. The men laughed.

"Nerves, Hugh!" someone said. "Too much fluff."

Morgan did not smile. Jim let him keep his hand there until the sweat rolled out of his pores like grease, and then with no conscious effort at speed he let the knife drop. He felt gristle parting; saw the dark blood well thickly where the blade skewered the big hand.

Morgan writhed but did not cry out; Jim brought the blade out with a quick jerk. The trapper wrapped a dirty head-bandana about his hand and took up his knife. "What're you waitin' for?" he demanded.

Jim pushed his hand out. He was not afraid of the big man's anger; he was enjoying the encounter, for the game was one in which a cool head and a quick hand meant everything.

Morgan took his time about getting set. Jim kept watching the gleaming eyes, but they lied this time, for without warning a foot struck him in the skin, beneath the table, and while he was still under the spell of surprise the knife flicked downward.

There was a sharp stab of pain which caused him to rise from his seat. He sat back, watching in a sort of amazement the way the blood oozed out around the blade of Hugh Morgan's knife. The trappers were shouting. Someone thrust a cup of brandy under the giant's nose, and he drank it before removing the knife. Then it was to bring the blade out with a cruel twist that caused Jim to bite his lip.

Morgan grinned. "Have ye the nerve to go another?" he demanded.

Jim picked up the knife and leaned forward. "Have you?" he countered. "Now that I know the rules by which you play?"

Morgan smashed his hand down on the table, to sit hunched

forward. Jim, knowing the real mettle of the man, again dal-lied over his thrust. And just as Morgan's mouth was begin-ning to twitch, he murmured: "Ten dollars I put the point through the first hole."

Rube Hammond shouted: "Ten you don't!"

"Twenty-five he does!" That was Old Black's bull-voice. Someone took his bet, and others were offered and taken. Jim watched Hugh Morgan through it all. Morgan was suffering as though the knife were already in him.

Finally Jim said: "The game is made. I am about to strike."

He saw Morgan tense. Yet for another fifteen seconds he did not move by the twitch of a muscle. Morgan released his breath and slumped; and Jim thrust the point of the knife precisely through the original wound.

Morgan shouted with pain. With the tavern resounding with laughter and swearing and men roaring for whiskey, Jim Smallwood stood up.

"You see," he said, "the game can be played fairly, as well. Good-night, Widow Parker. Good-night, Miss Allie."

In the morning Hugh Morgan and his wild crew were gone, and Jim had a steady ache in his hand to remind him of the trapper. After breakfast he and Allie and Old Black began to buy the endless list of things they would need. They rented ten freight wagons and bought a Conestoga to carry the daily essentials and furnish living quarters for Allie.

Old Black hired a couple of dozen trappers who knew the bottom was out of the fur bucket, as butchers, meat-getters, artisans and bullwhackers. As they turned back to the tavern that evening he looked critically at Jim. "You ain't going in them doin's," he said positively.

He brought him to a dark and odorous clothing shop where they fitted him out in buckskin shirt and trousers, the whole outfit trimmed with long fringes of leather. Jim smiled at this touch.

"How much extra to take off the fringe?" he asked.

"Be times you'll thank God you've got it, when you need a whang or a bit of waddin' in a hurry," Old Black said. He had sniffed at Jim's silver mounted pistol, and now he made him buy a pair of .44 caliber Walker model Colts as well as a Sharps .45-70.

The next day was occupied with packing and seeing to the welfare of oxen, mules and wagons. Axles were freshly tarred and tires tightened on the felloes. Just before dark, they left Widow Parker's Tavern to meet the wagon crew on the edge of town. They saw the widow waving, from the door, and Allie began to sniffle, and took Jim's arm.

The train was ready, bullwhackers and meat-getters lounging in the shade of the freight wagons, a bearded, hard-jawed crew of men in buckskin. Old Black seemed to expand. He rode up and down on his red mule, checking everything. Jim mounted his pony and waited by the lead wagon, Allie's white-tilt, listening to the bass-drum voice of the wagon boss.

A breeze had come up, blowing from the darkening west, laden, it seemed to him, with many strange odors and promises, and he understood why these men went back time and time again, risking their lives for a prize of only a few dollars if they won. It was a yonder call they heard, whispering of romance. It was the smile of a dark-eyed girl beckoning them on, and they kept following it until they found at last their nameless graves.

They traveled until midnight, making ten miles, and at dawn shoved on again. On their third day out they encountered a train of empty freight wagons lumbering across the dry wash of Dragoon Creek. Jim was riding a mile ahead of the train with Poke Harris and Old Black.

They stopped and talked awhile with the wagon boss, a

red-bearded son of the prairie. He talked casually about death and disaster in the mountains. He spoke of the long, dry stretch ahead of them. He told of increasing Mexican hostility in Santa Fé.

"Them greasers will have to be showed," he said darkly. "Likewise some of these renegade Injuns. Keep your eyes peeled if you cut sign on Gray Horse's Pawnees. They'll rob you blind or lift your hair if they like the color of it."

Poke Harris, the meat getter, took a chew of Mexican Twist. "Well, we won't have much truck with Gray Horse after we get into Colorady," he said. "We aim to set up a post on the Picketwire."

"Seems like everybody aims to have a post on the Picket-wire," said the wagon boss. "I passed a gent yesterday head-ing that way with six wagon-loads."

All three of the men stiffened in their saddles, but it was Jim who said: "Name of Morgan, maybe?"

"Why, yes. Hugh Morgan, him the Pawnees call Yellow Hair." The bullwhacker popped his short bull-whip over his oxen and the wagons lumbered on. "Keep your hair tied down, gents!"

They waited on the bank of the Dragoon for the wagons to catch up, none of them speaking the dark thoughts they had. Morgan had a day's lead on them, and he was encumbered with only half as many wagons. Once he had made claim to the spot on Johnson's Bluff he would be hard to pry loose. Even frontier justice would honor his claim if he put up his flag first.

Near sunset Poke unlimbered his long frame and stared long into the east. "What's keepin' that outfit?" he frowned. "It'll be dark afore they make the creek. Best head back."

On a rise of the prairie they found the train stalled beside the trail ruts. Whang Daniels, the blacksmith, had the wheel off one of the big freight wagons. He looked up when they dismounted, a slack-bellied man with ponderous muscles, given to greasy elk-hide shirts which he did not discard until they fell apart. He had eyes almost hidden by rough brows, a jaw like a saddlehorn.

Whang scooped a handful of lubricating tar from the inside of the hub and held it out to the wagon boss.

"Sand!" he said. "I put in A-Number-One lubricatin' tar in Indypendence. Somebody come along after me and put a handful of sand into each 'n! Spindles on three of the wagons are plumb burnt out."

"Morgan!" Jim said.

Old Black grunted. "Hugh don't like to be bested at his own games. I'm afeard, Jim, he's got us by the hair."

Jim said to Whang Daniels: "Can't we do something to patch them up?"

"Patched-up contraptions won't take us where we're goin'. We'll have to change the tar in all the hubs and repack the wagons we can still use. It will mean laying over a day."

Jim knew they were all watching him, wondering how the tenderfoot would take this first stroke of misfortune. To all intents and purposes, they were already beaten. Poke and Old Black seemed to expect him to say something, sitting there with their eyes hard as steel balls and their faces covering any emotion they felt.

"What's the word, Jim?" Poke said, finally.

"We'll repack tonight," Jim said. "I intend to beat Morgan, if we have to finish the race on foot!"

But after he had said it he had the feeling that the men were not satisfied; that they resented his decision. Were they afraid to go on? he wondered. Or was it simply the prejudice any veteran had against taking orders from a greenhorn? Whatever the reason, Jim Smallwood had set his course by a high and bright star, and he would follow it to the end.

Afterward, he passed by Allie's wagon and she called to him. "That was a nice speech, Jim," she said. "Do you know, I think I could learn to like you, even if you aren't as big as Hugh. You may kiss me if you like."

If he liked! Jim had her shoulders in his hard grip, drawing her toward him roughly; then he stopped, and, releasing her, turned away. "I—I mustn't, Allie!" he said.

Allie shook her head. "You're afraid, Jim!" she told him. "Of what? Of me? You weren't even afraid of Hugh Morgan that other night when you kissed me."

"But I wasn't in love with you then," Jim said. "At least I didn't know it. And now I am, and—I wish I weren't!"

With a woman's wisdom in such things, Allie Parker said: "I know. I wouldn't fit in Cincinnati, would I?"

"You wouldn't want to fit," he told her. "You wouldn't even like the people I know. You'd think them tame and stupid."

"And they would think me a barbarian. Maybe you're right, Jim. I couldn't go back with you. But you could stay out here with me."

Jim pondered, trying to phrase a thing that he could only feel. "No," he said. "I couldn't even do that. My father is alone, except for me. He has planned for years the time when I would take over his business. 'Smallwood and Son'—those three words mean the world and the heavens to him. And beyond that, I wouldn't fit here, myself. These men are all fine; but they would never accept me."

Allie did not deny it for a moment. "They can't help being suspicious, Jim. They live by mistrusting everyone. Even in their friendships, they keep their guard up until a man has proven himself."

"And how does he do that?" Jim asked her.

Allie frowned. "I don't know. But they can sense this feeling you have, that you don't belong. They know you don't love the same things they do. They respect you as a brave man, but—"

She didn't finish it, and Jim Smallwood went back alone.

Chapter Four

Gray Horse Strikes

Through that long night they worked at the task of repairing the wagons. When dawn roughed the horizon they rolled down the swale toward Santa Fé, the skeletons of three gaunt freight wagons on the crest behind them.

They nooned on Dragoon Creek and made Medicine Wash by night, digging in the sand until a barrel-form could be sunk to make a sort of spring. They began to set their needle by the water holes Old Black remembered, but not all of these were good. During the next week they pushed the mules and oxen hard. They saw a low range of hills come toward them, a fringe of trees along the base. They had been forced to cut down on the allotment of drinking water twice, and for the cattle and stock there was never enough.

On the eleventh day, Jim Smallwood saw signal smoke in the mountains and knew they had been sighted by the Pawnee. Poke Harris shook his head when he saw the signs on the horizon.

"It's Kitty-bar-the-door, now!" he said.

This was towards dusk; they made Brown's Rocks at dark. Here a scattering of ancient basaltic rocks protruded from the prairie in the shape of a crescent. In holes in the rocks there was a little green scum which the animals drank thirstily. For the wagon crew there was still some muggy water in the casks.

Allie did not seem to worry. She was brown from sun and

wind, so that her teeth seemed whiter than ever, and she gave Jim a smile as she started coffee for supper over the campfire.

"How'll you have it, pardner?" she asked him. "Boston?"

"No cream," Jim grinned. "The mud makes it thick enough."

Old Black and the rest finished bedding down the stock. They had brought the eight wagons around to complete the circle started by the crescent of rocks, but no one mentioned Indians or danger. Allie banged a skillet on a rock.

"Come and get it or I'll throw it away!"

Old Black sat on the ground against one of the big Conestoga wheels. "I give us ten days more," he said. "Then, with any kind of luck at all, we'll hit the Picketwire. . . ."

Jim had thought he was going to say something else, but he only made a kind of grunt and sat up straight, so that Jim's gaze was brought quickly to him. It was a moment before the Ohioan could realize that this was not a trick of his imagination; that the feathered shaft protruding from the trapper's shoulder was actually there.

Old Black was gasping and beginning to pull at the arrow.

Whang Daniels let out a bellow that seemed to blow the darkness apart. He kicked the coffee bucket into the fire and clouds of dirty steam arose while the fire guttered out. Poke Harris and the mountain men sprawled among the wagons. Allie sat there in the darkness, and Jim picked her up and deposited her in a cleft of the rocks. He gave her one of his Colts, then he ran back to help Old Black who was still sitting against the wheel.

The attack came now with a drum-roll of hoofs. Out there in the night the Pawnees were howling their gobbling war-cries. A few rifles rattled and a shower of arrows fell among the rocks and wagons. A shaft struck the spoke of the wagon above Jim's head as he knelt beside the mountain man, but

Jim was not conscious of fear, only of a driving haste to get Old Black to shelter.

The arrow had stuck in a spoke after it had traversed the bearded man's shoulder. With a quick snap Jim broke the shaft close to Old Black's chest. Gently, then, he drew him forward, until the ragged end had been pulled through his body and he was free. Old Black took a long breath and reached for his rifle.

"Thank'ee, Jim," he said. "Now we'll be showing them varmints how the stick floats with fightin' men!"

They found positions among the wagons just in time to meet the first determined attempt to break their fort. Jim saw the dark line of warriors sweeping toward them, saw the flashes from their rifles as they came and heard the bullets thud against the wagons and whine off the rocks. He got a paint-streaked brave in the sights of his buffalo gun and waited; when the line was within fifty feet he fired. The Pawnee went over the back of the horse, knocked loose by the heavy slug that was the size of a man's thumb.

Jim dropped the rifle and grabbed his revolver. Among the wagons other rifles and Colts were crashing. In the picket enclosure within the great circle the wagon stock were beginning to mill.

Jim kept cocking and firing. The Pawnees were close enough that he could see their feathered lances. But the sheer weight of lead thrown out by the wagon men caused the Indians to falter. A naked warrior in the middle of the line swerved his pony and curved back into the night; the rest broke and followed him.

Old Black's voice boomed, as hearty as though he had not had a scratch. "Allie, girl! All right?"

"All right, Black!" she called back.

Jim could see powder-flask and ramrod going to work and he hurried to reload his own weapons. For a moment he seemed to see the whole picture as if from a distance: Jim Smallwood, of Smallwood and Son, crouching on the limitless black prairie, living, perhaps, his last hour; Jim Smallwood, in buckskins, fighting for his life and yet not worrying so much about being killed as of harm coming to a girl he had known less than a month.

The Indians came back, this time from behind the rocks, and the bull-whackers and mountain men swarmed through the jagged buttress to meet the new attack. They let Gray Horse's men come to the fringe of the rocks before they fired. The impact of two dozen rifle-balls was a brutal thing. It knocked a dozen horses down and chopped wide holes in the charging line. Jim kept firing until they withdrew, and this time they did not come back.

Under the dim, sickle-moon, they cleaned Old Black's wound. He smoked his pipe and made not a sound, but once his fingers clenched and the clay stem snapped clean.

When it was finished, Jim walked over by himself among the rocks, looking out across the prairie toward the mountains. There among the scarps, like a ruby, he saw a campfire.

Apparently the Pawnees did not worry Hugh Morgan. . . .

CHAPTER FIVE

The Battle at Oak Creek

In the morning they found that all but one of the wounded Indians had been dragged away. This man lay just beyond the wagons, and even at a glance it was apparent that something about him was not right. He wore a beaded headband with single gray feather, and a breech-clout. But there was a margin of white flesh where his breech-clout had slipped down.

Old Black examined him, gingerly, as he would have a

dead animal. The body had been streaked with pigment which was cracking off. The hair was a little shorter than the Indians'. When the wagon-boss rolled him over, all the trappers exclaimed.

"Laclede!" the blacksmith said. "Kim Laclede!"

"Who's he?" Jim asked.

Old Black gave a snort and let the body roll back as though it were something repulsive. "One of Morgan's skinners," he said. "Morgan must have made a deal with Gray Horse to wipe us out. He sent Laclede, an' maybe others, to be sure they got the right outfit."

Again Jim was conscious that they were holding some silent communion among themselves while they waited for him to speak. This time he put it up to them. "What shall we do?" he asked. "Go ahead on the horses and have it out with Morgan? Or wait until we get to Johnson's Bluff and then try to run him out?"

"It's your party," Old Black said, not meeting his eye.

"All right," Jim snapped. "It would be risky to leave the wagons and the girl without adequate protection. We'll string along, but we'll double up the guard at night. When we reach the Purgatoire, Hugh Morgan and I will play another little game and settle it once and for all."

The sun came up behind them hot and yellow, laying a fierce hand on their backs as they rode. The stock, several days now without sufficient water, became weak and intractable. One of the oxen died and they butchered it, for buffalo were increasingly scarce. They stretched the unused meat on racks and dried it as they rolled on.

On the dry earth there was a scant fuzz of yellow burro grass, hardly good enough for sheep. Old Black rationed out a few gallons of corn to each bull-whacker to keep his animals going.

The mountains loomed close and high, promising water in

plenty at Oak Creek Tank. Here the ground tipped up, making it harder going for the oxen. Night overtook them still three miles short of the hills.

Jim rode ahead with Poke Harris, the Texan, watching for the slightest sign of an ambush. Poke seemed to sniff the air with his long nose. He avoided every depression and kept to the arroyo banks and the ridges.

When the hills were like a black wall directly in front of them, he pulled rein. "We'll leave the hosses," he said. "The tank's up yonder canyon."

It was hard going through the dry tangle of chaparral, for they must proceed as silently as possible. At length they came out on a bench above the barranca, beneath which could be seen a clearing beside the sandy wash. Wagons had cut deep ruts beside the stream-bed; and right below them a little rock dam had been stretched across the creek to dam up the runoff from the spring. Satisfied that the spot was deserted, they slid down the bank and went toward the spring, ready for a drink themselves.

Then they noticed the smell. Rank, nose-insulting, it permeated the still night air of the canyon. Poke Harris stopped by the edge of the tank, but all he could say was, "Lord!"

The carcass of an ox lay on its side in the shallow water, its legs sticking up like the legs of a sawhorse. There was a smoothed trough on the sand, as though the animal had been dragged into the water. Above all the small night sounds could be heard the buzz of blue-bottle flies.

Hugh Morgan, after the fashion of his kind, had taken care of Oak Creek Tank.

They met the wagons at the foot of the climb and gave Old Black the news. He took it in silence, signaling the train to make camp. "I ain't putting those brutes up the hill without there's water at the top," he said.

"We can dig a hole farther up," Poke said. "There's plenty of willows for rip-rappin' to shore it up. But it will take two-three days to collect enough water to put the animals back in shape."

"By that time, Morgan will have hisself a fort at Johnson's," Old Black said.

"Morgan's not going to build anything," Jim Smallwood said, and they glanced impatiently at him, as if their problem were too big to brook interference by an amateur. "Morgan's all finished," he repeated. "I'm going tonight, by myself. We'll finish that game we started."

Old Black shook his head. "He'd skin you like a jack-rabbit," he said. "And we can't risk splittin' the party, like you said yourself. We'll just water the brutes and go along when they're rested."

"And like you said," Jim retorted, "it's my party. My order is that you and the others stay with the wagons while I go ahead. If you don't hear from me in two days, you can do as you wish about it. Sell the goods and send my father what is left over, after paying off the men; or set up a post somewhere. But I'm sick of this cowardly, yellow-haired snake blocking us every time we take a step."

Old Black's eyes shone when he strode past them, but none of the mountain men replied. He stopped at Allie's wagon, where she was dragging out the supper things with calm practicality. She looked at him, fatigue in her face, and he thought a shading of anxiety. Her face was thinner, marked with small lines radiating from the mouth and eyes.

"Well, Jim?" she said.

"I'm going on," Jim told her. "Morgan and I have got to settle this once and for all. It's me he's making war on—not the whole train. But you suffer as much as I do, and I'm going to stop him."

"How are you going to do it?" Allie asked him.

– 173 –

"However it seems best when I find him." Jim took her hand. "I'm not sure I was right that night, Allie. I've thought about it since. It seems to me that every man must follow his star, and mine seems to hang over the West. If I come back, I'd like to follow it with you. If I don't, Old Black will get you back."

Allie shook her head. "You'll be back," she said. "Then we'll talk about that star of yours. Maybe all this has made you sentimental. But good luck, Jim."

Jim said: "No, Allie. But it's opened my eyes for the first time to some real values I was overlooking."

Jim Smallwood found the trail of Hugh Morgan's wagons and followed it until midnight. High in the foothills he made camp for the night, for weariness was in him and he wanted a clear head when he found the bourgeois. He reckoned that Morgan could not be far ahead. He had only a day's lead on them, and in the mountain country a wagon could make but a few miles between sun-up and dark. Sometime before dawn he arose and scrubbed his face with the palms of his hands to start the circulation. He saddled his pony and rode on, munching a handful of *panoln*.

He did not know just what he planned to do when he encountered the fur boss and his crew. But one conviction had come solidly home to him: In a life like this, where death lay always just over the horizon, a man wanted to live for the day at hand. He wanted to take what boons fell to him. And if Allie Parker meant happiness to him, he would have her.

His pony snorted, tossed its head. Instantly he was on the alert, pulling rein sharply and listening, searching the scrub timber around him. Now he heard, from the distance, an axe strike wood, and the scent of pine smoke touched his nostrils.

He tied his horse to a sumac and went through the scattered piñon and bull pines in the direction of the sound. Under his arm, the long Sharps was on half-cock.

He worked around so that he was on a little rise behind the wagon camp the grove among the trees.

Down there, mountain men were cooking breakfast over a small fire while the oxen were brought up to be yoked. But Hugh Morgan had a slab of red meat suspended over the fire by a stick in his hand, and his voice went up with the smoke in a bullwhacker's song:

"Beefsteak when I'm hungry, whiskey when I'm dry,
A redhead when I'm lonesome, and religion when I die."

Jim Smallwood began to crawl down the hill. You haven't got much time for the religion, Hugh Morgan, he was thinking. He dragged the Sharps along beside him as he went through the catclaw and sumac. He had only a ragged outline in his mind of what he would do, but the end was certain: Death for Hugh Morgan, in a fair fight.

From a point only thirty feet from the yellow-haired bourgeois, he watched him catch the beefsteak in his teeth and with his knife whack off a chunk. This, he thought grimly, was the frontier: A man standing in the fullness of life, relishing the strong spice of it, while Death brought the knot snugly up against his ear.

Then a weight landed crushingly on his back; his arms were pulled behind him in such a fashion that he thought they would break, and he heard Rube Hammond shout: "Got 'im, Hugh! Slick as buffler grease!"

Teamsters came boiling in upon him, tearing his weapons from him and stretching him flat on his back with arms and legs pinioned. Morgan strolled over, still tearing chunks of beef from the slab.

He said: "You're a long time comin', little man. I thought that Injun ruckus would bring you if anything would. I reckon you're shorter on guts than I figured."

"You mean you've been waiting for me?" Jim said.

Morgan waved the knife. "I know men, Jim. Even little curled and powdered specimen's like you, forever bowin' and scrapin'. I knowed you'd come after me, probably alone, to show your lady you were mucho hombre. So I've kept a guard out all the way."

"You're a smart man," Jim said. "But not tough nor so brave as you think. I found that out the other night, at Widow Parker's. Have you any more games?"

Jim's smile whipped a flush into the brown skin of Morgan's face. "That's why I had you took alive," he said shortly. "I got a real good game. I call it Beaver, 'cause the object is to skin your man out like a plew. Not much to it. All you need is two men, two knives, and a little clearin'. We got 'em all."

Jim got up, keeping his eyes on Morgan's face. "Will you make me a promise, Morgan?" he demanded. "That you'll have your men leave the others alone if I beat you?"

"That promise is easy kept," said Morgan. "Your hair is all I want. Do you know what, Jim? I'm going to have that curly black taw of yours after I kill you. I'm going to wear it on my belt, like a man does when he's kilt a Blackfoot chief."

"To make it even," Jim Smallwood said, "I'll do the same for you. I'll have my knife, Hammond."

Hammond flipped him the Green River knife. Morgan tossed his cap-and-ball revolver at the foot of a tree. The trappers spread about in a wide circle. For a moment Jim and Morgan sparred. Then Morgan sprang upon him, driving the long blade at his throat. Jim's knife clinked against the other's, but when he came against the force of Morgan's great forearm he was flung off his feet and sprawled in the dirt.

He lay there a moment while the bourgeois pounced after him, his blade held low for a stomach wound. Jim's foot came up and jarred against Morgan's knee, throwing him off balance, and as he rolled to his feet he lashed out at his body and felt the blade rasp across Morgan's ribs, cutting his shirt for a foot and laying open the white skin underneath. Hugh Morgan howled.

He came at Jim with his head tucked low, both hands working, the right making feints with the knife, the left grasping. Jim slashed at the free hand, saw blood gush from it. Morgan doubled his fist and struck at him, and at the same time he closed and stabbed straight and hard. Jim twisted, avoiding the clutch of his hand, but the knife went into his left bicep, coming out the inside to gash his chest.

Morgan, spurred by the cheers of his messmates, plunged on for the finish.

Jim Smallwood had expected this; he turned the trapper's over-confidence to his own advantage. He fetched a blow against the side of Morgan's head and caused him to stumble. With the big man dazed, he sank his Green River to the haft in his shoulder. Withdrawing, he lunged again, driving for the soft flesh beneath his ribs.

Morgan did something no trapper had ever seen him do: He backed away. Turning, then, he stumbled towards the tree where he had thrown his gun. There was blood all over his face and hands.

Jim called sharply: "Morgan! Are you afraid to finish it?"

Morgan turned from the tree, the gun in his hand. There was a look, a color, in his face which told Jim that he already belonged to the dark world beyond. His face was the color of old ash; his mouth was a twisted slash in the blood-spattered yellow beard. The barrel of the gun lined out unsteadily; Jim faced it with his feet wide-spaced and his clenched hands hanging.

Hugh Morgan reeled back against the tree. The roar of a Sharps pounded through the clearing, and Old Black's voice came with it: "You ain't fittin' to spit with mountain men, Hugh Morgan! Tell the devil we throwed you out!"

Rube Hammond and his mates were suddenly sprawling behind trees and wagons as Morgan fell, while the fire of a dozen guns poured in upon them. Jim grabbed his guns and ran low for the brush, diving headfirst into a manzanita. In amazement, he realized the woods were full of them—Poke Harris and Old Black, Whang Daniels . . . . and others he hardly knew. Men he had worked with on the long drag across the prairie; men he had fought with at Brown's Rocks; lean-jawed men who had made his fight theirs.

Jim cut down a renegade bullwhacker with his Sharps. Discarding it, he got the Walker pistol bucking, revelling in the power that was his for the turn of a finger. It came to him that his whole life, before Independence, had been a prelude to something important that would happen later, for moments like this when life was something you held to with both hands, fighting for it, cherishing it as you would a woman you loved. He could not think of Cincinnati as anything but a pleasant dream, nice to think back upon, but never to be lived again.

Back with the picketed animals, the survivors of Hugh Morgan's wild crew were mounting and striking into the woods.

Old Black let them go. When the camp was silent he came out. Jim went to meet him.

Old Black was not one for sentiment. He took a chew of Mexican Twist and offered the coil of black tobacco to Jim, who bit off a lusty chunk which he spat out when it was more politic.

"Jim," said Old Black, "I reckon the woods are safe for white men, now. We left Allie forted up with eight men to guard her and the wagons. We'll make Johnson's Bluff in four days and start a-buildin'."

"I've been thinking," Jim told him, "that I'd send for another couple of thousand dollars to do the job right. In this country a walled post is the only thing. And after all, a man wants a safe place to keep his woman and children."

"I reckon," Poke Harris said, "it takes more'n a walled post. It takes insides. You showed us you had 'em when you took the warpath alone ag'n Morgan's crew. You'll do to bait the stick with, Jim."

That was all they said before they rode back to the wagons, and back to Allie. But Jim Smallwood knew at last that his needle had settled West, and West he would go, where the world was yet new, and awaiting strong men and women to shape it to their desires.

The Seventh Desert

W H E N they had put the fifth desert behind them, Cole
Allan began to imagine he could smell California in the wind
coming out of the West. Old-timers called the southern route
to California the Trail of the Seven Deserts. Some turned back
at the first desert, in Texas; some struggled on to succumb to
the hot sands of New Mexico. And some reached California,
but they were not many.

Cole Allan was traveling what you might call heavy. He had
four hundred Texas steers, an aged cowpuncher, a spring
wagon, and a new bride. Between the bride and the wagon it
was a tossup as to which had lost more of its look of shining
newness on that last scrape across New Mexico.

Partly on Elly's account, Cole had swung northwest across
the mountains, instead of southwest, and around them;
and partly for himself, because no man hated heat and
thirst much worse than Cole Allan, and there was nothing
between Lordsburg and Tucson but sand and heat and
whirlwinds.

Tonight they bedded the cattle on a little stream that ran
through a pocket of rocky hills.

After the plains, this Arizona high-rolls country was cool
and pleasant. The sunset was a glory of gold and purple.
Elly stood a long time looking at it; Cole could see the tran-
quillity of the scene reflected in her face. It relieved him;
he had worried about her lately. Only eighteen she was, still
a girl in so many ways, and yet with a woman's quiet strength
in her.

Elly said softly, "I could live here forever, Cole. The trees, and the water—the mountains . . ."

Cole's arm was about her waist. "It's nice," he admitted. "Of course it ain't California, but it looks good after the desert. You wait till we hit the coast!"

Elly had heard it all before, but he knew she was not listening to him now. Her eyes were dreaming. "Right in those trees I'd want the cabin."

Cole glanced at her. She had never talked of quitting; he hoped she was not going to do it now.

"I'd better drive the cattle out of the creek before they founder," he told her.

Elly said hesitantly, "Cole," and he turned back.

"Cole dear, I think we're going to have to stop before we reach California. You see, we—we're going to have a family."

It hit Cole Allan between the eyes.

"I've known for quite a while," Elly told him. "I hated to tell you. I know how set you are on getting to California."

A mixture of gladness and disappointment filled Cole Allan. He said slowly, thinking his way, "Why, that's fine, Elly. Maybe it ain't like I'd have planned it, but we'll do the only thing we can. We'll throw up something temporary. In a year you and the baby will be fit to travel." He scanned her critically. "First thing," he said efficiently, "is to get you built up. I'll start weanin' Sudy's calf tomorrow. You'll need lots of milk."

Elly's eyes filled. "You're so kind, Cole," she said, "so understanding."

"No such thing," Cole declared. "You set yonder by the creek now, while I get the dishes washed up."

Cole cut wild hay to blend with the adobe mud he and Shorty mixed for bricks. They built a one-room cabin with an adjoinining lean-to. They laid out a stone corral. Looking the place over, Cole thought it wasn't so bad.

He tried to picture what it would be like around Los Angeles now. Cool, he bet; a refreshing shower every day that kept the grass green at all times. That was how the railroad pamphlets put it. Thousands of other folks were heading for California this summer of 1870. Cole didn't know how much land would be left after a year lost on the trail, but this California was a pretty big place.

One day, two weeks after they finished the cabin, four cowboys came through. They were pushing a bunch of steers down the ridge behind the cabin. Three of them stayed with the cattle, while the fourth jogged down to where Cole was milking.

The stranger stood down beside his horse and looked the layout over with a slow, appraising eye. He said to Cole, offering his hand, "Pete Hubbell. Figure to stay on here, friend?"

"Might," Cole said. He reckoned the man's age at about forty-five. He was thick-limbed. He had black hair which curled up under his hat brim. In a reckless sort of way he was pleasant-looking.

"It's a good country," Hubbell said. "How much of it you claiming?"

Cole thought there was amusement in his eyes. He said, "Why, about all I can cover with my hat—in a day's riding."

Smiling, Hubbell began to tap the palm of his hand with two thick fingers. "There's just two things wrong with your plans," he told Cole. "In the first place, the Apaches like this stretch too. They ain't always nice-mannered people. In the second place," he concluded, "this here range happens to belong to me—about sixty thousand acres of it."

Cole did not blink. "I thought it was government range," he

said. "Appears to me there's enough room out here for all the cattlemen in Texas."

"It's the water, friend," said Hubbell. His eyes could grow unfriendly without seeming to affect the rest of his features. "I've filed on Peach Creek, do you see? You're welcome to stop here four-five days and rest your stock; but I don't allow no squatters."

Cole said, "My missus is expecting, Hubbell. I'm not taking her over the mountains until she and the baby are fit to travel. But I'll gladly pay you range lease. I don't see that you're running many cows hereabouts. Haven't passed ten head in a week."

Pete Hubbell said, "I'm mighty careful about overstocking." He turned the stirrup to his toe and mounted. He moistened a forefinger to register the direction of the wind. "Southwest," he said. "Means the desert is a-frying. Means the Apaches may visit you. But they won't misput you any, because you'll have moved on by then. I'll be back from Tucson in a few days; it'll be best if you ain't around."

Elly heard it all from the window of the cabin. When Cole turned, she was standing in the doorway.

"It was my fault, Cole," she said. "I shouldn't have made you stop. We'll go on a ways. I'll be all right."

Cole held her by the shoulders. "We'll stay right here," he declared. "Hubbell was just testing his wind. Two Texans are equal to a parcel of Arizonians any day of the week." He said, "You get back inside and rest. You look peaked."

Pete Hubbell did not reappear that week, nor the week thereafter. Cole Allan spaced his cattle around so that the graze would not be cut back in any one section. He meant to play square with Hubbell so that he would have no possible grievance.

He saw the cattle begin to put on tallow. Elly seemed

pathetically eager to make him like the country. She picked berries and made jellies for him; she planted things around the cabin to give it a look of permanence.

Cole and Shorty were range-branding some late calves the day the man called California appeared.

He was a leathery little cowpuncher in his forties, riding a white-stockinged bay, with a pack animal in tow. He watched the Texans wrestle a big coming-yearling.

At the moment, Cole Allan was too engrossed in trying to flank the brute to pay much attention to the visitor. Suddenly the animal began to hump. Cole was deposited on his hunkers, while old Shorty, who was always more or less crippled up with rheumatism, swore ineffectively and threw a rock at the departing rump.

The stranger slipped his catch rope from the saddle, shook out a loop, and spilled the calf without running ten feet. This time Cole was sitting on the animal before it could rise.

Afterward, Cole said to the stranger, "You've worked cattle before, mister. Like to work them some more? Me and Shorty can't seem to be enough places at once."

The man looked up at the sky, as if the answer might be written in the weather. "I've got a little time," he said. "I'll see if I like it. You can call me California."

Cole's smile was as warm as his handshake. "There's nothing I'd rather call you," he said. "Matter of fact, I'm a-heading for the coast myself. But we're taking time out to have a family."

California shrugged. "Hope you like it," he said. "Some do." It wasn't quite clear to Cole whether he meant California or having a family.

As they rode in that night, Cole's conscience began to scrape. "Something I ought to tell you," he said. "I'm what you might call poaching here. The land belongs to a man named Hubbell. Until this baby is born I don't aim to travel. There may be bad blood between us."

California gave a short hard laugh. "Pete Hubbell owns all of Arizona, to hear him tell it. If you weren't new here, you'd know about him. He steals cattle in the States and sells 'em in Mexico. Then he brings back a herd of wet cattle to sell here. Thing of it is, he don't want anybody on his favorite holding grounds to check up on him."

Cole Allan nodded. "I figured it might be like that," he remarked. "He mentioned Indians, too. What about them?"

"That's another story," said California. "Some tribes will bother you. Some won't. Mostly they keep to the reservations. Just assume that they're all after your scalp and you'll get along best."

In his close-mouthed cynical way, California soon made himself indispensable around the ranch. A month after he arrived he moved his blankets out of the lean-to which he shared with Shorty.

"I've got the crawlin' fidgets," he told Cole. "I'll sleep out a few nights."

The next morning the Indians came.

A single gunshot planted Cole bolt upright in the bed beside Elly. There was a great rustling in the grass, and then a soft thunder of unshod hoofs. There was another shot.

He laid the barrel of his rifle across the mud sill. In the ghostly half-daylight he perceived a line of horses passing the window. But the moving file had no end — it was the rim of a wheel; the cabin was the hub.

Shorty's gun began to roar from the dark wedge of the lean-to. Cole shouted at Elly, "Get the carbine! Keep loading!"

He got into the rhythm of the spinning wheel. Fire between two horses and you would hit the second. The terror of his violent awakening had passed. He was proud, and a bit relieved, that he was able to live up to his own code of courage. He was proud of Elly, quietly, hurriedly reloading the guns as he passed them to her.

Out there in the dark a lone rifle spoke from time to time. It was California's .45-90 hacking holes in the line of riders.

Down in the bosque a flame broke out, flickered, and then flared brighter. Pitch fire, thought Cole; and the portent of it came upon him with a sense of horror that shamed his recent courage.

He watched the arrows arch across the corral and heard four solid thunks as they hit the roof. He looked at Elly. She was loading. She had not seen them. "Oh, God!" he murmured. He had meant to cover the riprapping of willow poles and cottonwood *vigas* with earth long ago.

He kept waiting for the heat. While he waited he fought, and up in the rocks California was fighting. From the lean-to Shorty's gun spoke with brash defiance. Suddenly Cole realized that there were quite a few Indians on the ground. The fabric of the noose was unraveling.

Elly said urgently, "Cole!" and tugged at his arm.

"I know," he said. "They did it with pitch-pine arrows. But they won't be around when we come out. They've about got their bellies full."

Elly obediently turned her back on the corner of the ceiling that was blackening, with tendrils of smoke leaking down and now and then a savage little lick of flame. She handed him the carbine.

Cole said, "Keep it. Start shooting when I say."

Elly put the gun to her shoulder. Under the redoubled fire the line of Indians swerved. California's rifle roared encouragement.

In the end, it was the thunder of his Sharps that convinced the Indians there was nothing in this small cabin worth dying for. They disappeared into the tall grass.

California kept guard while the others formed a bucket brigade from the horse trough. Luckily the roof timbers were still green. They burned reluctantly, finally subsiding into sullen steaming.

In the wreckage of her kitchen corner Elly started to cook breakfast. Suddenly she sat down and covered her face with her hands. She cried, softly at first, then with terrible, convulsive sobs.

"It was all my fault," she cried. "We might all have been killed. I'd have been to blame. Cole, I—I lied to you."

Cole said sharply. "No one's to blame. Get hold of yourself." Then curiosity crept into him. "What do you mean, you lied to me?"

Elly's fingers clenched whitely. "About the baby. I'm not going to have one, Cole! Only I couldn't cross another desert. Not then. I'm not a pioneer; I'm just a wife that wants to settle somewhere."

Her voice took on a small note of accusation. "I couldn't ask you to stop, because you'd say I was soft. You'd hate me. I thought I'd tell you later I'd been mistaken about the baby."

Cole got up. He stood in the doorway.

Elly said, "So now we can go on."

Cole would not look at her. "No," he said, "we're staying. Pete Hubbell is not going to brag to all Arizona that he scared a Texan. You got us into this, and you'll see it through with me."

Cole was angry and hurt; hurt because Elly hadn't trusted him with her feelings, angry because she did not possess the iron with which he had credited her. It troubled him because he knew a timid woman would be a stone around a man's neck out here.

At dinner that night Elly made her very last speech on the subject of pioneering.

"If some people wouldn't be so high-handed," she said, "it would be easier for a body to talk to them. I'd have let you know how I felt in New Mexico, excepting you were always

talking about the weaklings that never made it to California."
She sniffed. "How do you know this California is such a rose
garden, anyway? With you, California is just a frame of mind."

Some deep-rooted wisdom cautioned Cole Allan to hold his
tongue.

It was the weather which settled Cole's problem of whether
to go or stay. In the air the next dawning there was the first
taste of autumn. The heat would be going out of the lava-
studded plains between Phoenix and the Colorado.

He said to Shorty and California, "I figure to pull out next
week. By the time we get across the mountains the desert will
be fit to travel."

California licked a cigarette. "I'll help you across the mountains," he remarked, "but after that I draw my time. My com-
pass points east."

They rode down Peach Creek to South Fork, to start the
strays moving in. There was a purplish haze over the land. It
was a friendly sort of country, thought Cole.

They came onto a mesa and saw, below them, a train of five
wagons at the ford. Four of them stood on the east bank, but
the fifth was bed-deep in mud.

They rode down, watching the emigrants bend their strength
to the wheels of the mired wagon. The wagon boss waded to
the bank.

"Could shore use a pull, boys," he declared. "Don't want
to take the mules out of harness again if I can help it." Like
the rest of the men, and the women sitting on the wagons,
he looked pinched, tired, brown and dry as the earth itself.

Cole noticed that the sideboards of the wagon were weathered; the mules were no more than racks of bone and
hide.

They flipped ropes to the wagon and brought it out of the
stream. The wagon boss wiped his forehead.

"That's number two hundred and sixty-five," he said. "This stretch has been the worst since Californy."

That the caravan was heading east struck Cole for the first time. He noticed a faded "California, By Heck!" painted on one of the canvas tilts. "What's the matter with California?" he challenged.

"Why, nothing much," said the other, "providing you like land sharks and deserts, and coolie labor on the land you thought you were going to work."

Cole stared at the man, condemning him. "If trouble rubs the polish off a man," he declared, "he ought to stay home."

The emigrant colored, but not with shame. "I've seen my share of trouble," he retorted, "but I hadn't seen anything till I hit Californy. We're farming people. All the land except the deserts is owned by railroads and rich ranchers. They'll throw a squatter off before he can water his team. Some of the folks that went out there in '49 are still hunting a place to settle. The only free land is the deserts."

He stumped back to his wagon. Cole watched the caravan slowly lumber up the next hill. . . .

They found a few cattle on South Fork and got them drifting up the creek. But Cole was thinking of the face of the wagon boss—sour, pessimistic, defeated—and he was hating it. The man lied; his face lied. Cole Allan had seen the railroad tracts that told about good, cheap land in California; they wouldn't let them print stuff like that if it weren't true.

In the dusk they neared the cabin. Suddenly Cole said to California, "There's weak ones in any country. They make room for the strong." And for the first time he asked California about his name. "You ought to know California," he challenged, "being that you carry it for a name."

"Sure I know California. I lost an eye on the Mojave. Ran out of water, and there I laid till somebody found me. My hat covered one eye, but the sun did for the other."

"But the desert's only part of it!" Cole said desperately.

"California," said the cowpuncher, "is no better nor worse than a lot of places in the East. But the good land ain't free. And the free land ain't good. And to hell with the railroad and its pamphlets. Unless a man's well heeled, it's about twenty years late for pioneering."

Cole Allan had no answer. California was one man you couldn't call a weakling.

Gradually, as they rode, he took a good look around him. There were a lot of things he had been thinking about this country that weren't true. He liked its moods: the bright optimism of its mornings; the way the sun went down pensively at night, as if on a long sigh.

They pulled out of the bosque just below the cabin. And all in a moment fear caught Cole by the throat. Elly! Elly was alone, and there were horses before the cabin.

He rode the last hundred yards in a lope. When he realized that it was Pete Hubbell, he was both angry and lightheaded with relief. She'd be scared foolish.

But if she were frightened, she did not betray it. She stood blocking the door with one hand on her hip and the other holding her nutmeg mill by the crank. "These men," she told Cole, "think that they're going to set fire to our cabin. I think they've been drinking."

Pete Hubbell stared up at Cole Allan.

"You've had six weeks to get along," Hubbell charged. "Your cattle have stripped my graze down to bedrock. Now I'm telling you to pack and git."

If lying was the order, Cole thought, he could do his share. He told Hubbell, "I took the trouble to check up on your water rights. It seems like Peach Creek is still open. So I homesteaded my six hundred and forty and took a grazing lease on the rest."

"You're a liar," said Pete Hubbell levelly.

"What am I going to do?" asked Cole. "Swallow everything a cow-stealing borderhopper tells me? Cole Allan owns this land now, and you're saying *adíos*."

Hubbell said shortly, "I'll be back tomorrow morning. If your cabin ain't empty by then, I'll empty it."

Cole glanced at California. "It's these comin' yearlin's that are hard to flank, ain't it?" he remarked.

California showed that he got it by slipping the thong that held his catchrope. Hubbell moved back.

It was one of the men behind him who blew the tension apart. His right hand dropped onto the butt of his gun and the barrel tipped up without leaving the holster. It was a swivel affair, a thing only a gunman would own.

The report of the revolver was a jolt of thunder that hit Cole solidly. His pony reared with a cry such as he had never heard from an animal before. Among all the other sounds, Elly's scream was a high, sustained note.

The yard was in uproar, men dodging for shelter and horses beginning to fight their riders. Through his shock, Cole knew only that he must draw his gun. But even that he forgot when the pony went over on its back. He kicked out of the stirrups and threw himself sideways. He landed flat, pounding the wind out of his lungs.

Then he heard California yell. It was one of those ebullient cowboy shouts which defy translation but tell the world that somebody is about to do something. What California was doing was dropping a noose over Pete Hubbell's shoulders.

Cole found himself thinking: He can't do it this time. Hubbell will shoot him. . . .

He began to stare at Hubbell. What was the matter with him, anyway? Instead of pulling his Colt, he was rubbing his eyes! He was standing there like a fence post while the rope settled about his shoulders and California took his dallies, and raked his pony with the spurs.

Hubbell's feet left the ground; he came down with a grunt and skidded along behind the running horse. He caroomed off the man who had shot Cole's pony and knocked him rolling.

Cole Allan sat up to discover, with some amazement, that his gun was in his hand. Also he saw where Pete Hubbell had stood, a small wooden box marked the spot, as if in memoriam. He recognized it as the drawer to Elly's nutmeg grater. Hubbell's eyes had been as full of freshly ground spice as Elly had been of wifely fury.

Pete Hubbell's men did not work well extemporaneously. The two who were still on their feet stood befuddled; they had not drawn their guns, and it occurred to Cole that an empty-handed gunman was no more dangerous than any other man without a weapon.

He said authoritatively, "Lie down on your faces with your arms out straight."

The gunmen sank to their knees, hypnotized by the blue ring of the Colt's muzzle. They went down on their faces, and Elly Allan hurried to disarm them.

Down in the willows they could hear California whooping as he pulled Hubbell through the shallows. When he came back, Hubbell lay limp as a wet hide at the end of the rope. "Where did you want this strung up?" California asked.

"I'll leave that to the boys," said Cole. "There's a tree over yonder that could take care of four ropes and have a branch or two left over. Or there's plenty of trails leading out of here. It's their choice—this time."

Pete Hubbell's men departed at a lope, with Hubbell tied across his horse and his head flopping.

Cole went in and watched Elly put plates on the table. He kept waiting for her to break, remembering that last time the tears had come after all the excitement was over. Well, if she held up until the danger was past, you couldn't say she was fearful. But to his surprise she didn't break down at all.

She confronted him abruptly. "If anything had happened this time," she declared, "it would have been your own fault. I told you I was ready for the next desert. And I still am."

Cole Allan put his arms around his bride, and he saw her chin begin to tremble. "Pete Hubbell was the last desert we'll ever cross, Elly," he told her. "If so many people want this country, it must be worth having. Maybe California was just a frame of mind, after all."

Elly answered like a good wife and a wise wife, her eyes on the second button of his shirt. "Whatever you say, Cole. I think it's right nice of you to stay, if it's just on my account."

"No such thing," Cole retorted. "We'll just figure those first five deserts were put there to keep Arizona from getting overcrowded. As California was saying, it's a little late in the season for pioneering, anyway."

Plague Boat

A T dusk Ben Worden came up from the texas and took the wheel from Ord McDan'l. He scowled down at the opaque surface of the river, as thick and red as tomato soup in the sunset. Ezra Church arose from his plush chair at the back of the wheelhouse, and crossed to where Ben was standing. In the dusk, he loomed behind Worden like a fat, soiled ghost, his wrinkled white duck trousers and flannel shirt gray in the gloom.

He cleared his throat. "As I recall it," he said, "Whiskey Creek empties into the river about a mile above that shack, yonder."

Ben said curtly, "It's less than half a mile, and the mark's a burned stump on the near shore. Maybe you didn't know, but I've been up this river before."

Ezra Church, who owned a dozen steamboats four times the size of Ben's little packet, glowered at the back of the pilot's head. He said nothing, but the promise of an early explosion was in his purpling features and the small, shrewd eyes.

Night, sinister and full of dark portents, moved upon the river. Fear came out of the bayou and walked the wheelhouse, and its hard pressure was in the face of each man. Even Ben Worden, who had been at odds with danger before and had not moved one step out of its path, shared the general uneasiness.

Ben and Ord McDan'l and Ezra Church all knew that the shantyboaters of the Whiskey Creek region were more dangerous than rattlesnakes, because they gave no warning when

they struck. In the last month, three pilots had dropped beside
their wheels without knowing that they had come into a
shantyboat man's sights. They had slumped to the deck and
their boats had gone hard aground before the relief man could
reach the wheel.

They'd had their differences, the men who piloted the
gleaming white palaces that traversed the ol' Mississipp' and
the men who slept and fished and drank on their ramshackle
house-boats. But it was a bloodless feud which had become a
habit with each group. No one could have foreseen a war.

Shantyboaters' dinghies had been swamped by careless
pilots for generations. Trotlines were forever being cut by the
paddles of a packet working inshore uncommonly close. But
these were hazards of the trade, which were cursed roundly
and endured, like malaria and the spring shortage of good
corn liquor.

But when a shantyboat full of river folk was run down at
Whiskey Creek and seven men and women lost their lives, the
shantyboaters declared open war. No matter that the raft had
been in mid-river at midnight and jammed to the bull-rails
with river people celebrating a wedding, all of them more or
less drunk. *Murder had been done.*

The River Commission stewed over the sniping of steamboat pilots but did nothing, while cargoes mysteriously caught
fire, and snags, moored just under the river's surface, took out
the paddles of a dozen boats.

Ben's eyes, brown as the river at flood, squinted in a face
that was lean and hard with constant perusing of the river's
face—the book that a pilot must learn to read without stum-
bling. He strove for ease of mind and did not find it, for he
knew that old Catfish Clemens himself was likely in this
bayou. Old Clemens, who was to the shantyboat clan what
Neptune is to the deep-water man—part legend, part god,
mostly devil.

To Ord McDan'l, Ben said, "Tell them rousters to chunk that torch in the river and shoot craps in the boiler room. I'm gettin' a reflection on the bright work."

McDan'l, a stocky man in a blue box coat, grimaced at Ezra Church and went below. On the *Majestic*, flagship of Church's Red Star fleet, McDan'l was chief pilot, but he was only a humble relief man today on Ben Worden's down-at-heels little tub, the *Annabelle*.

Church's glance sought the wall clock. "Six o'clock," he muttered. "Too bad we couldn't have got here on schedule. We'll be crowded to get out of the bayou before sun-up. Flood'll be on us in less than twelve hours." His pendulous jowls worked like those of a bulldog. He bit the end off a cigar and his teeth locked upon it.

"I knew what we were getting in for," he went on. "The idea of personal safety is my last concern. I'm thinking of the men and women who are dying of yellow-jack at Bayou Grand. It's worth any risk if we can save as many as two or three of them. But as for being a hero—" His fat shoulders shrugged. He struck a sulphur match and twisted the cigar in the flame until it smoldered.

Ben Worden's hand shot back over his shoulder. He ripped the cigar from the boatman's mouth, slid open a window and hurled the cheroot into the night. "If you can't do any better than that," he snapped, "go down to the saloon. Maybe your pilots have to put up with your lightin' flares in the pilot-house. I don't."

Ezra Church came sputtering out of his stunned silence. All the indignities of the last two days were loosed within him. "By God, you won't ever make another payhaul if I can help it! I'll see that the commission blacklists you from one end of the river to the other."

At the companionway, he glared at the lean form of the pilot, framed against the rusty skyline. "You can put a shantyboater at the wheel of the biggest boat on the Mississip', and he's still a shantyboater," he said bitterly.

"That," said Ben Worden, "ought to be good enough for anybody."

He was glad Catfish Clemens and his long-legged daughter, Jolean, hadn't heard him say that. For in a way Ben was proud of his shantyboat ancestry, though he knew that there would be no more nights when he sat on the foredeck of Catfish's boat with Jolean, and talked and stole an occasional kiss. No more nights spent in spinning windies with other shantyboat men, while the air of the cabin thickened with smoke and the whiskey jug sat in the middle of the floor, and men's hearts warmed to each other.

All those things had ended two years ago, when Ben Worden had foresaken his father's honored calling to pilot his own packet boat. All Ben's kinfolk lived on the river. They said, "Trust a cottonmouth or the muzzle end of a gun, but never a steamboat man."

Ben's father had died like a good shantyboat man. He was setting his trot-lines after dark when the steamboat hove upon him. And because he knew he couldn't get out from under, he stood up and shook his fist and cursed the pilot until he was run down. But he was full of corn and out in mid-channel, so nothing much had been said about it.

There was plenty of talk, however, when Ben acquired the *Annabelle*. Her owner-captain had picked a night of hell and high water to tie up at Natchez, dismiss the crew, and get drunk. Ben found her on a sand bar, put in his claim for ten thousand salvage, and had it honored by the River Commission. Her owner swore she wasn't worth it and refused to pay. So Ben Worden gave his trot-lines to Catfish Clemens and went on the river.

He knew the smaller tributaries as he knew the palm of his hand. He was lean and tough, the way the river makes a man

who works hard and leaves whiskey alone. He was tall and his
eyes had small lines at the corners, pinched in deep through
reading the river's fine print.

The *Annabelle* was the smallest boat on the lower Mississippi. Thus she got a lot of jobs the bigger boats couldn't
take, when the river was too shoal or the haul was up some
small backwoods creek. And that's why the *Annabelle* had
been chartered by Ezra Church, heading a committee for the
relief of the yellow fever victims at Bayou Grand, to make the
trip to the flood-marooned village with medical supplies and
equipment.

Darkness came, and an ache behind Ben's eyes sharpened
. . . feud, and flood, and fever—three grim foremen to try
any pilot's heart. Ben knew he was risking his boat, for if the
oncoming flood took him out of the channel, he would never
find it again. Sniper's bullets, or the horrible death that men
called black vomit might do for him or all the members of his
skeleton crew, even after they reached the plague victims.

With the *wash-wash* of her buckets behind, the packet
poked her curious nose deep into Whiskey Creek. Glutted
with spring torrents the bayou was virtually a foreign passage
to Ben. The clock was bonging off eleven strokes when Ben's
eyes found a curious redness in the trees some distance ahead.
Hearing his grunt of surprise, McDan'l and Ezra Church came
forward.

"Grand Bayou," Ben frowned. "Though what—God in
heaven! The town's afire!"

They had come around the bend into full view of the town.
Great piles of flame poured a redness onto the water. Up this
carpet of liquid fire the packet glided with her paddles dragging. The town's outlines were starkly silhouetted by the surging light. Tumbledown shacks crowding the riverbank, wharves
leaning slantwise to the water, a mountain of baled cotton on
the dock.

"Them's sperrit fire!" McDan'l said. "Colored folks build 'em to keep the sick-devils off."

As they warped in to the dock, the dismal monotone of Negroes' voices came to them from the high ground back of town. The wailing traced a cold finger down Ben's spine. He sent the steamboat's shrill whistle through those mournful sounds.

Roustabouts threw the boat's stout hawsers over the mooring bitts. The flame-soaked streets were crowded with men and women hurrying toward the dock, and there was a medieval, plague-town malignance to the setting that made Ben's skin pimple with gooseflesh. In the noxious air he could taste horror and disease.

He raised his eyes from the wharf and let his glance wander down to where the flood-choked river had burst its banks and taken the south end of town. And there he saw Catfish Clemens' shantyboat.

He grabbed the speaking tube. His voice echoed harshly back from the engine room. "Keep them drums a-groanin'! We put out in an hour!"

The landing stage was run out and Ben was the first man on the dock. Lumbering behind him came Ezra Church, and at his heels Ord McDan'l, while behind timber and stanchion flashed the perspiring, scared faces of rousters.

Ben saw Church move busily among the piles of cotton, inspecting tags, counting bales, standing in the middle of it while he let his small eyes, quick and mercenary as adding machines, rove over the dock. Moving to the landing stage, Church cupped his hands to his mouth.

"Lay me a gangway! *Stir*, you scared louts! Stow those bales aboard!"

With his words, a slow wonder grew on Ben. But movement suddenly spirited his glance to where three figures were coming onto the dock. He strove for recognition, and when it came he stood with his spine gone stiff.

To Church, his voice coming with a quick thrust, he said, "Catfish Clemens. Watch him. When he's drunk he's tricky as a tinhorn gambler's left hand."

Catfish stopped within a few feet of them. He was tall and stooped and had a nose like a buzzard's beak. Malaria had yellowed his skin like an old hide and left his body a gangling rack of stringy muscle and bone.

"Of all the boats to get through," he said, "it had to be your stinking little tub. But it's any old port in a storm—"

There was corn liquor in his rusty-hinge voice and bloodshot eyes, but Ben answered coolly, "If you think I came up here to pull your damned raft to safety, you're drunker than usual. Where's those sick folks?"

"That's what Pop's saying." Jolean stood at Catfish's elbow, slim and straight in a white jersey and brown skirt, a slender, high-breasted girl with auburn hair caught back by a ribbon and eyes that were blue with flakes of gray in them. To Ben, her beauty was always as startling and as moving as the sun breaking through leaden clouds at sunset, after a day of storm. "We've got the sick 'uns in houseboats, but we can move them onto the *Annabelle* in an hour's time."

Ezra Church made a sound like that of a man strangling. "Move the plague onto my boat? Turn the thing into a pest ship? I reckon *not!*"

With Catfish and Jolean was a lean, rawboned young man in dirty white coat and trousers. He could not have been over thirty. He was tall and excessively slender, and his eyes were keen in dark pockets.

"Pest ship?" he echoed, with the trace of a smile. "I'd call it a mercy ship. By tomorrow Bayou Grand will be under three feet of water. We're evacuating the able-bodied to high ground and the sick to boats. But those dying men and women won't have a ghost of a chance when the flood hits."

Church looked at him coldly. "And who are you?"

– 200 –

"The shanty folks call me Young Doc. I reckon that'll do. I've escorted a dozen of those same shanty people out of this world in the last three days, not to mention a score of townsmen. The rest must be taken out quickly. When the black vomit strikes, there's not much I can do without medicine."

"Medicine—" Church's strained features relaxed a little. "Medicine, of course! Will you come aboard, gentlemen? We came for that very purpose."

Rousters were back-and-bellying the hemp-netted bales of cotton onto the boat as they ascended to the texas. Ben had said nothing yet, but his mind was busy, and he thought he had finally accounted for Ezra Church's unprecedented generosity in chartering a boat out of his own pocket to do rescue work.

The boatman lugged a box onto the deck and set it by a water barrel. He was sweating; his silk shirt stuck to his chest like a mustard plaster.

"You said medicine. There you are! I can't take your sick folk on board, but our supplies will insure that they get the best care possible."

Young Doc's knuckly fingers opened the box and removed a bottle. He read the label and nodded. "I'm grateful, Captain. But it will take more than medicine to save these people. I need clean beds, fresh food—pure water!"

Church's jaw set harder. He sopped his handkerchief in the water barrel and placed it folded across the top of his bald head. "I couldn't bring a whole hospital with me."

Ord McDan'l shifted on his stocky legs. "Reckon there'll be plenty of room, Captain, even with your cotton aboard. I don't see why—"

"Then I'll tell you why! No town on the river would let us land, with the damn' tub crawling with yellow jack! We'd be afloat for weeks, until the last man was back on his feet—or dead. What's more, my cotton would go begging after we did dock. Ten thousand dollars' worth!"

"You can stop right there," said Ben Worden. "Your own words damn you to hell. Cotton! I thought that halo was a size too big for you, Church. An angel of mercy grindin' a private axe under his robes. Don't you savvy, Young Doc? He bought this cotton on futures and knew he'd lose every bale if he couldn't take it out before the flood hit."

Church stood motionless, his eyes aflame with fury and desperation, "The cotton was a secondary consideration," he protested, almost shouting the words.

"You can prove that," Young Doc suggested, "by letting us bring the patients aboard."

Ezra Church's jowls worked. "I am under no obligation to defend my motives. I'm putting out in an hour. I have a feeling you'll make out quite nicely without any further help."

He dipped a tin cup full of water and was raising it to his lips when Young Doc rapped, "Captain Church!"

"Well?"

"Take my advice and don't drink that stuff. Call me crazy, if you like—plenty have. But I have a theory that yellow fever grows in contaminated water."

"Bah!" Church noisily drank off the brimming cup. Then he wiped his mouth and let it fall to dangle by the string. "I've drunk river water all my life and never caught a bug yet."

"I hope you can say as much a few hours from now—if you've been drinking that stuff all the way up."

His expression was somber.

There was a frowning interval of silence. Then Ben Worden said grimly. "I'm going down with you, Doc, and we'll load 'em on."

Ord McDan'l stared hard at Church, quite obviously undergoing an inward struggle to break from the manacles of convention. "I'm with you!" he said, finally.

Church pointed a swift finger at Ben. "Then it will be the last cargo either of you ever moves. I've got my rights. Until we hit New Orleans, I'm in command. If you men persist in mutiny, I'll see you both stripped of your licenses, and you, Worden, of your boat!"

Ben was conscious that Catfish Clemens was watching him, his amber eyes full of poison, his lips twisting in silent sarcasm. He knew Jolean was waiting to hear how an ex-shantyboater would answer Church's ultimatum.

It was McDan'l who first grunted response. "Bluff! With these witnesses you'd never touch us."

Ben's eyes were unsteady, touching in succession the faces of Jolean, Catfish, and Young Doc, and finally wandering to McDan'l.

"That's all right for you. You could apply for reinstatement if he did pull your teeth. But what about my boat? If I carry a plague cargo they'll tie her up at a bonded dock till she rots or wharf charges eat her up."

Catfish began to curse in a bitter monotone. "You yaller mudsucker! You misbegotten offspring of a rouster pappy and a she-wolf mammy—"

"Pop!" Jolean made it a command, and while Catfish got his breath she confronted Ben. "You haven't got this far away from the river, have you, Ben? To let folks die rather than risk losing your boat? Wash Gray's down with the plague, and Jube Milton's family. Remember them?"

Ben said, "I remember Wash Gray hammering a bullet under my nose last month, a mile above his shanty. Would Wash or any other cussed shantyman risk so much as a mess o' channel cat to help me out of a fix?"

"You know they would. We've taken aplenty from you high'n mighty steamboaters, but we can forget a grudge when there's a need."

"When you're a-needin' help, leastways," said Ben.

Jolean's face was tired and her shoulders were slumped under the thin sweater. She passed Ben without a word, and the heart of him turned sharply, so that he had to clench his fists to keep from reaching for her.

Catfish followed, pausing at the rail for a last thrust. "I've held 'em down as best I could," he muttered. "But I'm cuttin' the hawsers now. What happens from tonight on ain't on my conscience."

Young Doc went with them, carrying the box of drugs under his arm. In his very silence Bent felt scorn that was like a lash.

Church went forward. Ord McDan'l would have gone off the guard for a smoke, but Ben drew him into the shadows.

"A shantyman's pride is a sorry thing," he said. "It kept me from saying before those two what I'm going to say to you."

McDan'l filled his pipe without looking up. "I've called many a pilot many a bitter name, but never coward."

"Don't break the record for me," Ben said, beginning to smile. "Go catch Young Doc and tell him what I say—"

The older man listened; then smiled and struck Ben between the shoulder blades. "You've a fool's pride but a riverman's heart!" he said.

It was just after one o'clock when Ben Worden reached for the go-ahead bell and the *Annabelle* warped out into midstream. Ord McDan'l slumped in a chair in a dark corner of the wheelhouse, but Ezra Church was right there at Ben's elbow, seeing the job done right.

Sluggish under a wallowing weight of cotton, the steamboat swung a circle and headed out. Not until Bayou Grand was well behind did Church stir from his position. He rubbed his sweaty forehead with a moist palm.

"I'll grab a few winks," he said. "This cursed swamp air's given me a gadawful headache."

At dawn the *Annabelle* shouldered heavily against the tawny flood-heads of the Mississippi. Familiar landmarks along the shores were all erased, and where those guiding snags and cut-banks had been, the pilot's tired eyes found only the suck-and-boil of a brown blanket of water that lapped deep into the fields on each side.

Ben had hardly straightened up for the downstream haul when Ezra Church came charging into the wheelhouse like a mad water buffalo. "Worden!" he cried. "That damned shanty-boat is towing behind us!"

Ben tied the wheel and looked aft. A hundred feet astern, Catfish Clemens' shantyboat was throwing off huge bow waves like a harrow coming through a wheat field. She was loaded to the gunwales. Beds occupied every inch of deck space. Jolean was on her knees beside one of the victims, administering Young Doc's medicine.

It was right then that Young Doc himself came up from the saloon into the pilot-house, picking his teeth after a hasty breakfast. Ben gave him a quick glance.

"You know, I thought she handled mighty sluggish," he said. "I reckon Young Doc, here, must have tied on as we were leaving."

"You do, eh? It couldn't be that you thought you'd beat a mutiny charge by telling the commission they stowed away without your knowledge?"

Ben made his eyes round. "Captain Church! You don't trust me!"

The captain started for the door. "Have your little joke. But give an extra belly laugh when I cut that pest-raft loose."

Young Doc remarked quietly. "It would just about ruin a big man like you to have such a tale of cold-blooded murder bandied up and down the river."

Church halted, slowly turned around. He knew the doctor held aces. But he was not easily stumped. "Then I'll sure as heaven unload them at the first town we hit!" he muttered. "And if the townsmen cut them loose, it won't be my fault. Stand from the wheel, pilot. I'm taking over."

He thrust Ben out of the way. His face was flushed; his skin looked hot and dry, and he had ceased to perspire.

Seeing that, Young Doc stroked his chin. "Well, Church, you can't say I didn't warn you."

"About what?"

"About that river water. Why don't you admit you're sick? Your head's splitting with fever. Your throat aches. Your belly's tied in knots. Yellow jack!"

"Rubbish!" snorted Captain Ezra Church. "If you intend to stick with your outfit, mister, get back on the shanty. I'm cutting you off at Tobacco Point. McDan'l—send me up a bottle of brandy."

The little town of Tobacco Point had kept the plague out, thus far, and by the looks of the committee on the dock, she meant to remain healthy. Townsmen and shantyboaters stood close-packed, hats tugged down on their faces, jaws jutting. Rifle and shotgun barrels ran red, dipped in sunrise light, as the *Annabelle* warped in.

Standing between the chimneys with McDan'l, Ben Worden winced as he saw gun bores level off at them, and suddenly he and the other man both were sprawling on their bellies, as gunflame ran redly the width of the dock. Heavy duckload spattered the packet's windows. A rifle ball whanged off an iron chimney.

Up in the wheelhouse, Ezra Church shouted curses at the townsmen, and steered back into the river. Lead continued for some time to chew into plank and stanchion, and the yells of the Tobacco Pointers was their only farewell.

Ben got on his feet. "Maybe now he'll have sense enough to know he ain't going to land them that way."

"Don't you think it," said McDan'l. "He won't give up that easy and risk havin' his cotton burned at the dock."

Ben thought of that, knowing that a plague-fearful mob would not bother to take cotton off the boat before burning it. He had thrown his boat, his livelihood, his last penny, into the fight to save a boatload of people who wouldn't give a damn what happened to him so long as they got off safely.

At Brewster, four miles south, a group of armed townspeople met them on the jetty that ran out into the river from the little red-brick and clapboard town. Their shouts rang across the water.

"Keep a-rollin', pilot! You ain't unloadin' your pest-cargo here!"

Ezra Church thrust his head out the window. Through a leather megaphone he shouted, "We've a load of flood victims, neighbors! No yellow-jack aboard, you understand? Just let us drop this shanty—"

Someone bawled, "*Keep a-rollin'!*" and a bullet shivered the window beside his head.

Later, Ben looked back from the hurricane deck and saw something that chilled him to the marrow of his bones. Young Doc and Catfish Clemens raised a plank to the rail of the raft and let a body, wrapped in a sheet, slide into the water. It went straight down, and a trail of bubbles rose and was lost in the wake. But the remembrance of those bubbles remained as an image of horror in Ben Worden's mind.

Behind the locked door of the pilot house, Church steered a wild and perilous course. Two more towns drove the *Annabelle* off. They could see Church up there behind the wheel, sick, drunk, possessed of the blind fixation that he must unload his pest cargo at any cost.

The *Annabelle* ran full upon a dozen sawyers. Church barely missed them by climbing the wheel and each time the shantyboat rolled wildly, shipping waves that soaked the sick, lying on pallets on the deck.

Fear came into the packet, like a plague itself. Fearful roustabouts bunched on the foredeck, praying, wailing, terrified by the grim raft that followed like the shadow of death. The knowledge grew that Ezra Church was fever-racked, and half out of his mind. Young Doc told Ben that there was no doubt as to what ailed him. The full force of the yellow jack would hit him before nightfall.

The day wore on. A succession of river towns approached and were found hostile. There came a time when Church passed a town without making any effort to land. The significance of that put a cold weight in Ben's breast. But Ord McDan'l now seemed relieved.

"He's given up. Maybe he'll let us take over."

Ben went up with him, but he shook his head. "He ain't givin' up. He's too sick, too crazy to know when he's licked. I got a fear for what comes next, McDan'l."

Church grunted some response to their knock and they heard the door unlocked. The boatman had tied the wheel. He stumbled to a chair. Dropping into it, he let his head fall against the back.

"Take the wheel, Worden," he muttered. "McDan'l, fetch me a pitcher of water."

Ben took the smooth spokes into his grasp. He heard the other man leave and then, oddly, the grate of the lock. But the towering chimney of a Red Star boat took his attention right then as it moved past a near bend and into mid-river plowing north. Only a few hundred yards behind it came a second boat, pushing a string of tow-boats before it.

Until Church spoke, Ben did not realize he had come close. "Steer closer to her, pilot. Starboard to starboard."

"We'll risk the current sucking us together!"

A gun-barrel touched Ben's spine and Church croaked, "Spoke off!"

McDan'l was at the door with the ice water, pounding. The captain breathed noisily through his mouth and the pressure of the gun remained above the small of Ben's back.

"What are you trying to do?" Ben demanded.

Through the panels came Ord McDan'l's command to open the door. For a split-second the gun left Ben's back and the roar of an exploding shell pounded against his eardrums. Again there was the nudge of cold steel at his spine.

"Right close, now, pilot!" warned Ezra Church.

It was the *Henry W. Bean*, and they passed so close that their bull rails traded coats of paint. During the passage, Church lowered his gun and turned his back on the *Bean*. Ben saw the officers of the boat at the pilot-house windows. He could hear the captain cursing him, and a man shouting, "It's that shantyboater—Ben Worden! Full o' corn, I'll wager!"

In an instant the passage was completed. Ben reached for the tie-down, and with his hand still groping staggered against the wall and fell. Church's gun-barrel had struck him glancingly on the back of the head.

He was brought harshly back to consciousness by the sound of yells rising from below. Strongest of them was McDan'l's hoarse shout at the door. "Ben, for God's sake, stop him! He's fixing to wipe the shanty off on the tow-boat!"

Ben sat up, feeling blood move dully through his head. He saw a red chimney come into the square of a window. With the shock of that, he was on his feet and starting forward.

The *Annabelle* was cutting directly across the path of the big stern-wheeler with its string of tow-boats. The steamboat was so close that he could see the decks crowded with excited passengers, yelling and waving their arms. The forms of officers moved jerkily in the wheelhouse. The sound of the boat's whistle was a frantic, hoarse snore.

Ben staggered towards Church. Get away from that wheel!"
he ordered, his voice choked with rage.

Church twisted to fire. The muzzle blast of the gun was
deafening. But though it burned Ben's cheek the bullet passed
harmlessly. Ben stepped in, reaching for the gun. He gripped
the warm barrel and another shot ripped past him.

Ben tore the weapon free, and with a backhand blow
smashed the butt of it against Ezra Church's forehead. With
his foot, he shoved the ponderous body away and swung the
wheel. He hung on the steam cord. He was acting purely by
boatman's instinct, knowing that to try to swing upriver would
send the shantyboat crashing broadside into a raft; to try to
cross in front of the string would mean the shanty'd get cut
in two.

Ben headed down-river, hoping the shantyboat would follow
true. He came in beside the stern-wheeler so close that their
loading booms crashed together. A fancy scrollwork railing
was ripped from the bigger boat. He had a glimpse of the
captain in the pilot-house shaking his fist at him.

Then Ben knew why Church had made him pilot the boat
past the Red Star craft. There would be witnesses to swear
that Ben Worden had been piloting the *Annabelle* three minutes before the shantyboat was wiped off on a tow-boat—

At the last instant, he looked back. The shanty was
wallowing into the river giant's path. He climbed on the
wheel.

Ord McDan'l was yelling, "Hard a-starboard! Hard a-starboard!"

The *Annabelle* heeled far over, as if she would capsize.
Bales of cotton toppled like sugar lumps into the brown river.
And now the first of the tow-boats slid in beside the shanty.

Bow waves piled upon the shallow deck. Young Doc planted
a boat-hook against the sheer strake of the steamboat. The
force of that contact hurled him against the wall of the cabin,

and he slipped down and lay stunned, while Catfish ran past him to retrieve the boat-hook.

Then one of the heavy waves got under the raft and shoved her away gently, so that the protruding fan-tail of the steamboat grazed by her within a foot, and a landing stage crashed against the crooked sheet-metal chimney and toppled it into the water.

With clear water ahead, the *Annabelle* pulled her burden to safety and steamed on. Ben Worden tied the wheel and unlocked the door. His face was the color of a bloated channel cat.

"She's yours," he said to Ord McDan'l. "Like the feller says, I feel the need of a stimulant."

Sometime after midnight the *Annabelle* nosed into a berth at the foot of Canal Street in New Orleans. Ezra Church was not aboard. During the night yellow jack took him, and Ben and Catfish quietly gave him a river man's burial.

The sharp-eyed ferret of a man from the health department, who arrived in the morning, showed considerable curiosity regarding Church's death. He poked about the texas and finally came back to the wheelhouse where Ben, McDan'l, Catfish and Jolean waited on tenterhooks.

"Whichun's the room Mr. Church died in?" he demanded, and Ben thought, *Here it comes! They'll burn her before sundown.*

But Catfish answered, corking his jug of corn and setting it at his feet. "Matter of fact, Church died on my boat."

"On the shantyboat! Why in heaven's name did he set foot on that thing?"

"Well, you know Mr. Church. It was everybody else first, and him last. He was up all night, carin' for the sick. And when he knew he'd caught yeller jack himself and had to go, he said, 'Don't waste no medicine on me, Catfish. Save it for them other poor souls that has a chance.'"

Catfish choked a sob by taking another pull at the jug. The health officer gazed reflectively through a rear window at the empty shantyboat, from which all the sick had been removed.

"A pity," he murmured. "Mr. Church was a fine man. But it doesn't alter any the report I have to make."

He made a notation in a little leather book. "Mr. Worden," he said to Ben, "as your boat now floats, she's a menace to the health of the entire community. That menace must be removed. I shall send down a box of sulphur candles this afternoon, which you are to use to fumigate your boat from bull rails to whistle. After that, you may obtain your free-bill."

Ben sat woodenly, not trusting his ears. The ferret-eyed man froze Catfish's grin by remarking from the door, "I'll send a tug down today to tow that raft out to sea and burn it. Good day."

Worden watched Catfish's lean features twist and saw his eyes squint shut. "I'll make up for your loss, Catfish," Ben said quickly. "That was a right fine thing you did for me."

"For you!" sniffed Jolean. "If they'd burned the *Annabelle*, we wouldn't have had any way to get a tow back up the river. And now we haven't even got a shanty to go back in."

"You can have better than that, if you'll take it," Ben said. "I need a good freight clerk. I'll give you good pay, good grub, and rooms with real mosquito-bar screens. We couldn't finish this feud any better than by joining forces."

Catfish swore. "If you live long enough, you may see a steamboat sailing on dry land, but you'll never see Catfish Clemens working on a steamboat."

"You figure you've got to keep on feuding for the sake of your honor?"

Catfish scratched his head. "Didn't say so. After your bringing folks like Wash Gray and Jube Milton down the river, there ain't much we can do but admit a steamboater has his points.

I'll make you a proposition. You keep an eye out for trot-line jugs and dinghies and I'll see that the boys save their bullets for 'possum."

They shook hands on it. With Ord McDan'l, Catfish went out on the hurricane deck to smoke a sad pipe over the fate of his floating home. Jolean's back was straight and uncompromising as she stood at the window. Ben came quietly behind her. He slipped his arm about her shoulders and felt the tension go out of her body.

"Let's end this feud all the way," he said. "With a shanty girl on my packet, wouldn't be a man on Whiskey Creek could say a word against the *Annabelle*. If she was good enough for the daughter of Catfish Clemens, she'd be good enough for anybody."

Jolean turned, and put her hands on his shoulders, her eyes sober. "She's good enough for me, Ben. Do you reckon a shanty girl and a steamboat pilot could ever make a go of it?"

Ben kissed her. "I've still got corn-bread and catfish in my blood, and I reckon I'll never get so civilized but what folks will know I was brought up with the river for a backyard. And you'll find yourself lovin' the sound of the paddles and the songs the rousters sing down in the boilers on a cold night. We'll make out, honey. A few years from now Catfish will be showin' our kids how to set a weir and bait a fish-trap."

"And telling them how their daddy took a packet up a bayou during a flood and saved a whole parcel of shantyboaters. He's a stubborn old critter, Ben. But a lovable one when you get to know him."

"It's a failing of the whole family," Ben said.

The Green Moustache

THERE are a hundred canyons within a mile of Hangtown. Unfortunately for Stephens, he never reached the first one. The horse played out. Of all the horses in town, he had stolen a spavined one.

The miners dragged him to the jail. One of them threw a carpetbag on the floor. The others, rough men in rough clothes choked with the red dust of the mother lode, held the prisoner. "Noose bait, Sheriff!" one of them said.

Sheriff Hannaford studied the prisoner, a tall man, slender as a lath, with dark hair and pale eyes. "You don't look like a fool," he said. "How'd you come to steal a spavined horse? We don't hang them any higher for stealing a quarter horse than a jackass."

The miners roared.

"An oversight," the thief said. He could still smile.

Hannaford questioned him further and made entries in a daybook. *Name: Finn Stephens.* "Occupation?" he asked.

"Card sharp," said one of the men. "Amateur. Give the devil his due, Sheriff—he didn't have much time to pick and choose over the horse. He was in a hurry."

Hannaford, after locking the man in the end cell, went through the bag. He had a weakness for imagining dramatic backgrounds for the men he dealt with. This one, an Alabaman by his speech, he pictured on a fine white horse —his own—giving his darkies hell for not picking enough cotton. He saw him tall and graceful in a drawing room or bending over a lady's hand to pay a compliment. These things his parents had taught him. But they had neglected to teach him a trade. So when the crop failed and he lost the plantation—

Hannaford checked himself. Sometimes he thought he ought to have been a storyteller. He was a large, loose-jointed, yellow-moustached man in his middle years, with round silver spectacles. The moustache was patterned after General Custer's. Sometimes he would pose in front of a mirror with his hand tucked in his coat. He knew himself to be bashful and uncertain, but he had achieved a reputation for steadiness and courage.

He came across a flat box full of brushes and twisted tubes. He grunted. An artist! A famous one, no doubt; exiled for taking liberties with the wife of some nobleman whose portrait the artist was painting. He was tempted to ask about it. He refrained. It was harder to hang them when you had become interested in them.

The next day a west wind brought the choking fumes of the smelters into Hangtown. Grimacing at the nauseating taste of sulphur, Sheriff Hannaford carried the prisoner's dinner to his cell. Staring through the grilled window, he saw Finn Stephens hunched on his cot. Stephens was coughing. He arose in agony, gasping for breath.

Hannaford unlocked the door. "You didn't have enough grief havin' TB. You had to steal a horse, too!"

"Not—TB!" Stephens gasped. "Asthma. Damned fumes. Get me—every time."

"Asthma, eh?" Hannaford's ready sympathy leaped up. "Doc Jennings has a cure for asthma. Want I should call him?"

Dr. Jennings came in half an hour. The sheriff watched curiously while he sprinkled crystals on a bit of blotting paper in a saucer and touched a match to the paper. He placed it on a stool, told Stephens to kneel before it, and threw a blanket over him. In five minutes Stephens' voice said: "Good Lord, Doctor! What is this? It's remarkable!"

"Saltpeter," said the doctor. "Some European discovered that the fumes are good for asthma. I'll leave some in case you have another attack."

In thirty minutes Finn Stephens was breathing normally. He turned the crystals with his finger. "Saltpeter!" he said. "Ordinary saltpeter." He regarded the sheriff intently, frowning a little.

Hannaford cleared his throat. "Holler when you're through eating."

Stephens nodded. Then, as Hannaford was going out, he said quickly, "Sheriff!" He steppped close and ran a fingertip down Hannaford's jaw. "I have never," he said slowly, "seen such a jawline as that. Never."

Hannaford grasped the butt of his gun. "Hold on, mister! I ain't took in *that* easy!"

Stephens' hand fell away. "I—I'm sorry, Sheriff. Really, it was quite spontaneous. I'm an artist, you see. You have a fine jaw, what I would call a—well, a military jaw."

Self-consciously, Hannaford grinned. "It's a cavalry jaw. You can hang horseshoes on it." He smoothed the General Custer moustaches.

It was unfortunate for Finn Stephens that the circuit judge was in town. In the morning he was arraigned for horse stealing. Hannaford asked him, "You deliberately stole that horse? You weren't drunk?"

"I am afraid I wasn't," Stephens said pleasantly.

He was sentenced to hang on Saturday.

That evening the sheriff was surprised to find an excellent likeness of himself sketched in charcoal on the adobe wall of Stephens' cell. The artist had used charcoal from the sheet-iron stove in the corner. "Like it?" he asked.

"It's right clever," the sheriff conceded.

Stephens regarded it critically. "I have three days. I might be able to do some kind of portrait, if you like."

Suspicion's cool finger touched Hannaford's neck. "Sure," he said. "Only, of course, you'll have to do your studyin' through the bars." And he grinned.

"That's all right. I'll want my paints and some canvas."

Hannaford stroked his moustache. A tug of war began in his mind. It was his official duty to suspect Finn Stephens' generosity. But the dark hollow features were without guile. "All right," he said.

He brought the paintbox. The artist rummaged through it. "Damn! Completely dried out! And there wouldn't be any supplies closer than Sacramento." Then he snapped his fingers. "You've got assayers by the dozen. They'll have minerals I can use for pigments. It may be unorthodox, Sheriff, but we'll have a picture!"

Hannaford brought the minerals and a mortar in which to grind them. He had a frame made and stretched heavy duck over it. Stephens mixed his paints and daubed at the canvas. The sheriff's face emerged, moustache first.

Hannaford watched the likeness of himself come to life, the eyes bold, the jawline stark. It was not the man Hangtown knew, but the one who now and then posed before a mirror. The sheriff began to wish that, somehow, he could make it easier for Stephens to go, for go he must.

Yet the artist seemed to have forgotten about it.

"Waiting to swing doesn't seem to bother you like it does most," remarked the sheriff.

Stephens shrugged and put a tiny catch-light in the sheriff's right eye.

The portrait, when it was finished, was better than the

picture of the woman behind Finney's bar. The sheriff wished it were someone else he was hanging in the morning. This was a sincere and intelligent man who had lost sight of his star somewhere. . . .

At three thirty in the morning the dull stroke of an explosion awoke the sheriff. He thought at first it was an untimely shot among the mines. Then he knew it was too close for that. He heard sounds in the corral. There was a strong beat of hoofs in the alley.

Grabbing his trousers, Hannaford ran to the jail. Clouds of smoke churned in Finn Stephens' cell. By the light of the lantern, Hannaford discovered that two of the bars of the window and a section of the mud wall had been blown out.

Some men ran up the street from the saloon. They were too far in their cups to be of much help. "Stephens!" the sheriff shouted. "Someone must have slipped him some black powder! He's blown out half the wall."

This time the artist had taken the best horse in the corral—Hannaford's.

They found the horse some weeks later, but they never found the horse thief. Hannaford was secretly relieved. With an election coming up, he didn't want it to get around that the sheriff himself had supplied the powder for Stephens' escape.

It had been several days before he'd figured out that all the materials for black powder had been in Stephens' cell for two days. Saltpeter, charcoal, and sulphur. Sulphur that he himself had brought for yellow pigment. Ground fine in the mortar, tamped day by day into a hole a sharp stick could have drilled in the adobe wall, the powder had unlocked the door.

The sheriff was not an ungenerous man. He held only one thing against the artist. Stephens, just before he left, had impudently tinted the Custer moustache alfalfa green.

Dusty Wheels — Bloody Trail

M E N who play a waiting game need an accurate sense of timing. Clyman had this. They require boldness, and he had this. Originality is not out of place, nor capital, if they hope to sweat out the other fellow's game, and these things, too, were his. Jess Clyman, twenty-eight, unmarried, quiet but vigorous, knew he'd need all these attributes if he were to bull his way through this grandiose scheme of his, and he had decided, with a young man's vanity, that there was nothing he lacked.

For two weeks he had lain around El Paso, spending most of his time in a fuming little gambling and drinking place called El Sueco. He sat at a front window, with a view of the wind-harried plaza and the stage station across the way, watching the packing-in of a transcontinental log jam of stagecoaches, wagons, travelers and horses. Hotels bulged with frightened men and women. Saloons thundered with talk of war. Travelers journeying east were dumped here because the stages would go no farther for fear of running into bands of raiding Southerners or Black Republicans. Travelers following the western star were left high and dry because the Apaches had hacked to pieces most of the line between El Paso and Tucson.

El Paso was a cageful of terrified human animals who did eccentric things, who killed one another nightly out of sheer terror, with cards or women as an excuse. Jess Clyman felt himself aloof from the mood of panic. He had the indolent polish of self-sufficiency. He had a bag of gold, and when the time looked ripe he'd walk across the plaza to the depot of the

Great Southern Overland Mail and make his proposition to the division superintendent.

He was a dark-skinned, blond young fellow with blue eyes which looked pale in his dark face. He had been born in Missouri but raised in the Mother Lode of California. Given to figuring, it had not taken him long to notice that the men who had the gold were not the ones who dug and panned for it: They were the men who served them. When he was old enough, which was seventeen, he bought a span of mules and a wagon and began freighting on a small scale. By the time he was twenty-seven, he had run it up to twenty-five thousand dollars worth of animals and rolling stock. Then he got the urge to travel, and he put his money into gold and started east. He was one of the men who had been jettisoned at the El Paso depot. In three days he knew what he wanted to do.

He was at the depot the day the girl arrived from the east. She looked as frightened as any of them but was determined not to show it. Clyman saw her bags placed before her with an air of finality. She was small and neat and wore a gray poplin gown trimmed with blue ribbon, and a little feathered jockey cap on the side of her head. She kept waiting for someone to pick up her bags and escort her to a hotel, her chin going higher each minute.

Clyman was there to appraise horses. But he took pity on her and presented himself with his hat under his arm. "Jess Clyman, miss. Nevada City. I can get you a hotel room if you'd like. It'll be no trouble."

She brought her eyes coolly upon him. They were the gray of a smoke-tree, purplish and fine, and he knew at once that she was a member of the only class on earth he was in awe of—the lady. Highborn men or lowborn he could handle, but women of the upper class he did not quite know how to take.

"Thank you," she said. "There'll be someone to help me in a moment."

He set the bags down, sufficiently disciplined by her gaze, which came up from below him but managed to look down upon him. "Sure," he said. "Somebody will be bound to, if you wait long enough."

He went back to the saloon, not quite angry. Women, he guessed, had to be careful when they traveled, but that young lady was going to wish she had accepted his offer before night fell. There wasn't a hotel room left in El Paso.

The second time he saw the girl was two hours later, just before dusk, a cold, sweeping wind hurling grit at her as she came along the sidewalk. He was back in El Sueco, sitting with two Mexican girls. He had never drunk with more than one girl at a time before and he felt like a roué. But they had fastened themselves upon him in the hope, at the most, of acquiring a well-heeled friend; at the least, of acquiring a few drinks.

The girl stopped when she saw him through the dirty window panes. She was staggering along carrying her own bags. Chivalry was as foreign to the town as cold beer. Then she saw the girls with him and a look of confusion came to her eyes and she turned and hurried on. Jess left some money on the table and followed her.

He caught her fifty feet away, where she had set the bags down to rest. Once more he approached with his hat under his arm. "Still Jess Clyman, miss," he said. "Still from Nevada City. And I can still get you a room."

She wanted to accept in utmost gratitude, he knew. But she was afraid of him and couldn't forget things she had heard about men who drank with saloon girls. "Really," she said, "there must—I haven't tried them all, yet. There's one called—"

Clyman put on his hat and raised the bags. "That one's full too," he smiled. "The girls in there were after me. I wasn't after them. That's the way it is in this town. If you want this room—"

She raised her chin again. It was simply in her; she couldn't help it. "What makes you so sure you can find me a room? They told me at the depot there wasn't a room anywhere."

"I was going to give you my room. I'll catch a shakedown at the depot."

"Oh!" Her mouth was small and round and she looked as though she felt rather small herself. "Mr. Clyman, you're very patient and very generous, and . . . and I'm very sorry. But I can't let you do it."

He caught one bag under his arm, held the second by the grip, and had his other hand free to escort her along the teeming walk. "I don't know what else you can do, unless you want to share a stall with a stage horse. It isn't much of a hotel but it's the best in this place."

By the time they reached it he knew a few things about her. Her name was Susan Shelby. She was from Alabama, and sounded it. Her father was American consul-general in Mexico City. She was on the way to join him. She wanted to know what chance there was of their ever going on; she was trying to reach San Diego to take a boat.

"Not much," he said. "But we'll work something out."

"I hope so. The war *can't* last long, but if it should. . . ." She stopped abruptly.

He saw her settled and was granted permission to come back at seven to take her somewhere to eat where she wouldn't be poisoned by the food. . . .

Two more stages came clattering in, one from the east, one from the west. That brought the total to thirteen packed into the big stage yard. There were some hundred or more horses and mules in the corrals and mighty little hay for them. Clyman saw the division superintendent stomping back and forth between stables and station, a man crucified by his problems. The drivers sat around looking less important than usual. Going were the days when they could command four or

five hundred dollars a month to drive a stage fifty miles a day.
The time was ripe. The waiting game was over.

Division Superintendent Niscannon was barricaded behind
his desk when Clyman entered. He came in unannounced
and unwelcome. Niscannon was a bearish, sour-eyed man
with putty-textured skin rutted with harsh lines. For two weeks
nobody had brought him a word of good news. If anyone
wanted to see him, it was about finding a room or borrowing
ten dollars or demanding that the stages get moving. He made
a growl around his cigar as the younger man came in.

"You can sleep in the barn, if you want, but as for borrowing any money—"

"It's a hell of a situation, isn't it?" Clyman sat on a raw-
hide-latticed chair, crossed his legs and hung his hat on one
boot-toe.

Niscannon went back to mourning over waybills and express
vouchers. Jess Clyman was silent. The superintendent pivoted on the chair suddenly and exploded: "Look! If you want
to jaw, there's a dozen drivers sitting outside that door drawing
pay for doing just that. But I've got worries. I've got more
worries than any man in Texas. If there's anything I don't want
to look at, it's a man without worries."

"Everybody's got worries. I was going to Houston, but I got
sidetracked and stuck in this place. Isn't that a worry?"

Niscannon closed his eyes on the old, old story and went
back to his papers.

"And on top of that, I've got a peck-basket full of gold. And
that worries me."

Niscannon's bloodshot gaze came up. "Find yourself a girl.
You won't have it to worry over long."

Jess shook his head. "I'm going to invest it. Don't this seem
like the damndest time to be buying stagecoaches?"

At last the stage man perceived that his visitor was devi-
ously backing into a horse-trade. The vising of his jaws

ceased. "It sure does. What do you want with stagecoaches?"

"I'm speculating. I speculate that if I take a string of Concords into Mexico, I can sell them high. They're practically legal tender in the capital. Naturally I'd have to get them cheap."

"Naturally." Niscannon leaned back and rolled a cigar between his hands. "Why tell me about it?"

"You've got thirteen stages in the yard, a hundred stage animals and nothing to feed them. One of these days a couple of dozen Union or Confederate troopers are going to slope in, throw a handful of scrip at you and take them away. How's that going to make you look with the company? If there still is one."

"How does it make every agent and section boss on the Oxbow look, the way they're throwing up their hands and dumping everything in my lap?"

Jess Clyman shrugged, rising. "Well, it was just an idea. But I thought if you could sell those coaches and some of the wagons and stock, they might figure they had a good man out here. Maybe you'd be one of the ones they moved north with the line."

Niscannon bounced up as he put on his hat. "Sit down! Sit down! Clyman—by God, if you're joshing me—" But he quickly convinced himself Clyman was serious by peering into his face, and he pulled his chair around so that their knees were almost touching, and said, "All right. Let's talk turkey."

When he left the office Clyman walked the lighter for ninety-five hundred dollars in gold removed from his money belt. He did not know whether the stage man planned to abscond with it or turn it in to the company: It did not concern him. He had bills of sale on the coaches, ten wagons and seventy-five horses and mules. He had been given the name of Hugh Donovan, Fourth Division section boss, who would shake up a crew of drivers and hostlers.

Jess moved fast. He was anxious to scour the dust of El Paso in the Big River. The coaches were his worry now.

Hugh Donovan was another of El Sueco's partisans. Jess found him, by description, shooting pool with a sallow, spectacularly thin man. He watched Donovan sink the five ball, try for another, and presently pick up a glass of beer from the edge of the table. He drained half the beer. He belched. He was a very large man in a tawny buckskin shirt, dark pants and high, wrinkled boots. A sombrero with two matches under the hatband hung between his shoulders by a thong. His hair was crisp and short, blond going gray, and his eyes were deep and blue, set wide under the hard boneridge of his brow. He was about forty-five.

What Clyman liked about him was that he could play a decent game of pool in a time of general catastrophe. He made himself known to Donovan and the big man sank a couple more and then came over to stand by Jess while the other man shot. "You say Niscannon sent you?"

"He thought you could help me find twenty-five men overnight. Thirteen stage drivers and a dozen others. Two of them ought to be good shots with a rifle, for meat getters."

Jess saw him looking him over in the mirror behind the bar. "What do you want with thirteen drivers?"

"You guess. I want them by tomorrow noon. I'm not trying to fool anybody about where we're going. It'll be Mexico City, if we're lucky, and I'll pay two hundred a month to the drivers, a hundred to the rest. They can take five hundred pounds of freight apiece to sell in the capital. Guns, tools—anything like that. They'll all make a killing."

The lean, hollow-chested man playing pool with Donovan looked around. "Did somebody say Mexico City?" He stood leaning on his cue.

Donovan frowned. "Don't publish it, Doc. Clyman, this is Doc Bible. Maybe you'd like a sawbones along. Doc would give his right eye, the good one, to get out of this rat trap."

The doctor had a long, pinched countenance with a frazzled light brown imperial on his chin. His left eye had a peculiar yellowish-green cast and the pupil was too large: Jess suddenly realized it was a makeshift, probably a lynx-eye from a taxidermist shop. It caused him to smile as he shook Bible's hand, and Bible winked the other eye and said, "It's got all kinds of advantages. I'll hate to give it up if I ever get back to civilization. I can see in the dark with that one, you know. So you're going to Mexico—!" He said it with the greatest relish and curiosity.

Donovan glanced about them. "Clyman, if you want to get out of town, I'd walk soft and move damn quick. Let's go outside."

They left the saloon and walked in the plaza. A series of dingy alleys converged on the treeless square, where an endless procession of women and girls with *ollas*, or wooden buckets, balanced on their shoulders trudged to the stone well in the center of it. Bull teams jostled, horsemen spurred through the crowds of men and animals. Everyone seemed in a rush to go somewhere, though there was nowhere to go.

Doc Bible kept peering at Clyman. "I'd pay double fare to get out of here, Clyman, even to Mexico. I could get a boat from Topolobampo to 'Frisco. What are you charging?"

"It isn't a common carrier proposition; every passenger will make a hand. But you can go as company surgeon, and no charge."

The doctor grasped his hand. "I'll set you a broken leg or cure you a bellyache right now. Say the word."

Donovan's competent gaze was on the jam of dusty crimson coaches in the stage yard. "Twenty-five men. I'll make a deal with you: Twenty-four—and myself." He grinned.

"Can you drive a stage?"

"No, but I can shoot an antelope as far as I can see one. If

Niscannon's sold out, I've got no job to hold me. I'll pick up a load of junk jewelry and take over them brown-eyed women the way Cortez took Mexico."

Jess measured the section boss for an instant. The man's strengths were obvious enough — aggressiveness, confidence, leadership — but it was his weaknesses Clyman was interested in. These might be vanity and singleness of purpose that lapped over into stubbornness. "These men are all used to taking orders from you," he said. "Make it plain that they'll be taking orders from me on this trip."

Donovan looked at him steadily, his brown face flat. Then, grinning quickly, he struck him on the shoulder. "I'll have them call you Commodore if you say so."

With this done, the gun primed and ready to be fired, Jess thought again of Susan Shelby. He had only a faint notion that she'd be interested in a trip south. He wouldn't blame her. A delicately-reared young woman, if she had any imagination, would faint at the thought of the hazards and inconveniences of such a trip. But he meant to ask her.

He put in the afternoon buying supplies and seeing them packed. Flour, salt, powder and ball, hardware. Everything you could not pick or shoot on the trail. He inspected the stagecoaches for cut spindles and sprung thoroughbraces. He met the drivers and got their hands individually that they would stay with the train as far as Mexico City. He set departure for ten o'clock the next morning.

At seven that evening he went down the hallway of the hotel through a faint blue of whale-oil smoke and the conglomerate body-smell of too many people living too close together. He knocked at the door of Susan Shelby's room and waited. He waited fifteen minutes in the hall. Then he went to the noisy central room and listened to the racket of war talk and assorted complaints for another fifteen. At length she appeared.

She was unbelievably trim; she was contrite and vivacious

at one time. She wore the same gray gown with its touches of blue, but she had managed to get every travel wrinkle out of it, and the dark brown sausage ringlets at the back of her head were neat and shining as metal-turnings. She looked to Jess like something that ought to be under a glass bell to keep off the dust. She could have been two hours late and carried it off as well.

"I had so many things to do," she told him, "and then I slept . . . and then you knocked at the door. You don't know how fast I dressed."

Jess guided her through the raucous traffic of the sidewalk. She seemed to flinch from hurrying Mexicans. He led her past the stage depot where, for the first night in two weeks, the superintendent's office was dark. Niscannon would sleep for a week. Jess had had the coaches aligned, ready for teaming, and they bulked, freshly washed, in a gleaming dark line within the gate. He held the girl there a moment.

"How do they look to you?"

She shuddered. "I know how a pullet feels in a gunny sack, after coming all the way from Tipton in one of those things."

"Depends on what you're looking at. I'm looking at thirteen Concord stages, as saleable as ten-cent diamonds. I bought them today."

She turned her eyes up to his face in astonishment. "Jess! What do you want with them?"

"I'm going to sell them again."

"But where? Who else would be foolish enough to buy them?"

They came to the restaurant and he pushed the door open on a dimly-lighted scene of limber-legged tables and smoking lamps. At a tile stove in the rear a fat Mexican woman was dipping tortillas in grease, sprinkling ground cheese and onions on them and dousing the roll with earth-red chili. The old, familiar smell of Mexican cooking was as heart-arresting

to him as the sound of a sweetheart's voice. But he had to urge
Susan Shelby into the room with a promise.

"It tastes better than it looks."

He ordered, aware that she wasn't going to like it. On the
other hand, the food was safer than spoiled beef in an American café. She had a little difficulty getting back to the coaches
again. "I still don't see how you expect . . ."

"I don't. Not here. I'm taking them south."

"But there's nothing south of here but Mexico."

"That's right. Mexico City."

She caught her breath, started to say something, and then
frowned and looked down at the table. The food came, two
plates smoking with Mexican rice, frijoles, *huevos rancheros*,
and *enchiladas*. Susan pushed at the *enchilada* with an iron
fork. She took a bite and looked at him in distress. She got it
down and her eyes flooded with tears. It was incandescent
with chili, which was the beauty of it. Finally she ate the rice
and eggs and drank the coffee.

"Mexico City," she mused. "Did you know that was where I
was going when I was put off here?"

"You told me. You said your father was American consul."

"Confederate American consul."

She said it with pride, her eyes challenging him. He
scowled. Politics did not excite him, and the war still seemed
to be none of his business. He sidestepped a discussion of it.

"It isn't much of a road. I've got a map but I think a lot of
it's just a cowtrack. But what I was thinking, if you really want
to get there . . ."

She sat with her eyes beginning to lighten, waiting for him
to say it. Something slowed him down. If this were another
third-rate-café he was asking her into, he didn't want to be
held responsible. "I make no promises or predictions. But if
you want to go along you'll have your own coach and it won't
cost you anything."

"It frightens me but it frightens me still worse to think of staying here. Jess, it's fine of you to ask me. I'd like to go."

All the way back to the hotel he felt the lift of being with her. Yet there was a shading of intuition about it when he thought of the weeks ahead. She would have no maid, no pampering; her remembrances of the Oxbow would seem like a dream, Jess Clyman hoped she could take it.

At her door he said, "Ten o'clock. Get all the sleep you can. We'll travel fast the first couple of days."

And then, because she was the prettiest woman he had seen since he left San Francisco, and because she was provoking him with her eyes, he took her shoulders gently in his hands, bent and kissed her on the lips. She repulsed him without moving or speaking. It was like kissing a picture. She regarded him coolly.

"Have I paid my fare, now? Or will there be other installments?" She said that very slowly.

Jess said, "You're paid up. You were before. Good night." He was not so much contrite as angry and he didn't understand why.

Niscannon had said he could spend the night in the stage station, in a back room loaded with crated files and a cot. Doctor Bible was sleeping in one of the coaches, glad to be shut of a louse-ridden hotel room on the river. There was a barracks-like building at the rear of the stage corral where the drivers and hostlers bunked. Jess sat up late, studying his maps. He had the creeping fears of any man going into a dangerous gamble, not quite ready to back out, not eager to push ahead. It was after twelve when he snuffed the lamp and pulled off boots and shirt.

He was sitting on the cot rolling a last cigarette when he saw a light reflected on the wall. He glanced through the window. He saw only the dark corral with its throng of horses; and beyond it the low, pole-beamed facade of the employees' quarters. A wash of light ruddied the tawny adobe wall, reflecting faintly into Jess's room. He could not see the source of it. It was to the left, toward the stage barn. He saw the horses begin to move restlessly and all at once it struck at him.

He tugged on his boots, pulled his carbine from the head of the cot and strode through the dark freight room to the side door. He opened it and stood there a moment. His impulse to action ran down. Looking through it was like stirring up the lees of a nightmare.

Two coaches were already beginning to burn, and the man who had set fire to the second was already climbing a wheelhub of the third with a coach lamp in his hand, the brass lens-housing removed and the wick turned up high. A second man, four coaches ahead of him, pulled a lamp from its socket, drew the stopper and dumped the whale oil onto the floor beneath the driver's seat. Then he ducked on to the next in the compact line of coaches.

Jess pushed open the cheesecloth-frame screen door. A rusty spring squawked. Both men turned in alarm. Clyman set the stock of the gun to his shoulder and leaned against the jamb. He took aim on the man leaping from the wheel to the ground. The gunkick jolted him. The roar of the gun hit a dozen adobe walls and came rolling back at him in a cascade of sound. The hatless man with the lamp dropped it and lunged into the yard, reeled aside and fell across the tongue.

Jess saw the other man draw a revolver, balance there with his boot on the hub of a front wheel, clutching the brake with his left hand while he threw down on the doorway. Ducking back, Clyman heard the expanding report of the gun; the door frame was hit and wrenched from one hinge. He struck it open again and saw the gunman rushing toward the gate. Clyman's gun was a six-shot Dragoon Colt with a shoulder stock and a long barrel. He squinted at the indistinct, running figure through the sights, took his shot and knew at once he had missed.

Then there was another man in the gate. The running figure swerved, came up against the door of the baggage room, half raising his Colt. Jess heard him say in a gasp, "Hugh!"

Hugh Donovan, a tapered wedge against the faint lustre of the town, stood with one foot a little ahead of the other, his left arm hanging, his right slightly hitched back. A gun flashed. The bullet, crossing only twenty feet of ground, hit the man hard, nailing him to the door. He staggered two steps away and went to his knees. Then he went forward on his face.

Clyman lost the first stage. He saved the second. When they were through fighting the fire he went to the baggage room where Bible was tending the wounded men. The man Donovan had shot was killed instantly. The other was still alive, hanging to a thread of breath that sucked through the ragged wound in his chest. The bullet had driven a splinter of bone into his lung; Bible didn't expect him to live through the night. The man's name was Rice. He'd been one of the wagon drivers Donovan picked. The dead man's name was Naylor. Donovan stood with Clyman in the yard and swore.

"The dairty sons of Satan! Slave men they were, forever chattering about state's rights and low tariff and a parcel of other things I don't give a damn for one way or another. But I didn't see where it could matter what color a man's politics were, for this trip. They figgered, you see, there wouldn't be a trip. Maybe they thought you were taking these coaches north."

"Where would they get that notion?"

Donovan tugged at a shaggy blond eyebrow. "I don't know. Being you're a Californian, maybe." He scowled at the throng of drivers and hostlers about the door of the baggage room. "I'll be shakin' a few bushes tonight for any more Johnnies in

this crew. Get your rest, Clyman. I'll sit up with them Concords myself."

But Jess didn't rest the balance of that night. A hex had
been put on the trip. He wasn't superstitious but it bothered
him to put his foot into a room that had been quarantined.

Nevertheless, he went ahead in the morning with as much
confidence as he could display. He checked everything himself, assigned drivers to coaches and inspected the loads of
merchandise they were taking. He saw the teams watered and
grained and at ten gave the word to hitch. Then he hurried to
the hotel. He wanted to get out of town before all the frightened travelers who inhabited it realized a train was going out.
Clubs couldn't beat them off if they discovered it.

Susan Shelby called through the door that she'd be right
out. Twenty minutes later she appeared. Jess seized the bags
and hurried her out without listening to her excuses. She was,
he decided, one of those women born with their clocks set
back an hour.

Someone had shut the gate of the stage yard. Before it a
shouting mob surged. Men with suitcases, women with children, all trying to get through the cottonwoodpole gate to storm
the crimson coaches stirring restlessly under four-horse teams.
Jess pulled her aside. There was a door into the depot; he
rapped until Niscannon opened it. Niscannon was still half
drunk as a result of a celebration the night before. He bowed
low to the girl and barred the door after them. He said, "Ye're
a fool, Clyman, if you don't accept passengers at two hundred
dollars a head."

"I'd be a fool if I did. I may make it if I travel light."

He rushed Susan into the yard. The driver of her coach
was already on the box, a big iron-mustached man named
Ben Dallas. He was taking along a load of black silk bolt-
cloth, which he thought he could sell to women in mourning, which in Mexico included anyone over two. Jess put

Susan in and hesitated with his hand on the latch.

"Still sure?"

Her color was that of muslin but she smiled, "Sure, Jess."

Clyman slung up onto the box of the lead coach. The driver sat flicking his whip at pebbles. He was a leathery oldtimer named Gil Applegate. He wore a collar-band shirt with no collar, a wadded silk vest much stained with food, and buckskin pants. He glanced at Jess through the round silver spectacles he wore. "Know this is a crazy idear, don't you?"

"If it's too crazy, you don't have to go along."

Applegate spat tobacco juice on a wheeler's rump. He picked up a copper bugle from under the seat, decorated with a silk tassel, and wiped his lips. "As long as we've got Hortencia along, you don't have to worry. Roll 'em?"

Jess signaled the gate men to open it. "Roll 'em."

Applegate blew a sour little flourish which was his trademark. Other drivers sounded their calls, a brassy tangle of discord which somehow threaded a ramrod down a man's spine. The gate swung in.

There was a wild rush of would-be passengers into the yard. Men grabbed at the harness tugs and pounded on the panels. Applegate kicked off the brake and let the buckskin cracker of his whip singe a man's ear. The coach rolled forward with a grind of iron tires.

Jess heard a woman's shriek, "Murderers!" He saw a man hold up a chamois bag and shout, "A thousand dollars." He had to discipline himself, to recall that with loaded coaches on a trip like this he could hope for nothing but disaster. He could not feed them, bunk them nor tend the inevitable sick. He looked straight ahead and the team reared and lunged out onto the plaza. He stood up to look behind. The other stages were in motion, thrusting through the mob. Then they were out of his vision as Applegate hawed the team into the alley beside the station and let it run. There was a crowded vista of adobes boxing in a pot-holed street, then a glimpse of open land and cottonwoods along the river and finally they were on the river road, clattering along toward the ford, with the midnight-blue mountains of Mexico beyond the desert.

There was a desolate little store and cantina a few miles below the border, where border guards and riffraff made occasional stops for food and drink. Clyman stopped here and treated himself to a mescal while the others, except Applegate, waited outside. He talked to the proprietor, a fat *mestizo* named Corrales.

He bought Corrales four drinks and then backed into his subject. He was taking a train of stagecoaches to *la capital* for the Mexican government. Which government? Ah, the revolutionary government of Juarez. He wondered what he could hope for on the trail.

Corrales fished a fly from his drink with a fat forefinger. "Only the Indios, *capitán*, and the *reaccionarios*, and of course the *bandidos*. I know of no soldiers this far north, though in Sinaloa—" He shrugged. "But there is a gentle murderer by the name of Jesus Calzadillos in Chihuahua. He might have been here last week; how should I know? He has not the money for uniforms for his men, so he is still a *bandido*. He knows many tricks with ants and honey."

Jess stacked fifty pesos on the counter. "We know a few with rifles. But if you see him, tell him we were heading for Hermosillo, eh?"

They rolled steadily through the day, coming at sundown to the shore of Lago de Los Patos. Clouds of ducks and cranes rose at their approach; some of the men had loaded with birdshot and enough were brought down for several meals. They were on a dark plain reaching distantly to the east and running up against a chain of mountains a few miles to the west. Wild hay, green and young-tasselled, rustled hub-high to the coaches. The teamsters were to draw extra pay as stock handlers. They watered the horses and mules, grained them, and two of the men saddled to guard the herd through the night.

The wagons and coaches were drawn up in a circle, with the supper fires inside. Ben Dallas had appointed himself caretaker of the Shelby girl. He brought a leather seat cushion for her to sit on at dinner. He carried her a tin plate heaped with fried meat and potatoes. Jess bottled his scowls until the conversation came around to the war.

Dallas said, "Miss Shelby tells me it's a crime what them Yankees have already done in Kentucky. A disgrace. Farms pillaged with the crops just coming through the ground! Women and kids killed and—"

"So I hear tell," said Donovan seriously.

Applegate squinted at a cube of steak on his fork. "I heerd just the reverse. I heerd the Johnnies had raided into Ohio and burned a town clean to the ground."

Dallas leveled a finger at him. "Now that," he said, "is a damned—excuse me, miss—an everlastin' lie."

The word was on Dallas' tongue. But Jess came in sharply. "We're going to have a house rule on this trip. Anybody that talks politics gets his tongue hauled out by the roots. There's only one thing has caused more trouble than women, and that's politics."

The firelight had its sparks in Susan's eyes. "You don't approve of the South, Mr. Clyman?"

"I didn't say that. I said I don't approve of wrangling over things nobody knows anything about."

"I know something about the South. My father—"

"I know. If I wanted to know about the South, I'd ask a Northerner. If I wanted to know about the North, I'd ask you. Then I'd figure both were telling ten per cent of the truth, and I still wouldn't know anything."

He saw the watchful faces about the fire studying him. A throb of anxiety woke in him. He had suddenly the feeling that he was talking to a jury, that the things he said might come back at him from a prosecutor's mouth. He heard Hugh Donovan state, "You must have some feelings about it. It's pretty big."

"It's too big to decide in thirty days. When it comes to things like that, I like to grind on them a while before I make up my mind. I wish more politicians were that way. But the one thing I can tell you is that we're out here to drive some stages fifteen hundred miles south. We'll have Indians to fight, *bandidos*, and, like as not, fevers. But if I can help it, we aren't going to fight each other."

Dr. Bible nodded, glints of humor in his eyes, his long face gouged by light and shadow. "Spoken like a statesman. I'll be glad to perform that operation you spoke of, Clyman, on the first man who talks politics."

"Or woman?" the Shelby girl put in tartly.

Bible smiled. "A pretty woman has certain rights, one of which is not to turn a man's words back upon him."

Susan finished her dinner quickly and rose to go to her coach. Dallas started to get to his feet to escort her but Jess put a hand on the man's shoulder. "My monuments are built and my claim recorded," he said softly.

Dallas' broad, heavy-browed face watched him a moment and then turned away. Jess walked after her. He took her arm as they went through the grass. "Sue, I'm sorry. I'm on neither side. But politics could split this train right up the middle."

"Politics have split the country. Is your train more important than your country?"

"That," Jess said, "is one of the prettiest pieces of feminine logic I have ever heard. I have an idea if I were to put that question to you ten days from now, you'd say the train was more important even than whether Alabama keeps her slaves or turns them loose."

He saw the white anger coming into her face. He gripped

both her hands. "I said I was sorry. Let's leave it like that."

She turned away without a word and mounted the step of her coach.

In the middle of the night a shot split the prairie with a clean, echoless, spiteful crack. Jess, sleeping under the stage, rolled out of his blankets and began pulling on britches and boots, swearing. The sound wasn't close but it was followed immediately by the soft rush of horses' hoofs. Applegate was raising a profane clatter atop the coach. They heard the racket of horses falling and squealing; they were hobbled to make herding easier, and seemed to be falling all over themselves in the attempt to run.

There came another shot and a cry. Jess swerved around the rear boot of the coach and found his pony loosely saddled. He fumbled with the latigo, hearing Dr. Bible shouting, "Clyman! What in hell?"

"Horse raid!" Jess yelled.

Only six men had saddles, though there were saddle horses among the wagon stock which had been kept in the circle for emergencies. He mounted and rode over to where Bible, Applegate, Ben Dallas and three hostlers were saddling. For a moment his impulse was to order them onto a firing line beneath the stages: This could be a raid by *bandidos*, revolutionaries or Indians. It was not likely a raiding party of less than twenty-five or thirty. But it would merely be slow death to be marooned without stock.

The horses were making so much noise, about a quarter-mile west, that it was no trick to follow. Leading out, Clyman found the dark bulk of the herd. He pulled in. The others ranged in beside him. He told Applegate and Dallas to cut north around the tail of the herd and sent three others against the flank.

Then they heard a horseman hammering down out of the darkness to the north. The men deployed while Jess waited.

The man pulled in short of him and apparently was endeavoring to find the riders he had heard. Clyman recognized the stringy shape of Toll Breckwalter, one of the night guards. He called to him and rode forward.

Breckwalter was winded and his voice was high and stretched. "They knocked Ashley over. There was only a couple of them, it sounded like. I think the horses are just boogered."

They rode out and found the horses slowing, beginning to scatter. There was no indication of raiders. Jess left four men to gather the herd and they rode back to find Sam Ashley.

They came in with Ashley twenty minutes later. The fire had been built up, water was heating, and Bible spead a blanket on the ground and motioned the men to lay the wounded man on it. He worked without much sureness, it seemed to Jess, and the smell about him was not of disinfectants but of whiskey. Bible brought a mashed lead ball from the man's hip with tweezers. While he was cleaning the wound of the now-rousing patient, he pulled out a bit of wadding. He dropped it in the granite washbasin. Something about it caused Jess to pull it out on a matchstick to examine it.

He grunted and dropped it into the fire. It was the paper patch which had been wrapped about the ball. Evidently the gunman had fumbled in loading, lost the patch, and torn a bit of paper off something in his pocket to replace it. What he had wrapped about the ball was the corner of an American dollar bill.

Hugh Donovan came in a few minutes later. His horse had been worked hard and he threw a blanket over it before he joined the others at the fire.

Jess asked, "Where were you? Did they run you off, too?"

The firelight stroked the hard planes of Donovan's face. "I heard the horses moving before it happened. I didn't see any call to turn the camp inside out. I went out to see."

"What did you see?"

"Two jaspers sloping for the mountains, after the shot. They got Sam?"

Bible muttered, staring into the fire as he sat cross-legged. "He may live the night. He won't live the week." No one commented, and the lanky physician with his gray-green cat's eye glinting stared around the circle.

The party broke up. Applegate was grunting as he tried to make himself comfortable on his straw shakedown. Jess climbed to the box and reached under the seat. He kept his maps there, and suddenly too many things pointed to the fact that they might be as important to someone else as they were to him. He grubbed deeper among the tools and odds and ends: The long roll was gone.

Applegate heard him curse. "Now what?"

Jess sat on the seat, gazing into the darkness. Finally he turned. "Applegate, how do your politics run?"

The driver lay on his belly on the deck to stare at him. "You ain't going to start a political argyment with me, now?"

"Not if you're Union. Otherwise, keep still."

"I'm from Pennsylvania. Going back one day and likely join up."

"My plans, too, only I'm for California where I come from. Gil, the maps are gone."

Applegate groaned. "Maybe they shook out. We can ride back."

"No. Somebody took them tonight because I was tracing tomorrow's travel after dinner."

"You know how to git them back, don't you. Shake down every man in camp and shoot the sonofa—"

". . . There's a better way. We aren't lost because I've got a small duplicate in my boot. I think they'll be brought back if we keep still. Gil," he sighed, "this is a misbegotten outfit if there ever was one. A doctor that's turnin' into a drunk, a girl that's too pretty and Southern for anybody's good—and a traitor in camp."

Applegate's cheap vulcanite plates rattled hollowly. "How do you know that?"

"Sam Ashley was shot by somebody in camp. The bullet that shot him carried a paper-patch torn off an American bill. Would Indians or *bandidos* be heeled with American money? They couldn't spend it."

They both looked down at the sleeping circle of the camp with its surging red heart of dying coals. Applegate asked slowly, "Who do you reckon—"

"I think I can find out. But I can't go to shooting my mouth off too quick because he may have friends. He may have about twenty friends and nobody but you and me for enemies. We may know within forty-eight hours. We'll hit the cut-off to Texas at El Venado. It's marked on the map. If anybody else wants these stages of mine, I don't think he'll want to travel any deeper than that."

The morning was as many mornings would be before they reached Mexico City. Lame stock to tend, feed to dole out, running gear to tar. When Jess gave the order to stretch out, Applegate remarked drily, "They're back now."

"Did you see who returned them?"

Applegate let the lines slip through his fingers, adjusting them. "Yup."

"The girl?"

Applegate glanced at him. "You don't seem surprised."

"I'd have been surprised if whoever wanted them had the guts to do it himself."

He didn't let his emotions get into his voice but he couldn't keep them out of his head. It made him want to punish her before everyone. She was a damned brainless little tramp, a catspaw who didn't stop to look at end results when she went into a thing. But she was a lovely tramp, and she had her fingers on the strings that governed his life in a disturbing way. But if he had to sleep with every *chamaca* in every pueblo they passed, he wouldn't let her know she meant any more to him than she had when they left.

Through a morning of almost summer warmth, they wound deeper into the vast cattle empire of Chihuahua. Sam Ashley died without regaining consciousness; they buried him beside the road.

The stage trail to Chihuahua City was a deep trough in the tall grass along the base of the blue mountains. If it continued in as good condition, they would make the city in five days. They would reach El Venada, and the junction of the Texas trail, by the following evening.

Jess Clyman's gaze ranged continually along the foothills. These Tarahumare Indians were rough; Jesus Calzadillos, the *bandido* who aspired to be a general, might be even rougher. He could trade coaches for money, uniforms, weapons. A picket-like line of trees made a dark piping on the mountain-locked prairie ahead of them. Rio Tula cut its sharp scallops among the trees and emptied into a muddy seep far to the east. Jess and Donovan rode ahead to scout the trees before bringing the coaches on. It was safe, and Donovan lingered to study the land up west, toward the hills.

"I seen antelope rumps up there, Jess. We'd better git 'em whilst we can."

He looked back for approval, and found Jess' eyes on him in level, unfriendly scrutiny. Jess said, "You've got plenty of plans but not quite enough guts to shove them through."

Donovan stirred on the saddle. He cleared his throat. "What's got into you, Jess?"

"Too many killings. You sicced Naylor onto the coaches and then shot him. You killed Sam Ashley last night. Let me have your poke." His revolver came out with smooth, disarming speed.

Donovan's brows pulled. "A detective one minute, a highwayman the next."

"Let's see your purse!"

The stage man pulled a chamois bag with a clasp top from his hip pocket. He tossed it to Jess. Jess heard the dull clink of coins as he caught it. He opened it and pulled out a roll of bills that lay on top. He peeled off the top one and found a torn corner. He put the rest of the money back into the purse and tossed it to Donovan.

"Still a detective. Doc Bible pulled the other part of this bill out of Ashley's wound. What's your game?"

Donovan pocketed the leather purse and drew one boot from the stirrup and put his leg across the saddle swell. "You've got a lot of ideas. What's your idea about this?"

"Either you're a transplanted copperhead, or you think you ought to have the stages instead of me. Which is it?"

Donovan's wide mouth smiled. "Do either of those notions jibe with trying to burn the coaches?"

Jess had not yet reconciled it himself. He shook his head. "But I'll swear you had a finger in it."

Donovan smiled. "In a way. Rice and Naylor were good men, but crazy as hoot owls. I told them you were taking the coaches to Mexico to ship to California for the northern supply route. The same as I told them all. That was just to bring them along, but the damned fools got patriotic fever and decided to burn them before we left. Well, a burned stagecoach is no good to anybody, and I'm glad I came along in time to help you clean 'em out."

"What about the stock raid last night?"

Donovan wiped his mouth. "The sooner I can stall you, the better I'll like it. This is a harebrained idea of going to Mexico. You'll never make it. But I figure a man could cache these Concords down near Laredo and make a deal with the julep-merchants. In fact, now that you're in on it, I'll split with you."

Jess laughed briefly. "You can look down the barrel of a gun and make an offer like that!"

Donovan shook his head. "You ain't going to kill me, Jess. You can't afford to. The boys would lynch you. They're mine, every damn' one of them! Even the girl. Not counting the saw-bones and Applegate, of course. What are you going to do about it?" He didn't give Jess long to reply. He said, "Jess, there ain't nothing you can do about it. You came out with your guard down. I'm giving you your chance: Take off right now and keep your health."

Jess grunted and put his Colt away. "You're a pretty good chess player but you want to look in back of you as well as in front. If you took these coaches, you wouldn't dare go back to El Paso. They may be fighting there already. And you'll find getting to Laredo is more than tracing the route on a map stolen by an empty-headed little tart. Remember those greas-ers were trained to kill Yankees down there only ten years ago. A lot of them still make it a hobby. Donovan, if you got to the border I'd be as wrong as a man ever was. You'd ask about the next waterhole and they'd direct you to a salt sink. You'd try to shake out of them which Indians to trust and which not to, and they'd lie and then send somebody to let them start their dance. You're a hell of a fine schemer, except that you forgot something: You're in a foreign country that would still be at war with us if it had the money."

Donovan's broad brown face with its tough brows received it impassively. "I wasn't brought up in a ladies' seminary. I'll take on any fifty greasers you can pick."

Jess laughed in his face. "You're a good barracks fighter, but your guts will turn to water in the field. The Mexicans have a song that goes, 'For zarapes, Saltillo. For soldiers, Chihuahua. For women, Jalisco . . .' This is Chihuahua. Every peasant sucking sap out of a cactus dreams of being a soldier; and if you go along the way you think you will, a few of them are going to put their heads together and start an army."

Donovan's eyes scoffed. "What makes you better at getting through than I am?"

"Because I know them. And I've got letters. When I get into the danger zone I'll hire guides, on the strength of my letters." He shook his head, smiling confidently. "I'd hang you for killing Ashley, except for one thing: The boys might hang me. So we seem to be stalemated. You can't do without me, and I can't get rid of you—yet. We'd better try a few more moves until one of us thinks of a way to clip the other."

He turned his pony and rode back, showing Donovan the broad target of his back . . .

Reaching the train, Jess tied his pony on behind and climbed up beside Applegate. Gil took the Concord through the bright splashing little river. Donovan was out of sight, having gone after the antelope. And this was a tribute to Jess' dialectics, for about fifty per cent of what he had given the stage man was fancy. Donovan had him in the tightest spot a man ever squeezed into. How many of the wagoners he owned, Jess couldn't guess. He hadn't owned Ashley, that was obvious. And he didn't own Gil Applegate. But Ashley was dead, and Applegate and he made only two against twenty-four.

Jess looked back over the train. Susan Shelby, riding the box beside Ben Dallas as he brought the coach through the water, was leaning over to look at the stream. She appeared warm and uncomfortable in her heavy traveling dress. Suddenly she looked up at Jess.

"Mr. Clyman, will we hit another stream tonight?"

"Not for two days."

"Then I'm going to ask you to wait up ahead a few minutes

while I bathe. I haven't been so warm and dusty since I left the Oxbow."

"Go right ahead. The boys will enjoy it."

Some of the men chuckled. Susan put her chin up as color flooded her face. "Please stop and let me down," she said to Dallas. Dallas handed the team in. She closed her parasol with a snap. "You can go along for a mile or so and someone can come back after me." Imperiousness was out of place in someone six inches shorter than anyone else in the party.

Jess smiled. "You aren't afraid of the Indians or Calzadillos?"

"Not if you don't go off and leave me."

"I ought to. There's an old saying about an eye for an eye. Do you understand?"

She saw the double meaning and her lips parted. Before she could reply, Jess sent the cavalcade forward with a down-sweep of his arm. He signaled Dallas to drop the saddle horse trailing his coach. He glanced back a few minutes later and she was not in sight, but a white petticoat lay across a bush.

Everyone seemed to think it a good joke, except Dallas. The big driver drove in sombre displeasure. Finally he pulled out a silver pocket watch.

"Fifteen minutes," he said. "Dammit, Clyman, you'd ought to know better than that. There's danger of Indians; and in the second place she ain't dressed to fork a saddle."

"It was her idea. It'll do her good."

Dallas' eyes combed the back country. He turned on the seat. "I'm going back for her."

Jess dropped down and went to seize the leader's tug. "You're going to keep right on, mister."

Dallas stood up. "Leave holt of that tug."

"Swing those horses back in line and keep moving," Jess snapped.

He released the trace, but as he did so Dallas brought the horses around. Jess swerved to catch the tug. Dallas, still on his feet, sent the thirty-foot whip out in a savage cast. The cracker caught Jess on the side of the neck. The pain was swift and disarming; he felt blood sweeping down into his shirt. Dallas gave the whip to the horses on his next throw and they went lunging past the pony. Jess shook his head to clear it. Then he ran to untie his horse, mounted and started after him. Dallas had turned the horses loose. They were trying to climb through the collars; the coach rocked like a baby buggy on the uneven ground.

Crossing behind it, Jess loped up the off side, holding his pace until he could lean over and close his hands on the siderail across the seat from Dallas. He left the saddle like a bulldogger taking his ox, finding the floor with one boot and hauling himself up beside the driver. Dallas took a swift dally of the lines about the brake and, twisting on the seat, fired a looping overhand blow at Jess' chin. Jess took it on the shoulder, but it had the shocking power of a sledge.

Wild-eyed, Dallas lunged after him. Jess, slamming his punches aside, cuffed him on the ear. Dallas shook his head and scowled. He was a handpegged sort of man with the virility and homeliness of the country. He would not be taken to pieces by a few blows any more than a homemade saloon counter would collapse under a drunkard's fist. Jess' knuckles ached with a follow-up blow to the driver's forehead; but Dallas kept soberly about his business of pawing for a hold and clubbing with a fist like a bungstarter. He hammered the meaty edge of that fist into the muscle at the base of Clyman's neck. It locked him in an aching paralysis. Jess had to let his right arm hang and jab with his left. Dallas circled both arms about his neck, locked them with a fist clamped on his own wrist, and hauled Jess' head down. His knee drove up. Jess took it on the cheekbone. Staggered, he reached up and got both hands on Dallas' windpipe. He had the sense to hang on while the driver clawed at his face: man forgot everything when his breathing was tampered with.

Jess hung on like a badger. Now the hands muling over his mouth and eyes seemed to push more than to gouge. He got an urgent note into the snoring gasps he managed to force past the blockade of Jess' thumbs. Something was off-key. Dallas was not fighting. He was floundering.

Jess stared at him. The driver's eyes were focussed beyond the stage, off on the prairie. Involuntarily, Jess relaxed. Dallas gasped, "*Bandidos!* Bandits, by God!"

Out of a foothill barranca, two miles west of the stalled wagon train, lurched a winding string of horsemen. They were crossing rimrock, but making time. They wore the white pants and shirts of peasants. The sun struck blue glints from their rifles.

Catastrophe has a fascination, a beauty and balance, and Jess stood there an instant almost in admiration of it. A quarter-mile south were the wagons. A mile north was Susan Shelby, washing her body. There were at least forty bandits. Jess counted twenty-five in his outfit. Susan was in this spot despite his advice, but a woman was a woman, and, damn it, had to be protected.

A single shot cracked and the echoes poured down from the foothills. He saw a rider lope out of a brush thicket ahead of the outlaws and pound toward the caches and wagons waiting in a line as neat as a family of ducks on a pond. Applegate yelled something and hawed his team around to outline the circle.

The pony was back where Jess had left it. He shouted at Dallas, "Pull 'em in! Let me off to go get the girl. Blow your bugle and give her time to start dressing. If she gets stubborn come in without her. They may not find her."

Dallas was unable to stop the wild run of the team. He swung them and headed back toward Clyman's horse while they cooled off. They came out of their headlong run and Jess jumped. He seized the reins and made the saddle without touching a stirrup.

The grass was so deep a horse could run safely only on the road ruts, gouged by carts and the stagecoaches. This was an advantage over the raiders, and God knew he needed one. He glanced back as he knifed into the circle just closing up. Dallas had reached the river and someone in a white undergarment was climbing into the coach.

Donovan racked in about a mile ahead of the Mexicans. They were jogging in a switchbacking line down a rocky slope to the grass. They held their guns shoulder-high with one arm and manipulated the reins with the other, as if only this device could retain the horses' balance. Applegate and the others were cutting the horses off the poles and slapping hobbles onto them. Jess yelled at them to throw and tie the horses as well: He wanted neither to stage a battle with seventy-five crazy broncs stampeding around, nor to have them shot.

Most of the men had seen Indians in action at some time or other but there was no assurance that Mexicans would attack in the same fashion. Certainly not if they had any sense, for they didn't outnumber the wagoners sufficiently to take the risks of circling. Applegate said the only way was to lie under the coaches and wait. But when some of the men tried it, they found the grass was so high they couldn't get a shot at the bandits until they were close enough to strike straight through into the hasty stockade.

This gave Jess an idea. Measuring, he saw Calzadillos' men hitting the grass and letting their jughead ponies romp down across the flats. Less than a half-mile to go, now. But Ben Dallas, standing on the box with both arms extended across the clattering void between the dashboard and the wheelers' rumps, was bringing the Concord in at a full run. They had left a slot for him, and he rammed the coach into it and others piled onto the team and ripped the snaps loose.

Jess had to fire a shot before anyone tamed down enough to listen to him. "Five of you take positions on top of the coaches. The rest of us are going out into the grass. Donovan, you pick ten and I'll take the rest. Crawl about a hundred feet out. Stay down until you've got a sure shot. I figure they'll pull up about there to start peppering."

He looked around, taking a quick inventory. The horses were down with a couple of men to watch them. Donovan was tolling off his men, Applegate was jamming an extra Colt under his belt, and at the window of Dallas' coach Susan Shelby's face showed whitely. Dr. Bible stood with a long horse-pistol hanging from his fingers.

They crawled under the wagons and out into the grass. It was tender and moist and fragrant; it absorbed the sound of the running horses almost completely. Yet before he had crawled fifty feet, Jess heard the yells start: *"A bajo los Yanquis! A bajo los Tejanos!"*

He couldn't see the others. He hoped Calzadillos could not, either. A light desert breeze stroked the grass. His hands sweatily clenched the Dragoon pistol, the offbreed .44 with the barrel of a revolver, and the stock and firepower of a repeating rifle. He waited until his nerves were pulled out to a plucked tautness. His body throbbed to the hammer-blows of hoofs in the earth. He heard the men on the Concords begin to fire and a voice shouted something in Spanish so close he could hear the breathiness of it:

"Bajen ustedes!" Dismount. . . . Jess ripped out a rebel yell and came to his knees. The peasant army, uniformed in the garb of poverty, carrying weapons out of style for twenty years, was scrambling out of the high wooden trees. There was an Oriental cast to the faces Jess saw, the eyes narrow and wispy, with lip- and chinbeards marking most of them. He picked out a hatless outlaw who wore a red-and-gray poncho for his target. The man was about forty feet away. He put a shot into the out-

law's side as he left the saddle. Then he cocked the gun again and heard Gil Applegate's gun roar a few yards to his right. A second outlaw fell before he knew he had been fired at.

Heads were popping up all around, with every cheek against a gunstock. Gunfire crackled with the uneven tempo of pop-corn explosions. There was hardly a chance for a man to miss at this range. Ponies and their riders threshed in the grass; bandits came up on their stirrups and were pitched from the saddle.

Back about fifty feet was a lean, hawk-faced Mexican with a conical sombrero crusted with silver and a horse carrying forty pounds of it on his bridle. This man fired a shot from his rifle and suddenly wheeled and started back up the long slope to the foothills. As an afterthought he turned to shout, *"Haga a atrás!"* This merely made it official, as every *bandido* who was able to roll a spur was already falling back.

There was powder and ball in the downed outlaws' pouches, but the guns were cumbersome and rusty. Jesus Calzadillos must wait many months before he could call himself a general. He had left sixteen of his men on the ground. Bible took care of the wounded and they left them covered with their own saddle blankets. None of the Americans had taken a wound.

Darkness settled sootily over the prairie. There was not a peasant's *jacal* to break the limitless dark with a light, nor a town to glow beyond a hill: Nothing but their three cookfires, shining clean and clear as stars in the cold desert night. The men were exhausted with the aftermath of the fight. They ate hungrily, chewing poorly cooked duck, fried onions and camp bread burned on the bottom. Jess looked them over, trying to catch some indication from each man's face or actions as to how he stood—with him or against?

Susan he did not look at at all. Ben Dallas kept forcing food on her, and her good nature was wearing thin. He made a loutish boastful lover of the "feel-them-muscles" school.

Clyman made an offhand speech. "You've had your baptism. They may keep on baptizing us all the way. Things are apt to be tougher than I thought. The saloonkeeper at the border warned me that the Juaristas and the reactionaries are making trouble everywhere. It's a religious war, and there's nothing worse."

He saw Susan's eyes on him, dark and timid. He heard Breckwalter, partner of the man who had been killed the night before, say gruffly, "Anybody can start a thing. Not everybody can finish it."

Jess caught his eyes. "But nobody can finish it with a split crew." From his tin plate, Hugh Donovan's gaze rose slowly and with a dogged thrust. Donovan said nothing, but light ran fluidly along the browned barrel of his saddle gun lying across his lap. "Last night," Jess said, "somebody borrowed my maps. I got the impression he might be planning an excursion of his own. Maybe to Laredo. All I want to say now is that it's to that man's interest, and his friends', if he has any, to stick with the train. The Texas trail is suicide. Where we're going, we've got a chance. Make up your minds what you want: To die rich or to live well-heeled."

He went over to his own coach, stripped off his buckskin shirt and hung a lamp in a window and a mirror against a trim poplar panel. He got out his shaving things and worked up a crisp lather. As he daubed it on his jaws, he saw Susan's reflection in the mirror. He didn't turn. She stood there a moment.

"I'm sorry, Jess."

"About what?"

That stopped her momentarily, and when he looked down she was obviously trying to decide what he knew, exactly. "About . . . making you let me bathe," she said.

"That's all right. It would have been your funeral if they'd found you before they found us."

She sat on the sill of the door. All the pride and petulance was out of her face tonight. "You don't like me, Jess, do you?"

The razor whispered along his jaw. "It's your friends I don't like."

She frowned, "Ben Dallas?"

"No. Hugh Donovan."

"Donovan is no particular friend of mine. I've hardly spoken to him since we left. What do you mean?"

"You aren't friendly enough with him to steal a roll of maps for him?"

He heard the quick indraw of her breath. He turned with the razor loaded with lather peppered with stubble; suddenly he flicked it and the lather struck her on the mouth. "It was nice of you to bring them back. You'd make a dandy little spy, except that you haven't the sense to go with your lack of scruples."

She wiped the lather away, tears starting in her eyes. "I didn't do it for Donovan," she said, falteringly. "I did it for myself. For what I believe in."

He laughed. "What do you believe in: Susan Shelby? That she should never go hungry, dirty or unsatisfied?"

"I—I believe in the things the South stands for."

"What does it stand for?"

"For—for states' rights, and a low tariff, and—"

"One thing I would never make a thief and a liar out of myself for is a slogan. Those are the things they've told you. Are you sure enough about them to condemn Applegate and me to death, and take a chance of being massacred on a lost trail yourself?"

Susan looked up at him, earnest but confused. "I didn't do any such thing! Mr. Donovan told me you weren't taking these stages to Mexico to sell, at all. That you were going to ship them to California to use against the Confederacy. I wanted to know. I thought you might have traced the route on the map. . . ."

He examined her eyes and mouth, and all he could see was sincerity. Yet he remembered how stealthily she had stolen the maps, how completely selfish every act of hers that he had witnessed had been. He turned back to the mirror and placed the bright edge of the razor against a sideburn.

"I'm going to give you some advice. Get right with me or with Donovan damn' quick. We hit the Texas cutoff tomorrow, and it's just possible Donovan will call out the guard then. He can take nearly every man I've got. They may kill me, or they may just rob me. But whichever they do, they'll know they've been about the doing of it."

When everyone else had turned in, Clyman went out to inspect the stock, and returned in fifteen minutes, throwing his bedroll under the crimson coach and sliding into the blankets. He lay there about an hour, and then silently rolled out of them into the grass. He left the blankets tousled. He crawled about fifty feet and lay in the deep mat of wild grass. If an attack came, it would come with a shot at him.

He held to one fact: That Donovan had not had time before leaving El Paso to do a thorough job of hand-picking a crew. There must be some of the drivers with Northern leanings, or merely honest ones. Some men who could see through his pratings of Confederacy to the fundamental fact that he was acting for the good of Hugh Donovan. These were the men Jess hoped he had reached with his campfire preachment.

It was damp and cold in the grass, and the fire sank to embers and the stars burnished themselves on the black velvet of the sky. Horses moved in the yonder distance, scuffing over rocks. Jess was barely able to see them, moving across a ridge. His heart thudded. They were moving faster than grazing horses moved. Then from the camp he heard sounds carefully muffled; a man dropped silently from a coach and stepped through the ring of Concords to step into the grass. Another appeared with a saddle over his shoulder. They came like shadows from all parts of the camp, filing out into the grass: Ten, eleven, twelve . . . They did not gather, but moved in a broken line toward the horse herd. There were sixteen of them, and Donovan's massive shape led the rest.

Jess did some calculations. Sixteen moving out meant eight left behind. Assume these eight were loyal. They were still outnumbered two-to-one. Jess could throw down on them, drop a couple, and be killed with the rest when Donovan marshaled his men.

They walked with hardly a sound in a straight line from the stages toward the mountains. The horses had disappeared over the ridge. There were left nine men, a girl, and twelve stagecoaches with nothing to pull them. As the deserters crossed the ridge, Jess got up and walked into camp. He went around and glanced at each man, his Colt in his hand. They were sleeping, not lying there waiting for a signal to kill the dubious ones. Jess climbed a wheel and shook Gil Applegate. The old driver grunted and raised his head. A gun was in his hand.

"Get up," Jess said.

Applegate groused. "This is a helluva early start."

"The horses are gone. Along with Donovan, Dallas and fourteen others."

Applegate's toothless jaws sagged as Jess swung down. Then he began to mouth curses as he produced a pair of plates and jammed them into his mouth.

They wore out the night in vigilance. Susan Shelby awoke when the smoke of the breakfast fire drifted across the coach where she lay sleeping. There were sounds of her dressing, and at last she appeared and came toward the fire in the brisk early morning. She stopped in surprise and gazed about. There was no sign of saddle horses, and there was a grim handful of men squatting about the fire eating fried fat pork and thick slabs of bread.

No one looked at her. She got a cup and poured herself coffee. Then she stood by Jess. "There's something wrong," she said. "What is it, Jess?"

"Nothing, much. They've moved out, is all. We've still got all the coaches but they've got the horses."

She gasped and glanced westward at the spot where the horses had been pastured. Jess smiled. "A hitch? Were they supposed to take you with them?"

She looked at him in quick vexation but she held her anger. "No. Only—I don't see—"

"What they can do with the horses, if they don't have the coaches? Let's put it another way: What can we do with twelve Concords if we don't have horses to pull them?"

Breckwalter, the ponderous, frowning partner of murdered Sam Ashley, glowered into his tin cup. "Put rock foundations under them and start sod-busting," he said. "I tell you one thing: I ain't going to pull any stagecoach to Mexico City."

Susan sat down. "You mean we're—"

"Stranded is a good word," Jess remarked. "They took the precaution of packing out most of the food they could carry. Or probably what they did was to drop a sack of meal here and a flitch of bacon there, as we came along the last day. So we can't start hiking back to El Paso, a hundred and seventy miles, without grub. And we can't stay here. We'll have to hike for El Venado, the nearest village, and live on tortillas until we can get back to the States."

He started a cigarette. "Patriotism in action is a pretty thing. Patriotism to the Confederate States of Hugh Donovan."

Applegate had been mulling it over painstakingly half the night and still did not comprehend the strategy. "Why didn't they knock us off and take both, right then?"

"Because he was only sure of those fifteen, and we'd have been sure to knock off a few of them if he cut loose on us. But there was this other way that they could get the whole kit and b'iling without firing a shot. They're holding the horses some-where, and I've got a notion they're watching us right now. When we start hiking for El Venado, they'll come back pronto and hitch up. They'll by-pass El Venado and head for Texas."

Susan put the coffee cup down. "Jess, am I responsible for this?"

His eyes were calm and heatless. "Not necessarily. Not unless you got the map on his orders and let him see it. If you didn't, we'd have to assume he knew the trails anyway."

She stood up, looking at him in bewilderment. "I didn't know! I argued with him when he told me you were a Union agent. He said he'd prove it to me if I'd get the maps. I did, and he pointed out some marks I didn't understand, and copied the part of the trail to Laredo. Jess—all of you—I'm sorry. He made a fool of me, and I put you into his hands. I'll do anything you tell me to to make it up."

She waited, and still no one spoke, until Applegate slung his coffee into the fire and growled, "That's a hell of a pot of coffee somebody made. You'd better float a rag in 'er next time."

They puttered about, getting the feel of catastrophe. A couple of drivers commenced walloping dust off the varnished red panels of their coaches with long rags. Applegate removed a wheel nut and slipped the wheel to the outside of the spindle to dope it with grease. At the fire, Jess was molding ball-lead when he saw this. An idea entered his head, nebu-lous as steam. But he examined it from all angles, buttressed it with conjectures, and it began to acquire shape and force.

Jess walked over and looked at the wheel nut. It was large, hexagonal, slotted for a cotter-key. He said, "I'm going to borrow this," and walked around the coach. He compared it with nuts on the reach-and-bolster assembly; with the nut on the kingpin fastening the tongue to the hound. Carefully he went over the entire stage, but there was not another nut with which the wheel nut could be interchanged. Jess walked back. The driver had slipped the wheel to the inside of the spindle, and was waiting for the wheel nut.

Jess was beginning to smile. "Take a water bucket," he said, "and start taking all the wheel nuts off. I'll help you."

Applegate peered at him, not sure whether he liked the idea. He was one who held that a Concord stagecoach was not far from being divine, and it was sacrilegious to tamper with it. Then he seemed to perceive Jess' idea, and he chuckled and grabbed a wrench.

They went down the line of coaches, removing wheel-nuts and adding them to the greasy assortment in the bucket. They performed the same operation on the wagons. Then Jess summoned the other men.

"One of you dig a hole," he said. "We're going to hold a burying. Those coaches won't go far without wheel nuts, and there isn't another nut in the train that will take their place. We're going to bury them here and build a fire over the spot."

He retained the rest of the story until the bucket had been wrapped in a tarp and buried three feet deep. A fire was built on the spot. Jess occupied himself with making up a portable camp kit from the remaining supplies. They were going on a short trip, but it had to look like a long one. He gathered them at the fire once more.

"I'm taking for granted that Donovan doesn't like being out there in the hills on short rations and not knowing much about the Indians. I think he's watching us right now and waiting for us to leave before he comes back to claim the booty. Well, we're leaving. We're going to walk till dark, or until we spot them. Then we're coming back.

"They ought to make about a hundred yards before they break down. They'll go straight up, but when they come down they'll begin swapping nuts and bolts around trying to rig up something that will get them through. If it's night, they'll need light to work by. If it isn't, we still have the grass for cover. It's two-to-one, but we've got to chance it. Anybody got a better idea?"

Susan, standing back a few paces, said, "Yes. I'll stay here and get them away from the stagecoaches while you come in."

They turned to stare at her. She came forward, sober and defiant. Jess tucked his hands under his belt. "Aren't you afraid Donovan will talk you into telling where the wheel-nuts are?"

"That's just what I will tell him." She turned and pointed. "I'll tell them they're right up there on the hillside, about two hundred yards away. That will give you a chance to work back."

Dr. Bible pursed his lips. "If I could just open up your head, young woman, and see what's behind this. It's a twenty-four carat idea, Clyman. The only weakness of your plan is trying to get back in without being seen; because without the surprise element, we're gone goslings."

"And nobody," Jess speculated, "could do it but Sue. She's the only one they'd believe; the only one they wouldn't shoot on sight. All right," he said, "dig up the bucket and we'll take it with us."

It was the hardest slap he could give her; she did not wince. "You don't have to; but I can understand that you'd feel safer."

Gil Applegate brought a shovel but hesitated before commencing to scatter the embers of the fire. "Or you can kill two mallards with one charge," he told Jess. "You can find out by leaving it here whether she's really had a change of heart. Assuming it makes any damn difference to you."

They were all looking at him; all but the girl, who had gone back to the coach. In his heart, Jess put it on the scales: Applegate knew damned well it made a difference. It was the only way he could ever be sure of her, but it meant jeopardizing the whole operation to make the test. He shrugged.

"You boys take a vote. I'm ready to leave any time you are."

He walked over and shouldered the canvas roll he had made up for himself. Then he heard someone drop the shovel and the men went to secure their own bedrolls and their rifles. Jess walked to where Susan stood by the coach, her hand on the door. For a moment he stood before her. She bit her lip, but the tears crowded through. It could be the old strength-through-weakness gambit, Jess supposed, but it didn't seem to matter. He dropped the roll and caught her against him. She began to sob, her face buried against his shoulder, and Jess held her tightly. It went beyond politics, treachery or anything else, this feeling that bound him to her; and now he knew she was as helpless to fight it as he.

"I've been an empty-headed little fool!" she whispered. "Trying to be a gentlewoman, instead of the kind of woman you needed. Why didn't you straighten me out a long time ago?"

Jess' fingers were in her hair; he felt the softness of her bosom against him. "You were the kind of woman I needed right from the first. Sue, how am I going to leave you here?"

"It's the only way," she said. "I'll tell them I refused to go with you. Let's think about Mexico City and after that, California—We'll work something out of this."

Jess was thinking of those things—but Applegate, the doctor, and the rest were already tramping out a patch to the spot on the hillside where the wheel nuts were supposed to be buried. Under his belt he had shoved the revolver he had taken from Ashley's body. He made her take it. "You won't need this; but it will make me feel better."

"I'll need you though, Jess. Always!"

They set out in late afternoon in a brief file down the freight road. It sloped gently for a mile and then climbed a ridge and dipped again. On their right were the mountains. Eastward was a ghost of a peak. They made slow marching, not anxious to get far from the train. The coaches were out of sight in a half hour, but they left Applegate in a nest of boulders on the first ridge, from which he could observe anyone approaching and give the signal.

Before long they stopped to rest. They had made about three miles. Gil had given no signal. He was to come down the ridge if he saw anything and signal with a rag tied to his rifle barrel. The sun was close to the raggard skyline of the Sierra Lagartijas. Warmth was leaving the air. The long shadow of the mountains came across them and a cold breeze flowed down from the north. They marched again.

Jess began to realize how high a tower he had built on a foundation of speculation. Hugh Donovan might play it safe and remain out of reach for a week. The only argument against that was that he would be anxious to get out of the country without delay.

The swift desert night flowed over them. They camped and made a fire. But none of them ceased to watch the now lost ridge of their backtrail. The night signal would be a charge of powder burned on the ground. They boiled coffee, but no one had a hunger bigger than a hardtack could satisfy. They were sitting there sopping hardtack in coffee when suddenly all of them lunged to their feet and someone said, "By God, boys!"

The powder had flared too brightly and so briefly that it was difficult to believe it had happened at all. Donovan was coming back.

They left everything by the fire except their rifles. They set out at a jog and rested in twenty minutes. Did the signal mean Donovan was already there or merely on the way? They had to assume it meant he was very close. The road tilted again. They were on the long swale of the ridge. They stopped and blew, and not far off they could hear someone moving carefully among the rocks. They were closer than they had thought.

Jess eared back the hammer of his carbine, in case it was not Gil up there, and walked onto the crest of the ridge. The driver slipped out of the boulders, gripped Jess' arm and pointed.

"Horses are yonder," he whispered. "They only got here about ten minutes ago. Come down from the foothills."

As he spoke, a lantern wick made a small eye of light among the stages, growing until it was a golden puddle on the trampled earth near the dead fires. Men moved about confusedly. Harness rattled, chains clinked. Then the lantern moved from the camp in quick, swinging arcs. Several men were moving up the hillside.

Jess started down the hill. The plan was for Applegate to take four men and work around to the left, to a point near the false cache. They could ambush several men here, if they were lucky. Jess would take on the ones at the camp. The grass, deep and thick, muffled their boot sounds; not far off, on their right, the horses moved restlessly under guard. They walked slowly toward the dark ring of coaches. Applegate led off with his men, making a wide swing to the left. Jess signaled the others down. They began a slow crawl toward the coaches, fanning out to enclose half of it.

They were like this when the shot exploded. One of the horse-holders fired blindly into the loose pack of them and shouted.

"*Injuns, by God!*"

The shot screamed away over the prairie. Jess could see the man limned against the horses. He aimed and fired; the gun kicked like a mule and the man pitched forward. It was ninety per cent luck, but it was one man less to handle, nevertheless. He ran for the coaches and sprawled under the closest one.

Donovan was bringing his men back down the trail, bawling

caution. "Spread out! Git clear of them coaches!" But he himself was sprinting back into the area of danger. He had three men with him, revealed by the lantern. Suddenly he realized he was still carrying it and gave it a sling into the grass. It struck a boulder and shattered; whale oil spread over the rock and immediately there was a nightmarish illumination for the scene.

Gil Applegate's guns were hammering. Two of the men with Hugh Donovan staggered. Donovan darted into the ring of coaches. "Out this side!" he bawled.

Jess hadn't a clear shot at him, but he found big Ben Dallas and put the man's shoulders on his sights and squeezed the trigger. Dallas went to his knees, sagged forward on all fours, his head hanging. Behind Donovan, Applegate's heavy artillery was whanging again. It drove the stage man into the trap he had tried to bull the others out of. He sprawled in the litter of camp gear and tried to pick out a target.

Two men who had been trying to repair the tampered wheels dropped their guns and raised their hands. Donovan fired a shot into one of these men and shouted, "Damned chicken-livered sons! They ain't taking pris'ners tonight! Kill or git killed!"

He had emptied his carbine and lay over on his side to pull his Colt. It came out, and his eyes found Jess at last, ambuscaded behind a wheel. He fired two shots so swiftly that the rush of flame and the balls thudding into spokes shook Jess. But he steadied down and got a bead on the gunman.

Donovan pushed himself up as if to rise, stared at Jess a moment and quietly lay forward across his rifle. The rest of the men were shocked out of any semblance of defense. One of them tried to run, and fell. The rest stood congealed with terror.

Jess said, "Hold your fire, boys. I still need a few drivers. They'll drive hogtied and unarmed, and I'll dump them in the first *jusgado* I come to. But if you'd like that better than frying in hell tonight—"

They rolled toward Chihuahua City in the morning, sixteen men and a girl. Some of the men rode with irons on their ankles. They would be replaced by Mexican drivers at El Venado; and that, thought Jess Clyman, might not be a bad idea in this country.

Bibliography of Books
By Frank Bonham

WESTERN NOVELS

Lost Stage Valley. New York: Simon & Schuster, 1948.
Bold Passage. New York: Simon & Schuster, 1950.
Snaketrack. New York: Simon & Schuster, 1952.
Blood on the Land. New York: Ballantine, 1952.
Night Raid. New York: Ballantine, 1954.
The Feud at Spanish Ford. New York: Ballantine, 1954.
Rawhide Guns. New York: Popular Library, 1955.
Defiance Mountain. New York: Popular Library, 1956.
Hardrock. New York: Ballantine, 1958.
Tough Country. New York: Dell, 1958.
Last Stage West. New York: Dell, 1959.
Sound of Gunfire. New York: Dell, 1959.
Trago. New York: Dell, 1962.
Cast a Long Shadow. New York: Simon & Schuster, 1964.
Logan's Choice. Greenwich, Conn.: Fawcett Gold Medal, 1964.
Break for the Border. New York: Berkley, 1980.
Fort Hogan. New York: Berkley, 1980.
Eye of the Hunter. New York: M. Evans, 1989.

WESTERN SHORT STORY COLLECTION

The Wild Breed. New York: Lion, 1955.

MYSTERY NOVELS

One for Sleep. Greenwich, Conn.: Fawcett Gold Medal, 1960.
The Skin Game. Greenwich, Conn.: Fawcett Gold Medal, 1962.
By Her Own Hand. New York: Monarch, 1963.

YOUNG ADULT NOVELS

Burma Rifles: A Story of Merrill's Marauders. New York: Crowell, 1960.
War Beneath the Sea. New York: Crowell, 1962.
Deepwater Challenge. New York: Crowell, 1963.
Honor Bound. New York: Crowell, 1963.
The Loud, Resounding Sea. New York: Crowell, 1963.
Speedway Contender. New York: Crowell, 1964.
Durango Street. New York: Dutton, 1965.
Mystery in Little Tokyo. New York: Dutton, 1966.
Mystery of the Red Tide. New York: Dutton, 1966.
The Ghost Front. New York: Dutton, 1968.
Mystery of the Fat Cat. New York: Dutton, 1968.
The Nitty Gritty. New York: Dutton, 1968.
The Vagabundos. New York: Dutton, 1969.
Viva Chicano. New York: Dutton, 1970.
Chief. New York: Dutton, 1971.
Cool Cat. New York: Dutton, 1971.
The Friends of the Loony Lake Monster. New York: Dutton, 1972.

Hey Big Spender! New York: Dutton, 1972.

A Dream of Ghosts. New York: Dutton, 1973.

The Golden Bees of Tulami. New York: Dutton, 1974.

The Missing Persons League. New York: Dutton, 1976.

The Rascals at Haskell's Gym. New York: Dutton, 1977.

Devilhorn. New York: Dutton, 1978.

The Forever Formula. New York: Dutton, 1979.

Gimme an H, Gimme an E, Gimme an L, Gimme a P. New York: Scribner's, 1980.

A Note about the Author

THE WRITING CAREER of Frank Bonham (1914–1988) spanned more than half a century, beginning with his first professional sale to *Phantom Detective* magazine in 1935. His published credits include forty-five novels and hundreds of short stories in pulp-paper and "slick" magazines. The bulk of his output was in the western field, though he also successfully produced historical adventure stories, and mystery and young-adult novels. (One of his juvenile books, *Durango Street*, was an acclaimed YA bestseller in 1965. Two years after that, he received the George G. Stone Center for Children's Books Award.) He was also a frequent contributor of storylines and teleplays to such popular TV western shows of the 50s and 60s as *Tales of Wells Fargo*, *Death Valley Days*, *Shotgun Slade*, and *The Restless Gun*.